# PRAISE FOR
# THE GUEST BOOK SERIES

### *When The Daffodils Bloom, Charlotte's Story*

"Charlotte's story is one of determination, danger and transformation set against the glittering yet shadowy backdrop of 1920s Los Angeles. I love that she followed Ruth Landry and Annie Parker to begin anew in the Lake Arrowhead Mountains."

—Elizabeth Conte, award-winning author
of ***Finding Jane*** and ***Chosen Mistress***

### *The Man in Cabin Number Five*

"Masterfully written. An entertaining work that will keep the reader hooked until the end. Congratulations on an exceptional book."

—*Readers' Favorite*

"An engaging drama with a strong cast and a final surprise."

—*Kirkus Review*

### *The Girls in Cabin Number Three*

"With themes of love, family, friendship, new beginnings, and the complexity of life, readers will get hooked from the very beginning."

—*San Francisco Book Review*

### *The Starlet in Cabin Number Seven*

[The Starlet in Cabin Number Seven] feels like catching up with old friends as the narrative amiably revisits the highlights of Lake Arrowhead... A light and engaging read, with an enticing mountain setting."

—*Kirkus*

### *The Maidservant in Cabin Number One, The Beginning*

"*The Maidservant* is a poignant story of a young girl named Ruth Ann and her incredible life. Seeing the world events and history through her eyes is what makes this book impossible to put down. If you're looking for a book that will transport you to a different time period, pick up *The Maidservant in Cabin Number One: The Beginning*. It's quite lovely."
—*N.N. Light's Book Heaven*


### *Dear Noah, The Conclusion*

"**Dear Noah** is a story of love's timeless power, no matter a person's age. The descriptive and emotional narration makes Dear Noah a poignant and emotive read. The characters draw you in as the story unfolds. Chrysteen Braun's writing makes readers feel like part of the story. Dear Noah is an unforgettable read."
—*N.N. Light's Book Haven, Nancy Light*

THE GUEST BOOK SERIES  BOOK SIX

# WHEN THE DAFFODILS BLOOM

## CHARLOTTE'S STORY

### STARTING OVER WAS THE ONLY CHOICE LEFT

# CHRYSTEEN BRAUN

# ALSO BY
# CHRYSTEEN BRAUN

*The Man in Cabin Number Five, Book One*
*The Girls in Cabin Number Three, Book Two*
*The Starlet in Cabin Number Seven, Book Three*
*The Maidservant in Cabin Number One, The Beginning, Book Four*
*Dear Noah, The Conclusion, Book Five*


# COMING SOON

*The Storyteller*
*Table for Eight*

Design and distribution by Bublish

ISBN: 979-8-89989-001-7 (paperback)
ISBN: 979-8-89989-002-4 (hardcover)
ISBN: 979-8-89989-050-5 (eBook)

*Always for my husband Larry,
the wind beneath my wings.*

# CHAPTER ONE

We lived in a part of Texas they called Tornado Alley, where besides having tornadoes, it was mostly hot, humid and dusty. Main Street was still just a dirt road and only four blocks long. We had a small bank and a one pump filling station with stacks of tires out front. Our barber, Al Shipton, was also our photographer, and the musician at the bar where, even though I was underage, I sang on weekends. Our mayor was also the justice of the peace, the owner of the general store, the apothecary and the acting post stop, where we could send a telegram, mail a letter, or pick one up.

Like clockwork, every six weeks, the sheriff parked his old Model T in the same spot right in front of the bank to deal with the town business. One spring, he closed down a medicine man who'd set up a revival tent—he even deputized the mayor's nephew to carry out orders to run them out of town. I'd never been to a traveling show before and although I'd finally convinced my mother to let me go see the bearded woman and the trained dog show—certainly, they were the least offensive acts of the show, I'd argued—I never got the chance to see them.

And not long after that, the sheriff brought in men from the Bureau of Investigation when someone robbed Harold Johnson's filling station. They never found the thief, whom they reckoned was in another part of the country by then, and they had to declare the case closed.

Doc Brown drove his horse and buggy into town the first of every month to see patients and write prescriptions. He'd set up a room at the back of the general store, and one time, he brought a midwife with him to stay with farmer Morgan's wife until she delivered her baby.

Heading north and out of the town proper were the church, the cemetery and the two-room school with a baseball field. I'd once overheard someone say you could cause trouble in school in the morning, then go across the street to the church to be redeemed that afternoon.

There'd been talk of a railroad coming our way, but it never materialized; instead, it was built about twenty miles out of town, where the courthouse and theater were. When that happened, several of our biggest ranchers and farmers sold up and moved away. Unfortunately, one of them was someone I thought would have made a good husband for my mother.

In her day, she was beautiful. Oh, she was still the prettiest woman I knew, but even I could tell our life was tough on her. She had two photographs taken right after we moved into town. One was just her looking directly into the camera, daring anyone who saw it to doubt her, and the other was of her and me looking at each other. She had on the prettiest sundress that day, and she smelled so clean and fresh. . .just like spring. When I told her that, she gave me a big hug and said, "You smell like a young girl who's been out in the sunshine." Coming from anyone else, I would have been insulted, but I knew she was right.

Al Shipton made two sets of photos for us; one enlarged set hung on the wall in the photography corner of the barbershop, in amongst the other portraits he'd taken, and the second set sat on top of our dresser, in the beautiful wood frames he'd given us. After she died, I'd asked him once how he caught that glimmer in her eyes. He shrugged his shoulders, and the corners of his mouth lifted.

"I saw that glimmer in your mama's eyes the first time I laid eyes on her."

My mother worked at the only diner in town, and even though they didn't really need me, I came in after school anyway and helped wash and cut vegetables. I eventually learned to wait tables and my pay came out of my mother's tips.

The owner, Jasper Cook, was a perfectionist who ruled with an iron fist. In his late forties, he'd been running the diner since his father died. He constantly fidgeted with table settings, moving coffee cups so their handles were pointing in the right direction, and arranging silverware so it all aligned with the edges of the napkin. Every now and then, I'd sneak by a table and move a fork, and if he saw it, he'd wrinkle his eyebrows in thought, and turn to see who'd done it.

"If he ever catches you, you'll be in big trouble," my mother would say.

"If he does, you'll be there to protect me," I'd say back.

He had a way of clearing his throat that drove me crazy, and sometimes I could tell it annoyed customers, too. Jasper Cook was headstrong, and he didn't take any guff off anyone, unlike his parents, who went out of their way to please their customers.

"No substitutions," he'd say matter-of-factly when someone wanted tomato slices instead of potatoes. Sometimes, I wondered why people kept coming back in.

He told one woman that, and she walked out. She told my mother she was on her way to New Mexico, and would just find somewhere else to stop and eat.

Mondays were our slow days, so I'd sit at the back of the diner and do homework or just daydream and doodle in my notebook. When Mr. Cook went to the bank, my mother would have a cup of coffee and sit with me.

"You know, you're going to have to figure out what you want to do when you graduate," she'd say.

I liked school, but I was bored, and I had no idea what I'd even be good at. I'd have to go away to college, and just the thought of leaving my mother made my stomach ache.

I could tell Jasper Cook had an eye for Mama, and although she never said anything to me, I knew she wasn't the least bit interested in him. One time when he wouldn't leave her alone, I told her if he kept bothering her, I'd tell the sheriff when he came to town, but she just smiled and said, "He's harmless."

I always thought he was a whackadoodle. I'd heard that word on the radio once and while I wasn't sure exactly what it meant, it seemed to fit Jasper Cook perfectly.

Some nights, after we changed into our pajamas, if we didn't feel like reading, we'd both lie there in bed waiting for sleep to find us. I would either talk about school, or Mama would talk about her dreams. Once, when a new young man made the fruit and meat delivery, she said, giving me a nudge, "He's kind of handsome. I'll have to learn more about him, though, before you talk to him."

"I don't need a boyfriend," I said. "And so far, you've gone through three delivery boys, and in your mind, none of them were right for me."

"I'm just looking out for you," she'd say.

"When I'm ready, I'll start looking myself."

Eventually, we'd both drift off to sleep, only to wake the next morning and start the day the way we always did; with one of her muffins and a glass of freshly squeezed orange juice. While I wasn't a fan of baking, I loved watching my mother as she measured, sifted flour, and poured batter into her tins or made her delicious brownies.

One day, she brought a couple of batches in and offered them to her favorite customers. Once Mr. Cook saw how much they liked them, he took it upon himself to charge for them.

"I think we should sell these," he said. "No need to give them away for free. In fact, you could bake them while you're in the diner. Folks would love the smell."

I gave him a look, and he added, "Of course I'll pay you extra."

I wasn't interested in doing any baking myself, so I offered to be the baking manager. I ordered all the dough and paper and calculated how much additional Mama would get paid. Since he still wasn't paying me, he couldn't complain, and in no time we were selling muffins and brownies by the half dozen.

One night when we couldn't sleep, my mother got up and took an envelope out of her dresser drawer. She climbed back into bed and handed me five dollars.

"For helping me bake."

She pulled the covers back up and said, "You know, Charlotte, one day, I'd still like to open our own place. Just you and me. We'll call it Flo's Diner."

"I wouldn't mind getting rid of Jasper Cook," I said.

Where that diner would be was anyone's guess. There wasn't room for two eating houses in town, even though we'd have had the most satisfied customers.

Little did we know that in a split second, everything was going to be different and there was nothing we could do about it.

My mother would never have that diner.

My name is Charlotte Hayes, and I was sixteen when Mama died.

While crossing the street to make a deposit at the bank, she accidentally spooked Eldon Lowell's horse, and it kicked her square in the chest. They told me she fell to the ground and died right there. Townsfolk gathered around her, and the banker, Aldon Buford, came out and covered her body. Since we didn't have a funeral home in town, he put her in the back of his wagon and I rode with him in silence to the church.

The pastor's wife tried to shoo me away, but I sneaked in while they were cleaning her up, and that's when I saw the bruising from the horse's hoof on her chest.

"Oh, honey," the pastor's wife said as she rushed over to me. "You should never have seen your mama this way. You need to remember her like she was—like the last time you saw her. A beautiful, loving woman."

I pushed away from her and ran outside, where I could breathe.


We were never churchgoers, but the pastor didn't seem to hold that against me. He offered to preach a sermon that next Sunday, but I told him I was sure Mama wouldn't want a big deal made of her death. He sold me a casket and a plot for twenty-five dollars, and we had her service there at the cemetery. I think everyone in town attended, which at first surprised me, but then when I thought about it, everyone had known my mother from the diner.

I stood there, numb, as they lowered her pine coffin into the ground. I tried to keep from crying in front of everyone, but when Mama's best friend, Moira MacDonald, started talking about how wonderful a person Mama was, I couldn't keep the tears from coming. When she finished, she came and held me, which almost made it worse.


Jasper Cook offered me Mama's job, and as much as I hated the thought of being around him every day, I knew I had no other options. I wanted to stay in the tiny one-bedroom house my mother and I rented— it was the only home I'd known. So I quit school and took him up on his offer. I made enough money to pay the rent and still have something to tuck away into my savings account. A couple of times a week, Moira brought over a casserole, and between that, the canned food from the storm cellar and the leftovers I brought home from the diner, I had plenty to eat. In those days, no one really paid attention to someone my age living alone.

I wanted solitude, and I got it. It took me a while to get used to the quiet. . .no pots and pans clanking on the stove as my mother prepared meals, no cooking and canning the apples and peaches from our trees or the vegetables from our garden. And no mess to clean up afterward.

I'd never been afraid of the dark when my mother was alive, but suddenly I found I dreaded putting out the kerosene lamp at night before

I made my way to the bedroom. The pitch blackness always startled me until my eyes grew accustomed to the only source of light left—that of the moon. It didn't take me long to figure out that if I brought the lamp into the bedroom at night, I didn't have to walk from the living room into the bedroom in the darkness. I could change into my bedclothes, then keep the lamp on my bed table for emergencies.

I'd also never given much thought to the howling and barking of the coyotes at night when my mother was alive. But now, they jarred me awake with a pounding in my chest before I realized what the sounds were. And sometimes, no matter how hard I tried, I couldn't go back to sleep.

Not long after I started full time at the diner, I could smell Jasper Cook coming from a mile away. He started slicking his hair back, and until then I hadn't realized just how big his ears were. He never touched me, but sometimes I'd turn and unexpectedly find him standing right behind me. I'd jump, and he'd laugh. I'd give him the evil eye, but it only made him laugh harder.

# CHAPTER TWO

Three weeks after Mama died, out of the blue, the pastor's wife came to my door and asked if I was ready to clear out her things. She said it just like that. No 'I'm sorry about your mother' or 'Are you doing okay?'

"We're here to help," she said, referring to herself and a two other ladies who followed her around. "It just so happens, we're getting ready for our annual church rummage sale and we could certainly use a few more things."

I hadn't even gotten used to my mother not being around, so I hadn't given her clothing a thought. I wasn't sure what to say, so I agreed, and the next day, the three of them showed up on my doorstep with muslin bags and wooden crates in hand. As if I wasn't there, they started going through her shoes and clothing, acting like they'd found buried treasure. Sometimes they'd even hold a dress up to themselves before putting it in a crate. I listened to their idle chatter and watched them pack her things up for about a half hour before I realized they were just vultures.

"Stop!"

I yanked my mother's dresses out of their hands, and they just stood and looked at me like I'd lost my mind; maybe I had. Within minutes, they'd removed almost every trace of her from the room.

By then my blood was boiling, and I screamed, "*Leave!*"

They looked at one another, then decided the best thing to do was indeed to leave me be.

"I'll pack up what I don't want, and bring it to the church," I said.

The pastor's wife asked sweetly, "Are you sure, honey?"

I was tempted to tell them all to get the hell out, but I said nothing more.

"We'll leave these here, then," she said, referring to the bags and crates. "And when you're ready, you can bring them over."

They packed up their coats and purses and as they stood on the front porch, the pastor's wife said to me, "It's really a shame about your mother. I was hoping she could have made some of her lemon squares... I don't suppose you could bake something?"

The next time Moira came by, I told her what they'd done, and after hugging me, she asked if I'd like her help.

"We can do it together," she said as she touched my face. She tucked a strand of hair behind my ear.

Coming from her, the task sounded so much more respectful and less daunting. I'd already emptied everything back out onto my mother's side of the bed and slept that way for a week. In a way, it made me feel like Mama was still there in bed with me.

Now, we got started. Moira instinctively knew which things to keep, and which to donate. I went to our dresser and there on top was Mama's mother-of-pearl comb and hairbrush set, and a bottle of cologne that she hadn't worn in years.

"She used to tell me she was silly to keep it," I said, showing Moira. "It's just that the bottle was so pretty."

I picked up a tube of lipstick, her favorite shade called Forever Red, and put a dab on my lips; I pressed them together the way my mother used to, to even out the color.

Moira caught me looking at myself in the mirror.

"You look beautiful," she said. "You remind me of your mother."

"I do?"

"Yes, sweetheart. You do."

I continued to go through my mother's half of the dresser and decided to keep all her underclothes and socks. There was only one small drawer left, under the round framed mirror, and in it were some coins, her mother's bible and the locket with photos of herself as a young child. I picked up an envelope and inside was my birth certificate, my parents' marriage license, and a wedding band.

With the envelope in hand, I sat on our bed and just sighed.

"A penny for your thoughts," Moira said. She stood there with one of my mother's dresses draped over her arm.

"I have their wedding license. I haven't thought about my father in years."

"Ah. I see."

"Mama never talked about him."

Moira scooted a stack of clothing aside and sat down next to me.

"Well, it's really not my story to tell, but I'll tell you what I *do* know."

"Please."

"Your mama moved here right after your daddy decided to head west to seek a better life. Land was cheap, cities were growing, and he thought for sure he could make a new life somewhere else."

"Well, that sounds reasonable," I said.

"But, honey, he never intended to take you and your mama with him."

"Did he *tell* her that?"

"He didn't have to. One day she came home from work, and all his things were gone."

Moira hugged me close, and just the feel of someone being there made me cry.

"That's when she packed you two up and came here."

"But what if he would have come home to find us?" I sobbed.

"That was the point. If he left you both once, she figured he'd probably do it again if he saw another opportunity down the road."

I didn't even remember my father, but now I cried harder. Moira got up and handed me one of Mama's handkerchiefs so I could wipe my eyes and blow my nose.

I think that's when I finally grasped it. . . I was alone.

I finished packing up what I would not use, and in doing so, I couldn't help but feel I was somehow chipping away at my mother's memory. I'd tried to hold on to the past, to keep everything the way it was, but I felt like my life with my mother was slipping through my fingers. And that's because it was.

There was still plenty to take over to the church for their rummage sale—if they didn't keep some things for themselves. Thankfully, the pastor's wife wasn't there when I stopped by, so I dropped it all off at the back door and left.

I spent my days drifting; physically present but mentally somewhere else. Even conversations with Jasper passed by in a blur, which was a blessing. Most of the time, I didn't even pay attention to what he was telling me, and I found it wasn't hard to do. I remembered what Moira had told me to do when I felt like I couldn't go on.

"You just have to take one step at a time. Pretend no one's watching you and take giant steps; eventually you'll be back to walking normal."

I could never do that when I was around people, but sometimes when I was by myself and felt so overwhelmed I didn't know which way to turn, I'd remember what Moira said to do. I'd pick up one foot, like I was a clown at the circus, and take a giant step forward and wave at the imaginary crowd cheering me on. Then I'd take another step, and another, until I felt the weight of the world lift off my shoulders. If I was feeling silly, I'd wave to the crowd again as I walked on.

A couple months after my mother died, the old banker, Aldon Buford, started coming into the diner, acting like he was interested in me. I wasn't sure how old my father would be, but Mr. Buford seemed like he was older than that. He always said he was sorry about Mama, and he'd leave me a nice tip.

"If you ever need company, all you have to do is say something," he'd say.

And then farmer Morgan's oldest son, Jeb, came in to the diner a few times with his hair slicked back and smelling clean and he reminded me of Jasper Cook's new look. He turned beet red every time he tried to talk to me, but I pretended I didn't notice him.

I could see the rage brewing in Jasper Cook every time a man came in and paid attention to me. He never came out and said anything, but he acted like he owned me. I could never be interested in him, and I wondered by the way I reacted to him why he was such a fool to not see it.

Besides, I wasn't interested in marrying anyone and having babies just yet. I was lonely, but not that lonely for the slim pickings our town offered. Even though I sometimes felt I'd lost my way, I was learning how to be more independent.

When Al Shipton's sister died, her son Tommy came to live with him—Al was the only one who didn't already have a household full of children. It was close to Thanksgiving, and I hadn't given the holidays much thought since my mother died. Other than Moira, I didn't have anyone I could think of to share it with.

Moira and I asked Al and Tommy if they wanted to do a supper, and I was surprised when they jumped at the opportunity. Cooking with Moira brought back memories of my mother, and I felt comfort in having people around me who cared. My mother always hummed when she cooked, and more than once I swore I heard her voice—but then I realized it was just Moira.

We cooked a turkey and made mashed potatoes, biscuits and bean casserole. Since I didn't bake, Moira made a pumpkin pie and chocolate chip cookies. Tommy was a shy kid, but he brought his fiddle and the minute he plucked his first string, he was like a caterpillar coming out of its cocoon. He turned into a handsome butterfly. He and Al played duets, and I sang.

In the past, for Christmas, my mother always put up a small tree in the diner, complete with lights and empty boxes wrapped like packages. I couldn't imagine who'd even send Jasper Cook Christmas cards, but as they came in, she'd hang them on string garland. One year she made and decorated stockings with our names on them in glitter, and she'd clip them on too. Without asking me, the first week in December, Jasper brought in the ugliest small tree I'd ever seen and, after stringing the lights on it, he said, "You do the rest. I want it all done up like Flo used to do it."

I hated him for other things, but I especially hated him for that. I figured I'd show him by doing a crappy job of decorating it, but when I stepped back to look at my work, I realized that by doing so, I'd unintentionally been disrespectful to my mother's memory. I ended up taking everything down and re-doing it, and suddenly I felt much better.

When Moira asked me if I wanted help putting up a tree at the house, my first thought was to tell her the same thing I wanted to tell Jasper—that decorating for another holiday was the last thing on my mind. But I knew she was just trying to get me out of my doldrums and encourage me to keep going.

I thought Christmas without my mother would be impossible to bear; I couldn't help but think of us decorating the tree, or cooking something special for dinner, even if it was just for us and Moira. We'd listen to Christmas carols on the radio, and we'd pretend we had microphones and sing the choruses we all knew. There was always something special for me under the tree, and although I was no longer a child, I'd come to look forward to it; almost expect it. It didn't matter what it was; I knew my mother gave my gifts a lot of thought.

I got to open one present on Christmas Eve—a new pair of pajamas and a pair of socks—and the minute I opened the package, I'd run to our room and change my clothes so we could spend the rest of the night snuggled in blankets, sitting by the fire.

I didn't expect anything with her not there, and I knew it would be hard for me to just sit by myself, staring at the fireplace, looking at a tree my mother didn't help decorate. But in the end, I relented to the tree idea, and three weeks before Christmas, Al and Tommy came over with one from Al's property. Once they set it in the corner of the room, Moira came over and the four of us did quite a dandy job of decorating it with strands of popcorn and cranberries. Tommy made a twig star for the top, and I unwrapped the boxes of handmade ornaments my mother and I had made over the years. I tried not to cry with every new one I took out and hung. Moira tied red ribbons on candy canes she found at the general store, and we hung them, too. We promised not to eat any of them until Christmas Day.

We cooked a small turkey and a ham and had biscuits and gravy. Moira baked an apple pie and made whipping cream for the top.

Santa brought Tommy a harmonica, which we all regretted the minute he unwrapped it.

"You're going to need some practice," Al said, shaking his head.

I was wondering if Al was getting sweet on Moira, for she blushed when she opened her gift; he'd gotten her a pearl hair clip.

"It's lovely, Al," she said, going into the bedroom to check it in the dresser mirror.

Al got some new barber towels for the shop, and Moira gave me a handmade journal with a note written on the inside of the cover.

> *To a wonderful young woman. You have your whole life ahead of you,*
> *and I know you'll find love and happiness.*

> *Love, Moira*

Taking one day at a time, I managed to get through the holiday, and then somehow, one year turned into another.

A dull ache was still a weight that never truly lifted, and when I began to realize that life had moved on when I couldn't, I sometimes couldn't tell when sorrow turned my memories into a type of rage. Why did my mother have to die? How was I going to live my life by myself and alone? There were days I wanted to make the world hurt as much as I did, but even *I* understood that if I let the hurt control me, I'd be angry all the time and hate everything .

And then, some mornings I woke to appreciating a new day, vowing I would do my best to just keep taking one day at a time, and trying to cherish the memories I had.

To say I was conflicted was an understatement. I would have to figure out how to cope and find a way to see a path through the storm. . .

# CHAPTER THREE

I once read in the newspaper that Texas got over a hundred tornadoes a year, and that some people swore they could smell one coming. I knew that afterward, the air smelled like dirt and water. Greenish clouds turned dark and rotated, moving in circles. That spring, I was by myself in the house when the tornado hit, and although I knew what to do, I'd never had to head for the storm cellar without my mother. Our cellar was really just a hole in the ground with wood beams and plank floors. It normally had shelves filled with canned jars of food, but I'd eaten most of them.

The minute I heard the familiar sounds of the storm coming, I grabbed a candle, an umbrella, some blankets and clothing, and then headed down to the cellar. I pulled the wooden doors closed behind me and tied them shut, hoping the storm wouldn't rip them off their hinges.

There was enough air down there to light the candle, and then I sat and waited. Rain turned into hail, and then the wind died. All of a sudden I heard the deafening rumble of what sounded like a freight train roaring by, and then what must have been a tree branch scraped the wood doors above me. The storm didn't last very long; and before I knew it, the wind calmed down and then all I heard was rain. I waited a few more minutes, then untied the cellar doors to peek out. Sure enough, the tornado had passed me, but I could still see it off to the west, just outside of town; right where the school and church were.

I climbed the ladder and threw the doors open, and the stench of sulfur filled the air. It was still raining pretty heavily, but I gathered everything I'd brought down there and climbed back out. A wheel barrow had overturned and some garden tools that hadn't been there before were about ten feet from me. I quickly glanced toward the house, and thankfully, the glass in the windows was still intact, so I didn't have to worry about the rain getting in and drenching everything inside.

I grabbed the umbrella and by the time I walked to town, I was soaking wet. My mother and I had never left the house right after a tornado, so I didn't know what to expect. I was surprised how people were just standing around, like it was an ordinary day. They were chit-chatting about how lucky we were to have escaped with so little damage, and I wanted to scream, "Do any of you have a lick of brains?"

Instead, I walked out of town to the school, and I could see it hadn't fared well. Half the roof was gone along with one side of the building and most of the windows were broken. School desks that hadn't been blown away lay on their sides, and wet papers were scattered everywhere. Outside, the swing set still stood, but the swings had wound themselves around the poles. You could tell where the tornado left its trail and incredibly, no other buildings were damaged.

The rain let up as I walked back into town, and I couldn't believe the same people were still standing around, yapping.

Suddenly, it struck me that we all just seemed to accept this was the way we lived. Drought, rain, hail and tornadoes were the norm. What was wrong with these people? Why didn't they get it and move away to a better place like my daddy did? What if someone had been injured or had lost their house or business? What would they do then? Then it dawned on me; what would *I* do? I didn't own our house, so there was nothing for me to sell, and if the tornado had taken it, I wouldn't have anything left, anyway. I had nothing.

I crossed the street to the diner, and the bell rang as I opened the door. Jasper Cook was there, mopping the floor, acting like nothing had happened. Then he turned on me.

"Where the hell have *you* been?"

He rubbed his hands through his slicked down hair and then stood there looking like a moron.

"First of all, I was at home and second of all, I was down in the storm cellar where everyone else should have been. And then I came into town and people are just standing around like nothing has happened. I went by the school, and it's a disaster."

"Who cares? It's over." He shrugged. "Get over here."

Something had gotten his craw, and I must not have responded quickly enough, for he let the mop fall to the floor, and then came to where I was standing. He grabbed my arm and I could smell a sickening sweat. He gave me goose bumps of revulsion.

He said, "Finish cleaning this floor. Customers are going to be here any minute and we need to be ready."

"Get your hand off me," I said, but he didn't release me. "I *said*, let me go! You repulse me."

I knew he was in a mood like I'd never seen, and the hair on the back of my neck stood up. I involuntarily shivered.

"So you don't appreciate your job and everything I do for you?" With that, he shoved me aside.

Jasper Cook was a scumbag, and he was finally showing his true colors. For some reason, he'd gone off the deep end, and there was no way I was going to stay there and work for that creep. Then suddenly it clicked. There was no way I was going to stay there, period. I wasn't sure what came over me, but like a petulant child, I shouted, "I hate you and I can't stand working here!"

I *did* know I hated my job, and I hated Jasper Cook; I hated my town and aside from a few, everyone in it.

The moment I started walking toward the front door, he rushed to block my way. But when I looked past him, Jeb Morgan was standing there, pounding on the door to get in. Jasper Cook turned to see where I was looking, then realized he needed to pull himself together. He stepped aside, and I opened the door.

"No one was at your house, so I came to see if you were okay," Jeb said, panic-stricken.

I raised my shoulders high and took a deep breath.

"I'm fine," I said. "I was just leaving."

Both Jeb and Jasper Cook stood there and watched me walk across the street to the bank. It hadn't opened yet, but a few minutes after I knocked, Aldon Buford came to the front door.

"I'd like to close my account," I said.

I don't know what I expected would happen by my outburst, but the minute I got home, I took my mother's revolver out of the closet and made sure it was loaded. I carried it with me everywhere I went in the house, ready to use it if I needed to.

I found two old suitcases and put them on the bed and I carefully folded everything so I could fit as much as possible into them. I dumped Mama's drawer of mementos into a carrying bag made of old carpet, along with my money, extra bullets, and her lipstick.

When I was finished, I dragged the blanket off my bed, wrapped it around me, and I sat in the chair in the sitting area off the kitchen, waiting and listening for sounds of footsteps. Throughout the night, I could feel my eyes drooping, but then I'd wake back up, alert as a fox.

I sat there all night in case Jasper Cook showed up.

Would I be able to pull the trigger if he broke into the house?

I believed I would have.

The next morning, I splashed water on my face and quickly dressed in one of my mother's best dresses. I felt I owed Al Shipton, my music partner at the bar, some sort of an explanation. He was busy getting ready for the day when I showed up at his door.

"Well, look who's here. You're up awful early," he said, chuckling.

I couldn't think of any way to tell him about me leaving than to just come out and say it.

"If I can get a ride to the train station, I'm leaving this morning."

"Whoa now, girl. Where are you going?" he asked, scratching his head.

"I'm headed for California."

"Ah. Going to be a movie star?"

"No, I just need to leave, and there has to be a lot more places I can sing out there. I know I'll find something."

"Well, I don't know what to say, but if you're sure about this, then I wish you a lot of luck. You'll need it, but you're one determined little lady, and if anyone can do it, you can."

He came around from the back of the barber chair and opened his arms to me. I gratefully stepped closer to him, and he gave me a big hug.

"You know my address if you get into trouble, but I'm sure you won't need me," he said.

"Thanks, Al. I really appreciate the opportunity to sing with you at the bar. That, and knowing I need to go, has given me the courage to take a chance. Look for a letter one day. I promise to write if you don't tell the whackadoodle where I am."

He looked at me like he was going to ask what that meant, but changed his mind.

"You know, I don't know that I have anyone coming in this morning for a haircut, so why don't I drive you to the train? At least I'll know you got that far without getting into trouble." He smiled.

"Thanks a bunch, Al. I really appreciate it."

He put the closed sign in the window, and while he hitched the horse up, I loaded everything into his wagon.

I didn't even take a last look at the town as we rode off.


By the time we got to the station, it was noon, and I was afraid I'd missed any outgoing trains to Los Angeles. But it was turning out to be my lucky day; there was one departing at 1:15. Al helped me carry everything to a bench and stood guard while I went to the ticket counter. Train fare was $40.75! And that was with no food.

I made thirty cents an hour working for Jasper Cook, which came to about twelve dollars a week, plus tips. I had five hundred dollars, including my mother's savings, and I could see it wasn't going to get me very far.

I must have looked as devastated as I felt, for Al saw the ticket, and then dug around in his pocket; he handed me ten dollars.

"For food," he said.

I shook my head at him and said, "Thanks, Al."

"Well, I'll leave you be," he said as he put his hat back on.

"Oh, Al, could I ask you one last favor? Could you give this letter to Moira when she comes looking for me?"

"You mean to tell me you didn't say anything to her?" He shook his head.

"I was afraid she'd talk me out of leaving," I answered with a weak grin, acknowledging I was a coward.

Al just shook his head again as he took the letter.

*Dear Moira,*

*By the time you see this, I'll be on my way to California. And yes, you're right, I didn't have the courage to tell you in person because I was afraid you'd convince me to stay.*

*I have no idea what I'll find, but I need to give it a try. I'll hopefully get a job singing somewhere until I can find a place I want to call home. I promise to write and let you know where I am.*

*Please try not to worry about me.*

*With much love,*
*Charlotte*

# CHAPTER FOUR

Four very long days later, we pulled into the busy train station in Los Angeles. Passengers scrambled to get off the train, then I waited for a break while they wrestled with their luggage. I was grateful I only had two suitcases; some people looked like they'd packed up a household. I was in awe, as the first thing I noticed when I stepped outside the station was that the streets were paved and filled with vehicles of all types and sizes. A crowd of weary travelers waited ahead of me, and it took forever for me to get a cab.

I desperately needed a bath, so I found a boarding house and took a room for the night. Even though the mattress was lumpy, it felt wonderful to sleep in a bed with no strangers in the same room, plus they offered a reasonably tasty dinner. At breakfast the next morning, I asked about transportation to Hollywood, and one of the other tenants drew me a map to where the streetcars ran. It was definitely too far to walk with my belongings, so I took my second cab ride.

I waited in line, again, with other passengers, and eventually the streetcar arrived. I wasn't sure where I was going, so I told the operator I wanted to go to downtown Hollywood. He looked me up and down, then shrugged his shoulders.

The journey wasn't long, and yet I had a chance to see all the modern buildings and what looked like hundreds of people rushing on foot to their destinations. One thing I knew for sure, I was going to have to adapt quickly to the fast pace of life in Los Angeles. It was obvious I'd been sheltered in my small town, where people could cross the road without worrying about getting run over. Here, motor cars shared the roads with electric streetcars and horse-drawn wagons.

About ten minutes later, up on the right, I saw a beautiful large hotel like something I'd never seen before, and asked if we could stop there. After giving me another look of disapproval, he stopped the streetcar, and I jumped off.

I stood in awe in front of what I wondered was originally built as a mansion for some rich movie star or as a palace for a king. Iron balconies and railings stood out against its stone and stucco exterior, and I could see the arched windows with carved detailed moldings and cornices and columns. I'd never seen such lush landscaping with beds of colorful flowers and palm trees in Texas. A costumed man greeted guests at the entrance and I thought I'd die of embarrassment when I tripped on the cobblestone drive. I caught his eye, but straightened myself up and remembered I was here because I was starting big.

I wasn't prepared for actually walking into the hotel, though. Ornate rugs covered the polished floors and large sparkling chandeliers hung from the high ceiling, giving the lobby a warm, golden glow. People sat quietly talking and drinking coffee or tea on sofas and chairs, and off to the right was a large built-in counter where guests were checking in.

Another uniformed man stood at a much less dramatic counter, and I asked him where I might find a nightclub.

He, too, gave me a stern look and pointed to several across the street.

"Do you have a nightclub here in the hotel?" I asked.

He thought for a moment before saying they did.

"It's off to the left," he said with hesitancy.

"Thanks," I said, trying to sound more confident than I felt.

I thought I'd try here first, then go across the street if there were no positions open. It was late morning, and the door to the club was locked. I went back to the grumpy man behind the counter and asked if there were any positions open in housekeeping. I figured I'd need a place to stay, and with any luck, I could find a job here first and hope they offered lodging.

With a tilt of his head, he motioned me to a hallway, and grabbing my things, I made my way down to a door marked Housekeeping. I knocked gingerly, not knowing if I could just walk in, and when no one came to the door, I took a chance and opened it. A heavyset woman looked up as I stepped inside.

"What can I do for you?" she asked, looking at my tattered suitcases.

"I've come to see if there's an opening?" I asked tentatively.

"Hmm," she said, scratching her ear. "Do you have any experience?"

"Well, I've worked in a diner and I've sung at a bar in town."

She looked at me like I'd sprouted a second head, but I patiently stood there.

She sighed and looked in a journal of some type before answering.

"We have an opening for a laundress and a bellman, but you look more like a laundress to me." She chuckled like she'd told a joke.

"And what would the job pay?"

Now she looked at me like I was being impertinent.

"We start at twenty-eight cents an hour, and then if you work out, it goes to thirty cents."

"Hmm," I said. Now it was my turn to think. "Does that include a place to stay?"

"Nope. We do have apartments, but it'll come out of your pay. Ten cents a day, and meals are five cents."

That was highway robbery! But then I remembered I was also going to try to get a side job singing, so in the end, I'd probably have a few extra dollars a week to survive on.

"I'll take it. When can I start?"

"Hows about tomorrow? Have a seat and I'll figure out where you'll be staying," she said, looking at a chart of some sort.

After what seemed like an eternity of shuffling papers, she called me back up.

"You'll start at seven every morning and finish around eight at night. You'll alternate washing and ironing with the other women, making sure the housekeepers have enough sheets and towels to do their jobs. We'll see how you do, and if a different position opens up, we'll talk about it then. You're staying with three other girls in the apartment building behind the hotel. Here's your key. And the name's Mrs. Beckett."

"I can't thank you enough," I gushed. "You won't be sorry you hired me, Mrs. Beckett."

"Let's hope not,"

I found the building and my apartment and quietly knocked on the door. If anyone was home, I didn't want to just barge in. When no one answered, I let myself in and I couldn't believe my eyes; the place was a disaster. Dirty dishes were piled in the sink, and a milk bottle was lying on the counter along with an empty cereal box. A pan with dried eggs in it sat on the stove, and a loaf of cut bread was just sitting there getting hard.

Clothes were strewn around the living room and bedroom, and three of the four bunk beds had their covers thrown back like someone had just gotten out of bed. The fourth bed, no doubt mine, was piled high with clean laundry that needed to be folded and put away.

To the left was a built in dressing area covered in cosmetics, and inside the tiny bathroom, stockings vied for hanging space on the shower curtain rod over the claw-foot tub.

I knew *I* could be sloppy, but something had to give. I crammed my dresses into the closet and found a space in the dresser to put my things away. Unsure who the laundry belonged to, I folded it all and left it on my bed. When I finished, I went back into the living room and gathered the rest of the clothing and dumped it all in a pile. The girls would have to sort out their clothes when they got home.

Apparently, the living room was also where everyone ate, for there were dirty glasses and dishes covering the coffee table and end tables. I brought them all back into the kitchen, then ran warm water in the sink and washed everything up. I cleared the counter and filled a trash can. As soon as I was finished, I found the exterior rubbish bin and dumped the trash.

I'd certainly make an impression on my roommates when they got home, and that was fine with me.

I was hot and sweaty when I finished, so I washed my face and changed my dress. I still had time to look at the nightclubs across the street and leave my number. Within walking distance from the hotel, I found two clubs that looked reasonably respectful and went inside. In both, I made sure there was a stage for performers, and even though there were no customers, the bartenders were busy preparing for the afternoon and evening.

There was no manager I could talk to in either club, so I wrote my name and the name of the hotel on napkins and left them with the barmen. On both, I added that I'd be back to talk to someone about a job.

On the way back to the apartment, I stopped at a little corner grocery and picked up some fruit, bread, butter, and peanut butter and jelly. I hadn't checked the icebox when I was in the kitchen, but I assumed there was room enough for my few groceries. I made a mental note to make sure it was clean before I put my food in it.

That night, I wrote a letter to Moira. I wanted her to know I'd arrived safely, and that I had a job and a place to stay. I told her not to worry about me, I think more for myself than her, and I wanted her to know everything was going to work out fine.

# CHAPTER FIVE

My first day in the laundry was all that I expected and worse. It was downstairs in the basement with only small casement windows cranked open to allow for air movement.

I arrived exactly at seven, and a woman with a clipboard gave me the once over before she looked at her pocket watch.

"Here," she said, handing me a starched white uniform. "Put this on, and come in prepared to work from now on. Your time doesn't start until *you* start, and we'll dock your pay for every minute you're late.

I found a quiet corner and quickly changed into a uniform that was way too large and it made me feel like a child playing dress up—but I kept my thoughts to myself, knowing no one would care. I was already sweating from the hot and humid air and I quickly nicknamed the laundry the broiler.

"You'll start each day doing an inventory of what you have on hand, and you'll end the day doing the same so we can make sure you have all the soap and lye that you need for the next. Today you'll sort the towels from the bed linens," the woman said, pointing to a large laundry cart on wheels. "And from there, you'll bring them over to the women operating the agitating washing machines. Once they're done, you'll load the wet towels into the machines over there that dry them. And when that's done, the women there will fold them. We operate like a well-oiled machine down here, and everyone pulls their own weight."

The sight of machines that washed and dried clothing was completely new to me, and I was fascinated as I watched women running the sheets through a wringer. At another station, they went through a hot press of some sort to remove the wrinkles.

"What're you waiting for?" the supervisor asked, giving me a nudge.

I fell into line. By the time we had our lunch break, I realized I hadn't thought to bring something to eat. My muscles had started cramping, and I was feeling a little light-headed. I joined the other women in my group while another team took over for us at the machines. I asked where I could get some water, and one of them nodded to a cart over in a corner. At the rate I was perspiring, I'd turn into a shriveled prune in no time.

A young woman named Clara noticed I hadn't brought anything to eat and offered me a part of her sandwich. Once I got back to the table with a cup of water, I took advantage of her offer. I ate and drank too fast, and within minutes, my stomach started cramping too.

"You need to take it slow and easy," Clara said. "Don't worry. You'll catch on."

And eventually I did.

For two weeks, I ate nothing but the cheapest thing I could make, peanut butter and jelly sandwiches, and with my first paycheck, I bought a thermos jug and filled it with water.

It was 1927, and for my eighteenth birthday, I treated myself with a cake from the bakery down the street from the hotel. I put a candle in it, made a wish for a call from one of the nightclubs I continued to visit, and then blew it out. I left a few pieces of cake for my roommates and took the rest down into the laundry.

"You should have told us it was your birthday," Clara said.

While we couldn't talk during our work, we worked the same hours and spent our breaks side by side, eating and sometimes sharing our lunch.

"It changes things up a little," she said, handing me half of her sandwich..

Clara was living in one of the other apartments, and a couple of months after I began working, one of my roommates got fired for dating one of the other workers. We had an extra bunk, and I immediately thought of her and asked if she'd like to move in with us. She asked Mrs. Beckett in housekeeping if she could transfer over, and we soon had a new roommate. In the meantime, the nightclubs across the street never contacted me, but the club at the hotel did.

I had an audition as a singer.

Maybe my birthday wish was coming true.

# CHAPTER SIX

I tried to tell myself that auditioning with the musicians at the hotel was no different from applying for any job, but it was. Other than applying for the laundry job, I hadn't really ever put myself out there based on my talent. When I began singing at the bar back home, I'd just started coming in and I quickly picked up the tunes. Al thought it would be a kick to ask me to sing and when the customers liked our music, the rest, as they say, was history.

But this was different. I was so nervous the night before, my mind played out every likely scenario—I'd never sung with real musicians before and I was sure my voice wouldn't be strong enough for them. I'd have to memorize the songs, and it was possible I just wouldn't fit in. I wished I was a smoker, so I'd have something to do to calm my nerves. I didn't think I'd ever get to sleep, but somehow I managed to.

The first thing Clara said to me when she saw me that next morning was, "Boy, you look exhausted."

"Thanks for that," I replied defensively.

I took one look at myself in the mirror and agreed.

"I hardly slept."

"Let's put some cold towels on your face. It'll perk you up. And before you go in for the audition, you can do it again."

The workday itself was a disaster. One girl in the laundry didn't show up, another passed out from the oppressive heat, and there'd been a large convention over the weekend, so laundry was piled up twice as high as normal.

Somehow I made it through the day, and the minute the work bell rang, I rushed back to our apartment so I could take a bath and try to relax.

I did my makeup and put on one of Mama's dresses. In my drawer, I found an old pair of her stockings and when I pulled them on, one was snagged! They looked dreadful. I couldn't go out looking like a floozie! Just as I was about to burst into tears, Clara came to me with her hands behind her back.

"These are for you," she said, handing me a box with a ribbon tied around it.

Inside was a brand new pair of stockings.

"I've been saving them for tonight."

She offered to come with me to the audition, but if I failed, I didn't want anyone to see me. So, instead, she walked with me to the door of the lounge and gave me a hug.

"Break a leg, or something like that," she said.

"Thanks," I said.

Miles was on the saxophone, Finn was on base, and Reggie was practicing his scales on the piano. They introduced themselves, and when they handed me a stack of music, my stomach dropped. I'd never read sheet music before; Al just played, and I sang.

Reggie, the piano player, looked at me and said, "You can read, can't you?"

He wasn't unkind, but I could tell I'd turned deep red with embarrassment.

"Yes," I said, somewhat defensively. "I can read."

"Good then, let's get going," he said.

Thankfully, I'd heard the songs before, so I found I could sing to the words without having to read the notes. An hour later, Miles said, "Well, I'm good with her if you guys are."

"I'm fine too," Finn said.

"Good for me," Reggie said.

"I understand you work in the laundry?" Miles asked.

My face flushed again. "Yes," I answered, somewhat hesitantly.

"Okay, get here as soon as you can so we can keep practicing. You'll be fine."

The moment I opened the door to leave, Clara got up. She'd been waiting for me all that time!

"I got the job," I said, needlessly.

I was on top of the world.

Clara had been working at the hotel longer than I had, and not long after I got the job in the nightclub, she was promoted to housekeeping. I was thrilled for her, but disappointed I hadn't had the same opportunity. I had to remember so many things had gone my way lately, and I tried to hide my disappointment. I was still down in the broiler, but I couldn't forget that I was now making more money. And after sharing tips with the guys, I was able to tuck away a pretty sizeable amount of cash each week.

Another roommate moved on, this time for being insubordinate, so a new girl moved in. Clara took this opportunity to switch to the top bunk over me, so that we could talk to each other at night, without disturbing the other two girls. Our goal was to eventually find a place for just the two of us, but the timing wasn't right, yet.

Just before my nineteenth birthday, I got my promotion to housekeeping. I would start where everyone did, on the lower floors where the less important guests stayed. Clara was getting promoted up to the higher floors, but I was able to shadow her until I got the lay of the land.

While I was no longer in the sweat pit, I quickly learned housekeeping had its own challenges. Not only did we have to be invisible and discreet, I had no idea how physically demanding it was going to be. We bent, stooped and stretched, lifted mattresses to change bed linens, cleaned bathrooms and swept carpets. We became privy to private conversations and affairs, and I soon learned the wealthy were not immune to loneliness, betrayal, and sorrow.

I began looking after a woman named Adele Rochester who lived on the first floor. I'd never heard of anyone living in a hotel before, but Clara told me there were several guests who stayed there full time. They were mostly widows, obviously with enough money to pay for the luxury of residing there. We still cleaned their suites daily while they went out and shopped, had their meals, or played cards with other long-term guests.

I guessed my lady to be in her mid to late seventies, for she had slightly stooped shoulders, and she walked with a cane. Her thick hair was snow white, and I knew she had it done in the hotel salon every week. I tried not to snoop, but sometimes she left a stack of letters out on the writing desk, and I found myself drawn to them. They were all addressed to Mrs. Albert Rochester to an address in Los Angeles. I wasn't familiar with any of the neighborhoods in the area, so I had no idea if she'd lived in a big, fancy house, but that's how I imagined it.

One time, when I was feeling bold, I read parts of a letter Adele had left out. I wouldn't have dared to open any of the envelopes, but it was almost as if she wanted me to read something about her life.

My heart raced as I skipped to the end of the letter to see who it was from. His name wasn't Albert Rochester, it was Jonathan, and I immediately understood she must have had a lover!

It was dated June 11, 1889. By my guess at her age, she would have been around thirty.

*My dearest Adele,*

*The many miles that separate us make me long for you more every day. If you were free, I'd ask you to marry me. I'd never be able to provide you with all the comforts you have become accustomed to, but I can always dream that you would be happy enough with just the love I have to offer.*

*I'll continue to write to you, unless you tell me to stop. And I'll remain
forever hopeful someday you will make me the happiest man alive.*

*Forever yours,*
*Jonathan*

I put the letter back, then worried I hadn't left it exactly as I found
it. My heart was pounding in my chest, and I half expected the door to
her suite to open unexpectedly. I quickly started cleaning the bathroom
in the event she came back early. Hurriedly finishing, I opened the door
and, after checking in both directions to make sure no one was there,
I pushed my cleaning cart out into the hallway. Would Mrs. Rochester
know I'd read the letter? How would I face her the next time I saw her?
I knew I shouldn't have done what I did, but she knew I'd be cleaning
the suite—had she intended me to read it? But why? There was no way
I could go back now.

Twice a week, when her laundry was delivered, I'd carefully unwrap
the brown paper packaging and if it wasn't too wrinkled, I'd neatly fold
it up. At the end of my shift, I'd bring both the paper and the string
back down to the laundry so it could be reused. When I first started
cleaning for Mrs. Rochester, she put her own things away, but not long
after meeting me, she asked if I could fit this extra job in to my schedule.

I knew her instructions to the laundry were to hand wash her
undergarments, and I could see why. I'd never seen silk fabric before,
and it was so much more beautiful than the cotton I wore. I'd gently
place her chemises, garters and hosiery into her dresser along with the
rest of her luxurious things, and each time I did, my mind wandered
back to that letter. If she'd had a lover, of course, she'd have wanted to
wear nothing but the best when she saw him!

Every week, Mrs. Rochester would leave a dollar on the dresser.

I finally told Clara about Adele, and she told me about a man she
cleaned for on the seventh floor. Every morning, he'd have a pot of
coffee brought up to the room and he would drink it while reading one

of his many books. After he dressed in one of his finest suits, he'd have breakfast downstairs and read his paper.

He always left an extra pair of shoes out to be shined, and twice a week he'd leave a bag of laundry for her to take downstairs.

"His routine is pretty predictable," she said. "Sometimes I can tell he's out for the evening when I turn his bed down, but I've never seen him in the company of other guests. And if you haven't figured it out yet, you can always tell if a guest had a visitor in the night by the messed up sheets on the other side of the bed."

I'd had no idea that was one way to tell, and from that time on, the first thing I did when I opened the door to a room was check the bed!

Clara lost her parents to the Spanish flu in 1918. Even with strict quarantines, it quickly spread across the country, and Chicago, Clara's hometown, was hit hard.

"I lived with my aunt until I moved to L.A.," she'd told me.

I introduced her to Miles and Finn, and when the four of us had time off, Finn would drive us around in his Model T four-door sedan. At Grauman's Chinese Theater, we saw *The King of Kings*, by Cecil B. DeMille, and *The Jazz Singer* at the Avalon Theater. On other nights, when we didn't play in the hotel nightclub, we went to speakeasies downtown where we sometimes danced until dawn.

I'd learned Miles had come to Los Angeles from a small town in Canada where he lived with his mother and sister. He'd struggled with leaving his close-knit community, but he wanted to explore the world more and play the saxophone. He came to New York first, thinking he'd make it big, but soon realized he was just another one of the thousands of people looking for work.

"I hated to admit I felt lost in the crowds," he said once. "I played a few gigs, but nothing permanent, and short of playing on street corners, I realized I didn't belong there."

"But isn't that where you met Finn?" I asked.

"Yes, so it wasn't a complete dog's mess."

I'd never heard that term before, but I could figure out what he meant. *Dog's mess.* I'd have to remember that.

Finn came here from Ireland. He didn't talk much about it, but his mother remarried after his father died. His stepdad made it clear he thought playing any kind of musical instrument was a waste of time, and more than once, he'd said, "as long as you're living under my roof," (which was actually his mother's), "then you need to get a real job."

His mother didn't back him up, so he left the small coastal village where he grew up and sailed to New York to prove them wrong, and make a good living playing base.

"We met at a hostel. I heard him playing one day and made my way towards the music. 'I play the sax,' I said. 'We should practice together.' And from there, everything just clicked."

That summer, Miles fell madly in love with a girl who was staying in the hotel with her parents. Josephine was her name, and the way *he* explained it was the moment she came into the nightclub, he knew she was the one. She was eighteen, but her parents were very strict with her. When she told them she'd met someone, and that he was a musician, they didn't approve of his profession, and they were not interested in meeting him.

"Someone like that can never provide for you in the manner in which you've become accustomed," her father told her. "Plus, we'll be going home soon, and I don't see how anything can come of it."

While her parents visited friends and went to fancy dinners, Josephine and Miles saw each other after our performances each night, and whenever they could during the day. Then suddenly, she was gone. They'd checked out of the hotel and disappeared.

Miles was devastated, and for weeks, we couldn't convince him he'd get over her. He refused to join us on our nights out, and more than once, I caught him looking up whenever he saw a woman come into the club, hoping it might be her. I could always see the beginning of a smile on his face quickly fade. Never having been in love, I didn't quite understand why he couldn't just bounce back. He hadn't even known her that long. I never said that to him or anyone, because just thinking about it made me feel insensitive and unsympathetic. I hadn't realized how sensitive some men could be.

Thankfully, by the end of summer, the old Miles came back to us. We knew it when he said, "Where should we go tonight?"

# CHAPTER SEVEN

In 1927, alcohol was still illegal, and while the hotel never openly served it, I'd seen customers continue to pass around flasks of what I was sure was whiskey or bourbon during our shows. And the barman still kept a few bottles of liquor behind the bar for vetted customers who wore either a white carnation or a red rosebud on the lapel of their suit coat. Otherwise, customers drank specialty drinks with sodas and flavors, olives, cherries, and twists of limes.

I'd also heard from other housekeepers that the hotel, like many other establishments at the time, often looked the other way when the mob rented ballrooms and hosted what they called house parties. Guests had to arrive at a certain time, and then the doors were closed until the early hours of the morning. Beer, bourbon, and champagne flowed freely and only a select few servers were ever assigned to the events.

While I was on my break one night in the lounge, a big burly man stuffed into a dark suit came up to me and asked if I'd like a drink. It was so obvious he was a mobster, he could have been wearing a sign around his neck. He pulled a silver flask out of his suit pocket and took a drink and then wiped his mouth with the back of his hand.

"Thanks," I said, "but I need to get back on stage in a minute."

I'd seen men like him in the hallways and I always made sure I was busy with my laundry cart if they looked my way.

"Want a drink?"

His liquor breath was foul, and he made my skin crawl. I'd never become accustomed to alcohol of any kind, and I would never have taken a drink after he did.

"You've got quite a voice, doll," he said.

"Thanks," I said, hoping the guys were ready to play again. And as if on cue, Miles stepped back up onto the stage.

I said, "Oh, that's my cue."

As I walked away, I felt the man's eyes boring into my back, and I wanted to turn to see if he was still there, but I was afraid to. In my haste to get away, I tripped on a chair leg and almost went down. The man sitting there quickly got up to make sure I was all right.

Once I stepped up to where my microphone was, I casually wiped the perspiration from my upper lip with a napkin, and asked Miles, "Is that big guy still at the bar?"

He casually looked around the room and said, "I don't see anyone."

I turned to see for myself, and indeed the man was gone.

I quit holding my breath.

"Thank god."

I didn't know very much about the mob, and I didn't want to.

The housekeepers all had stories to tell about our special guests.

The first time I saw Samuel Williams was when he opened the door to his suite to let the bellboy in with his luggage. I was in the hall, having just left Mrs. Rochester, and I caught a glimpse of him. He was a well-dressed, handsome man, tall, with dark hair and a thick mustache. I was surprised there were only two bags, considering I been notified he was going to be a long-term guest. I saw a gold wedding band on his left hand as he reached into his wallet and tipped the boy.

He gave me a quick glance and then closed the door.

He wasn't in his room when I turned his bed down at the end of my shift, and when I made a quick sweep of his rooms before I left, I couldn't help but notice he'd left his wedding ring on the bathroom counter.

"Hmm," I thought, my mind working overtime.

I didn't give him another thought as I rushed home to change into a new dress for the evening's performance. After quickly powdering my face and applying lipstick, I smacked my lips and declared myself ready for the evening. Since moving to Hollywood, I hated walking even a short distance once it got dark out, and tonight was no different. I quickly checked to make sure no one was there, and then fast-tracked it to the back entrance of the hotel. Once inside, I could take a deep breath and relax.

Miles and Finn were warming up when I came into the club, and not long after I got there, Reggie sat at the piano and played his scales. Frank the barman brought me a glass of water, and I took a sip.

The doors opened a few minutes later, and people made their way inside. We started our first song, *Everybody Loves my Baby*, and just before our break, I saw what looked like Samuel Williams walk in with a beautiful brunette. From the stage, I watched as she snuggled up close to him, and then he whispered in her ear. She laughed as though shocked, but loving every minute. Something told me she wasn't his wife, but what he did was none of my business.

Traces of a woman's fragrance lingered in the room the next morning when I cleaned up what I started calling their love nest. Mr. Williams was gone, as were his luggage and his wedding ring. I called down to the front desk, and confirmed he was still registered as a guest, then I made up his room like I would have any other time.

A week later, he showed back up in the suite, so I put a towel swan on his bed, and then that night, he was there in the nightclub once more with the same woman. Two days later, he was gone again.

Months went by before he came, and then he and the woman sat cuddling in a booth during our show. The next day, he disappeared again. One of the other housekeepers heard from her friend at the front desk that his wife showed up after the nightclub closed, and demanded to know where her husband was staying. She got a key to his room and caught him red-handed, or as the housekeeper said, caught him with his pants down. And boy, was there a ruckus.

The next morning, Mr. Williams and his wedding ring were gone for good.

# CHAPTER EIGHT

In 1928, President Coolidge awarded Charles Lindbergh with the Medal of Honor for his first transatlantic flight, Mickey and Minnie Mouse made their movie debut in Steamboat Willie, penicillin was discovered, and I celebrated my nineteenth birthday.

We celebrated at Philippe The Original in Los Angeles. Their claim to fame was inventing the beef dip, and that's what Miles, Finn, Clara and I ordered. None of us had ever been to nearby Chinatown, so after lunch, we decided it would be our next destination. I was surprised to see hundreds of residential and commercial buildings in a predominantly Chinese community. There was an opera theater, several temples, a newspaper and I later learned it had its own telephone prefix.

Unbeknownst to us, it was also the Moon Festival, and the streets were crowded with spectators. While we snacked on delicacies offered by restaurants and food stalls, we watched in awe as almost a hundred people performed in the dragon dance; a symbol of China's culture and a sign of good luck. We bought a few souvenirs in the curio shops, and then we made it in to a performance at the theater before we headed back to the hotel. We were exhausted, but we all agreed we'd had a great day.

"it was the best birthday ever," I said truthfully.

A letter from Moira was in my mail slot at the apartments when we got home. I'd tried to keep in touch, letting her know how everything was going with me, and asking how everything was back home. I'd only been gone two years, but in that time, Jeb Morgan, the farmer's son, married the daughter of a rancher, and old doc Brown had been thrown from his buggy when it hit a big rut in the road. He was fine, but had broken his leg, so he'd been out of commission for a few months. Mrs. Morgan had another baby, so they called the midwife in. You'd think someone her age would figure out how to stop having children. Those were my thoughts when I read the news, not Moira's words.

I couldn't help but wonder what I'd be doing if I'd stayed back home. I was certainly nowhere I wanted to ultimately end up, but I knew there were a lot more opportunities for me here in Los Angeles.

I'd invited Moira to come out and visit, although I knew she'd hardly be able to afford it. The train ticket itself was expensive and the cost of staying in the hotel was high; Plus, there were rules about outside guests staying in the apartments, so there was no way she could have stayed with us there. I'd often wondered if anything had come of her friendship with Al, but she'd never mentioned him. I missed her terribly, but almost every waking moment of my life here was filled with something to do.

The four of us always managed to find new places to explore. When we had a rare two days off in a row, we took a trip up to Big Bear and Lake Arrowhead in the San Bernardino Mountains. On the highway up, we discovered a large white hotel tucked into the hills and acted like we owned the place as we sat at an umbrellaed table and ordered a cocktail.

"It's a hot springs," Miles declared after reading their brochure.

As if on cue, a strong whiff of sulfur wafted our way.

"Phew," I said.

"Let's finish our drinks and head out of here," Finn said, gulping his drink down.

We eventually continued up Hwy 18, also known as the Rim of the World Scenic Byway: if you followed it further up, you could drive almost a hundred miles through the San Bernardino Mountains. But we turned off onto Hwy 173, which took us into Lake Arrowhead and ended up in a Norman style village complete with red roofs built along the lake. We'd packed a picnic from the hotel kitchen, and found a park-like setting used for the outdoor movie theatre, and laid our blanket down. By the time we finished our lunch, the air had turned crisp and cool, and Finn went back to the car and brought us our jackets.

"I'm ready for a nap," Miles said, stretching out on the blanket.

"I could do with one too," Finn added.

"Well, I'd like to walk around before we find a place to stay tonight." I said.

"Me too," Clara said.

With that, she and I walked out to the edge of the lake. I'd never seen boats pulling people on skis before, and I couldn't figure out how they managed to stay upright. To the right, there were spaces where boats could tie up and we watched as a man wearing a straw hat effortlessly brought his boat in. Once he climbed out, he turned to his passenger and helped her out. She wore a red scarf tied around her hair, and I caught a glimpse of a brightly patterned dress under what looked like a long coat. She had a blanket wrapped around her shoulders, and I knew she must have been frozen out on the lake.

I was engrossed in watching them when Clara nudged me. She pointed to what looked like a large home built along the water on the opposite side of the lake.

"I think that's a house over there," Clara gushed. "Can you imagine living there?"

"I can't imagine being able to look out at the lake all day. They must be terribly rich," I added. "I've heard they make movies up here. Can you imagine? It's probably some movie star."

"It is quite beautiful, even from here."

"Well," I said, breaking the spell. "We need to figure out what to do. I thought I saw a cluster of cabins as we drove in. It's back a way. Should we check there?"

"Let's go get the guys and see what they want to do. I don't want to be driving around all night looking for someplace to stay."

Miles and Finn were dozing when we made our way back to them.

"Wake up sleepy heads," I said. "We need to find a place to stay."

Once we packed everything up, we made our way back down the road and found the cabins. We pulled into a gravel drive and the guys went in to see if there was something available. The plan was they would get a cabin and Clara and I would sneak in. We'd get the bed, and they'd get the floor. About twenty minutes later, they returned with a key in hand.

To save money, we shared dinner at the local diner overlooking the lake. Except for a few ripples, the water was still, almost like glass, and I was mesmerized by the way the light of the low moon almost shimmered with each movement of the surface. The shadows of the surrounding tall pine trees turned darker as the moon rose.

Clara had to elbow me when we were ready to leave.

The next morning, I was certain we'd be caught trying to sneak out of the cabin, but luckily, the cabin owner was gone before we left. After a quick breakfast, we headed east to Bear Valley, then known as Pine Knot, which was a small cluster of camps. None of us had been there before, and it was almost the opposite of Lake Arrowhead. Everything was in town, instead of being at the end of a road. There were shops, places to eat, and handmade signs that indicated places to stay. We passed an open area to our right, and Finn pointed out a spot where visitors could ski during the winter. Just looking at the wide open space, it was almost impossible to imagine how snow could turn it into a ski area. But then again, I'd never actually seen a ski slope or a snow-covered mountain before.

At the end of the main street, we saw a zoo and pulled in. They were just opening for the day, and a woman greeted us as we came up to the gate.

"Glad to see you all. Come on in," she said cheerfully. "We have special food for the animals if you're so inclined to feed them. But remember, they aren't pets. They're wild animals and they can be unpredictable. That being said, enjoy yourselves."

We took turns taking photographs of each of us by the cage of the bobcat, red fox, black bear and mule deer, and the woman who let us in took one of all of us by the sign. We weren't ready for lunch yet, but the zoo had a snack area where we bought popcorn and sodas before we headed out.

"I'm not sure what else there is to see here but the lake," Finn said, looking at a map. "It looks like we can drive around and go home from there."

We headed east again and passed an airstrip, and as we followed the road around the lake, we passed several cabins and a small general store. Eventually, we made our way back onto the highway and headed down the mountain, where we all complained of plugged up ears from the altitude. Over two hours later, we were once again back in Los Angeles.

For another trip, we headed southbound to San Diego and gorged on hot dogs, popcorn and cotton candy before we rode the Giant Dipper Rollercoaster at the Mission Beach Amusement Center. I thought for sure Miles was going to upchuck after that, but he didn't. I didn't feel so well myself, and afterward, we walked on the beach until our faces turned pink from the sun. We decided against having dinner at The Hotel Del Coronado when we looked at the prices on the menu. Instead, we drove until we found a small diner and had hamburgers.

I always thought it was interesting that the four of us were never romantically inclined. Both Miles and Finn were nice looking, but I never felt any real attraction to either one of them. I'd asked Clara once about it, and she felt the same way. They were wonderful friends, and they would have done anything to protect us, but I never saw them as a love interest. It was best that way, for a failed relationship would have ruined our friendship.

Miles and Finn had dalliances with a few young women, but then men could do that and it was considered manly. Women had to be much more proper. At the hotel, I saw a few interesting men, but dating staff was forbidden, and I wanted someone with loftier aspirations than a lifetime of hotel service. I knew I'd never meet a doctor or lawyer—

someone with a profession. Men like that usually had their wives and families with them.

I also often wondered what my mother would have thought of me right now; on my own, and cleaning up after people. I knew she'd be proud of my singing. . .it was one thing she knew I always loved.

In the springtime, Clara met the nephew of one of her long-term residents, Mary Kelly. More often than not, with most of the hotel's residents, the housekeeper's responsibilities often overlapped with that of being a caregiver or confidante. The hotel charged the guests accordingly, and since the guests no longer had domestic staff, they willingly paid for the service just to have someone there for them.

Mary Kelly moved in not long after her husband passed away. For years, she'd been actively involved in her woman's club, and now that she no longer had a household to run, she found she had more time to devote to her club's charity activities, the arts and the theater.

One morning, when Clara knew Mrs. Kelly had a social function, she'd helped her decide what to wear. She'd laid out her clothing and when she came back to check in, she was surprised to see a young man in her room.

"Jeffrey's going to accompany me to the gala tonight," Mrs. Kelly said brightly.

"Nice to meet you," Clara said to him, reaching out her hand.

"Likewise," he'd said, taking it.

She told me later his eyes lingered on hers, and she felt herself growing warm.

He was tall and a little too slender—but still on the handsome side. He still needed more years to fill out his lanky body. He quickly moved to help his aunt into her coat, and then said nothing more to me when he held the door for her. In the end, he hadn't seemed the least bit interested in me, and I hate to admit it was the first time I felt insignificant around someone else. How will we ever meet Mr. Right?"

I sighed. I'd often asked myself that same question. Back home, I would have been considered an old maid by now.

On our breaks, a group of us ate together in the staff kitchen. We'd sit around an old table with mismatched chairs, and mostly grumble about the guests we served. Most guests that could afford to stay in an expensive hotel could afford to leave tips, but not all of them did. Next to having to clean up a disgustingly dirty room, receiving nothing for your hard work was almost a slap in the face. Of those who did tip, some were more generous than others. I looked at it this way; like the tips from the nightclub, they all added up. I'd learned how to leave a freshly made bed with towels folded to look like elephants and swans and I folded a washcloth into a pocket where I tucked a wrapped bar of soap. I turned under the toilet paper tips into a point, and I made sure the tissue coming up from the box was clearly standing erect. The next time we had our break, I showed the other girls how to do what I did, and in no time, they found the sizes of their tips increasing.

Gossiping about guests was discouraged, but some of the girls always had interesting stories to tell. Several told about men who were on business trips, who brought different women back to their hotel every night. Another housekeeper complained how she always got guests who partied and left alcohol bottles, dirty ashtrays, disgusting sheets, and vomit on the bathroom floors. "And they leave nothing," she added.

The worst one was before my time. A man who was apparently smoking in bed caught his room on fire. Another guest smelled smoke in the hallway, and they sounded the alarm. They found his body on the floor, determining he died from smoke inhalation, and thankfully, no other guests were injured.

Within the week, workers came in and, after relocating the other guests on the floor to new rooms, they replaced the carpeting and drapes and repainted the damaged suite. A cleaning crew then sanitized and deodorized the entire floor.

In October, Finn got a letter from his mother. His stepfather had died in a harvesting accident while working his neighbor's land. He told Miles and me before we started our first set, and if you didn't know any better, you would have thought he was okay. That was one thing about showmanship; you always had to be "on" even if your world was collapsing around you.

After we finished playing that night, the four of us went to an all-night diner where we could hear ourselves think.

Although his mother insisted he shouldn't come home, Finn still felt torn. He knew she was grieving, and part of him wanted to be there with her. His sister and her family lived nearby, so he knew she'd be there to help with all the funeral arrangements.

"If my mother sells the property, she can move into town and finally live comfortably," he said, fiddling with his soda. "A trip back home would take almost all my savings," he said, running his hands through his hair.

"How do you think your mother would feel if you didn't go back? You said she wrote you didn't need to," Miles said. "And if you just sent her money, it wouldn't deplete your account and it would benefit her, too."

"I'm sure she could use the money," he said, sighing.

While the three of us devoured our burgers and fries, Finn only nibbled at his. "Just the thought of stepping back into that house after my stepfather and I argued for the last time makes my stomach flip. And my mother just stood there and didn't defend me or try to persuade me to stay. No matter what I decide, I'll always wonder if I did the right thing."

After our dinner, Clara and I saw the two of them off, and we walked back to our apartment.

Clara said, "That's a tough one. I would feel the same way if my stepmother died, although I hated her. I'd feel bad for my dad, being alone again."

# CHAPTER NINE

Sleep evaded me that night as I thought about Finn and the decision he was forced to make. Only he knew how he'd feel if he didn't go home again. No matter what, he still loved her, but I couldn't even imagine my mother not sticking up for me, regardless of who she was married to.

The sound of Clara's soft snoring made me think about her and how she came to California. We'd just started having our lunch breaks together, and I'd only known her for a week or so. I told her about my mother dying and me leaving Texas after the tornado.

"I just couldn't live there anymore," I said. "Everywhere I looked, I saw her, and I hoped starting over would make me miss her less."

"Does it?"

"It does. Nothing here reminds me of her—but out of the blue I'll think about her, especially when we play music she used to listen to. Or the holidays bring back a lot of memories. I miss her laughter, and when I go to the bakery, I'm reminded of her cookies and brownies."

"I know what you're saying," Clara said.

"I still think of her all the time, but in a different context, if that makes any difference. I wish she was still alive, but there are no ghosts."

Clara chewed the inside of her cheek in thought.

"For years, my mother struggled with tuberculosis and it got worse after we moved to Atlanta. My father found a job in a furniture factory and it was amazing he didn't end up with some illness too, breathing in all that dust.

"We lived in a crowded apartment building with basically no sanitation. I quit school to work in a food processing plant, so I could contribute to the family. Once I figured out no one was keeping track of my wages, I started tucking away a little money so I could eventually leave."

"How old were you?" I'd asked.

"Sixteen."

"Eventually, my mother died, and within months, my father remarried. It happened so quickly, I couldn't help but wonder if he had someone lined up and ready to take her place. I could see he needed helping care for the seven of us, but all I saw was that he replaced my mother with someone who brought two more children into the household. Her name was Myrt, and she was a tough one."

Clara finished her meal, then burped.

"Excuse me. I eat too fast," she said.

"I do too," I admitted.

"So what made you finally make the trip to California?"

"One day, I saw Myrt when she didn't think I was looking at her, and she was pregnant. It was naïve on my part, but I couldn't believe my father had sex with her, and now there was going to be another mouth to feed. I counted my money and one day after work, I went to the train station to see how much a ticket was. I had a little more than I needed, so I bought the ticket. It was good for a month. I kind of feel bad now about how I left them. High and dry would be what I call it. I packed an old suitcase and hid it in the back of a closet, and then one day when they thought I left for work, I went directly to the station and took the next train out."

"Wasn't the trip dreadful?" I asked, recalling my own train ride.

"Let's put it this way. I'm not planning on traveling anywhere soon."

The next night, Finn was at the nightclub early, and even though we'd become close friends, I wanted to wait for him to talk to me first. He'd finished setting up, and he was sitting at a table nursing a Coke.

"I'm not going home," he said, leaning back in his chair. He let out a heavy sigh, then hunched over and rested his arms on his thighs. "I knew my mum felt like she had to make a choice between me and my stepfather. I could have left anytime, but then she'd have no one besides him. It sounds harsher than I feel, but when she made that choice, and when I made the decision to come to America, I knew I'd never be going back."

When he stood, I stepped up to hug him. Miles walked in, and in jest, said, "Hey you two."

We stepped away from each other, and when Finn laughed, I could tell in a way that some of the weight of the world had been lifted from his shoulders.

"Let's get those doors open so we can earn some tips," Miles said.

Clara met Charles Robinson in the shoe department at The May Company department store. She was looking for a new pair of T-strap high heels to wear when we went dancing, when he approached her.

"These just came in," he said, holding up a pair for her to see.

"I took one look at him, and he was so handsome, I almost fainted," she told me later. "I would have bought any shoe he showed me."

"Let's just measure your foot," he said, taking her hand and leading her to a chair.

"I could feel my heart almost beat out of my chest just waiting for him to return, and when I stepped on the measuring device, I instinctively steadied myself by touching his shoulder. He looked at my hand, then at me. He had the most gorgeous green eyes, and he actually winked at me!"

"I'll be off in about a half hour if you'd like to join me in the Tea Room upstairs. We could have coffees?"

"I tried to act nonchalant when I said, 'That sounds great, Mr. Robinson,' but I could tell I'd turned beet red. He told me to call him Charlie."

They began seeing each other on lunch breaks, and in no time, Clara was madly in love. At the time, she didn't think it odd that they never had a proper date—one in the evening where they could have dinner or see a movie. Charlie told her he had a second job in the shoe factory, and by the time he got home, he was usually exhausted.

"He told me he lived with his mother and cared for her. I thought he was a wonderful son, and I told him so.

"We used to find places where we could go to kiss, and I even let him touch me outside my blouse. We talked about what we wanted out of life, and I just knew he was the perfect man for me."

One afternoon, about three months in to their relationship, Clara stopped at the bakery across the street and bought Charlie's favorite cookies.

"I thought I'd surprise him by stopping by the shoe department after my shift. I surprised him all right, and myself, when I saw him with a woman and three small children. The youngest one was tugging on his suit coat.

'Stop it,' he told her. 'I'm working and I can't have you climbing all over me. Do you want me to lose my job?'

"I just stood there like the fool I am, and it was almost as if I couldn't move. I wanted to scream at him and tell him he was a cheat, but I couldn't find my voice. His wife looked my way and just smiled, totally oblivious to any possibility I could know her husband. I finally composed myself, then turned and left. I dropped the cookies in the trash bin just outside the store."

She paused, then said, "I hate him."

The silence that stretched between us was heavy. I wasn't sure what to say at first. My heart went out to her. While I'd never given my heart to anyone before, I could understand her feeling betrayed and foolish. A hundred thoughts went through my mind; most of all, how Charlie was a total bastard, and wondering how she hadn't realized something about their relationship was off.

I could see it in her demeanor; her self-esteem was deeply wounded, and I didn't blame her for hating him. No advice I offered would make her feel better right then, so I said, "I'm not judging you in any way. I'm here for support."

I pulled her into a hug and said, "You'll move on and eventually you'll find Mr. Right. We both will. "

The three of us did everything we could think of to cheer her up, and even though I knew time would take care of things, it was heart-wrenching to see her in pain. But like Miles before her, she eventually came around.

When she was ready, all she said was, "I was such a fool," and we didn't talk about it again.

I knew then she was going to be all right, and it was good to have her back.

Fall weather in southern California was almost perfect; warm enough to still dress lightly, with only bursts of cool air on days when you had to wear a sweater. The days grew shorter, but unless you traveled out of town, there wasn't a lot of seasonal color change. There were few deciduous trees left after so much building, however, I never stopped being amazed at how California was such a wonderment.

You could pick up any newspaper and read about how the 1920s were prosperous years for Los Angeles. The film industry became famous worldwide, job openings attracted immigration, especially from Mexico and the Midwest, and the population tripled—it became the fifth largest city in the U.S.

Soon it also became the aviation capital, and petroleum became a major industry in Long Beach, Santa Fe Springs, and Huntington Beach. Real estate boomed. With all the growth came innovation; for some, refrigerators instead of iceboxes, vacuum cleaners instead of sweepers and other electrical household appliances. On the negative side, it brought water supply issues, traffic congestion, pollution, labor unrest and segregation between the Negroes, Mexicans and Asians. It seemed the wealthy got wealthier, and the poor got poorer.

The stock market boomed, and stocks soared beyond their values. Some investors borrowed money to purchase more stock, and then panic set in when people began selling. Prices plummeted, and the market lost billions of dollars in value.

On October 29, 1929, the market crashed, and while we didn't see the shift immediately, everything was going to change. We were in The Great Depression.

You wouldn't have known it the way Los Angeles celebrated the holidays that year. The hotel was extravagantly decorated with a twelve foot tall lit Christmas tree in the lobby, plus smaller trees in each banquet room. Fresh garlands with red ribbon bows twined up the main staircase, and there were strands of lights everywhere. The four of us drew secret names for gifts, and on Christmas Eve we ate at The Highland Park Bowl. After dinner, we opened gifts and tried to guess who drew our names. The only rule was that the gifts had to be something someone would use. Miles got a new neck strap for his saxophone, Clara got a Kodak Brownie camera, Finn got a new driving cap, and I got a bottle of *Coty L'Aimant,* my favorite cologne.

We rented bowling shoes, and once a lane opened up, we bowled a foursome, and after a long ten game tie, Miles and Clara eventually won. Finn and I had to buy them desert.

The hotel never referred to them as the Mafia, or the mob, but I called them gangsters. And for New Year's Eve, they booked their private ballroom again, and like last year, all the guests had to be inside by nine; then the doors were closed and locked. Liquor was still prohibited, but it flowed freely.

We played that night in the club, and Clara spent the evening in a comfortable booth in the corner. I watched as a number of men asked her to dance, but she never obliged them. Everyone sang Auld Lang Syne, and after quick kisses, we blew party horns and in no time, the floor was covered with popped balloons.

It was after three in the morning before we got out of there and Clara had fallen asleep. We started the new year by going to the all-night diner and having our usual burgers and Cokes and afterward, Clara and I splurged and shared a root beer float.

"I guess we'll start dieting tomorrow," I said, slurping the last of the root beer.

# CHAPTER TEN

After the holidays, there was always a slowdown in guest check-ins—it was to be expected. Families that had come to town returned home, and holiday business celebrations had come to an end. Weekend registrations were also down, but the hotel kept all the decorations up throughout January in order to keep the festive atmosphere alive a while longer. In contrast, the housekeepers who took care of the full-time guests saw their work flow increase. More affluent individuals were selling their homes and opting to stay in luxurious hotels that could offer them the same comforts they were accustomed to while still keeping their cash.

At the end of January, I was promoted to the ninth floor, where two more permanent guests checked in. Mrs. Rochester in Suite 201 asked if I could remain her housekeeper since I'd been with her for so long. Management approved her request, and even though logistically it wasn't very efficient, I somehow fit her and my new guests in to my busy schedule. The reward was they all tipped me well.

Mrs. Rochester had two newspapers delivered; The Los Angeles Times, and The Wall Street Journal. It was through her I was able to skim the papers every day—I could tell she'd already read them by the way she folded and left them on the coffee table. Headlines jumped from the front pages.

## UNEMPLOYMENT REACHES 25 PERCENT!
## LOSS OF JOBS FUELS ECONOMIC DECLINE!

The paper criticized Congress of being a major contributor to the current economic downturn—when they voted in Prohibition, no one had taken into consideration the ramifications of making it a law. Alcohol taxes were a major source of revenue, and now the government was spending millions of dollars trying to enforce the law.

Farmers hadn't been able to sell their grains, distilleries and distribution lines were closed down, and unemployment was higher than it had ever been. Organized crime syndicates prospered, smuggling and selling alcohol illegally, bringing in unheard of amounts of profits, while legitimate employment opportunities and government tax revenue suffered. Corruption and violence escalated, reducing resources that could have helped ease the burden of combating the effects of The Great Depression.

The first few months of the year, I didn't see a major change in people on the street and I wondered if the depression had somehow passed us by.

But when I saw Mrs. Rochester a few days later, she asked if I'd read about the man who lost so much money in the stock market, he jumped from his lawyer's office window and landed on a car parked on Wall Street. There was my answer.


In February, our head housekeeper suddenly disappeared. Two rumors were going around; one was that she'd overheard something she shouldn't have from one of the gangsters upstairs, and the other was that she made off with a diamond necklace in the lost and found. Of course, management would never confirm either one, and within a week, we had a new head of housekeeping; a man named Henry Ellsworth. His name sounded very proper and indeed he'd originally come from England.

"Pardon me as I get to know you all," he told us with his heavy accent. "We will continue to operate without interruption. I need to be kept up to date and I want to know all details about anything you encounter that needs to be addressed. I run a tight ship, but a fair one."

In March, Clara's oldest full-time guest died in his sleep and she helped his daughters pack up his belongings. She said the way they sorted through his possessions, she was sure it was with an eye for value. They constantly bickered over even the smallest of items, and they made sure that when one got something, the other set aside something of equal value.

One night, Clara said, "When they called me into their father's bedroom, one of them held a torn envelope. The eldest daughter grumbled, 'I assume you knew about this?' I told them I had no idea what they were talking about, and truthfully, I didn't. Both girls barely hid their disdain for me; they obviously hadn't intended for their father to recognize me after his death. I refused to give them the satisfaction of watching me read the contents in front of them, so I immediately tucked the open envelope into my uniform pocket and gave them what I hoped was a quick neutral smile. After we finished packing, the first minute I was alone, I re-opened the envelope, and the only thing inside was Mr. Hopper's brief note. He thanked me for my services and I was certain they took out any money he would have left me."

Within a week, Clara was assigned to care for a husband and wife who moved into another suite. They complained about everything; how the towels weren't soft enough, how it took so long to get room service, and how they had to put most of their belongings into storage because the hotel suites weren't adequate.

"It's amazing how some people with money are so disrespectful, as though their wealth entitles them to superior treatment," she said when I saw her. "It makes me wonder how people get to be that way. Are the material things in life more important than being happy, or do they just not know the difference?"

I had to agree with her, but I was surprised at the extent of her bitterness.

In early march, I'd begun to notice a pleasant-looking man in the club. He came in by himself and always sat in booth five. He was more appealing than overly handsome, and he looked to be in his late twenties to early thirties. Sometimes he stayed for one set, and sometimes he stayed for the entire evening. He drank club soda with a twist of lime.

Over the next few weeks, he bought the four of us sodas, and we thanked him by nodding in his direction. He never came up and spoke with us, but seemed content sitting by himself. And then we didn't see him again for a while.

I rarely worked the evening shift in housekeeping, but in April, I began filling in for a girl who'd been fired for being pregnant. My twenty-first birthday was drawing near, and while no one would tell me where we were going or what they had planned for the evening, I knew something special was in the works. When I found out I was needed that night, I begged the head housekeeper, Mr. Ellsworth, to let me trade with someone else, but he wouldn't budge.

"You're the one they want," he said.

"*What?*" I asked. "Why would someone I don't know request me?"

"I have no idea, Miss Hayes. We just do as we're told. Here's the suite number, and you'll start tonight."

I knew I was being childish, but I left his office in a huff. I didn't even go home to clean up and change my uniform. Instead, I said aloud, "they're going to get me just like I am, and if they don't like it, so be it. Maybe I won't be called back."

Another woman got onto the elevator when I did, and the elevator operator turned to her, looking for direction.

"Oh, I see the floor I want is already pressed," she said, somewhat flustered.

I tried not to keep glancing at her, but I couldn't help but notice she fidgeted with her bracelets and took several deep breaths. She was pretty, and I could smell the shampoo in her freshly styled hair. She wore it in a bob, which was the current style, and her dress was fashionable and elegant. Suddenly becoming aware of my soiled apron, I turned away from her and tried to smooth it out. I picked off a crumb of something and watched it fall to the floor.

"Oh, dear, I'm going to be late. Can this go any faster?" she asked.

"No, ma'am. It's set to go at a certain speed," I said.

When the elevator stopped at a different floor, I thought she was going to burst into tears.

"We'll be there in a minute," I said calmly.

When the bell for the fifteenth floor chimed, I thought she was going to jump out of her skin. What on earth would make her so nervous? The door opened, and she frantically scrambled out, only pausing to find the number she was looking for. It seemed we were going to the same suite; number 1512.

"Here, let me," suggested, knocking. "Room Service."

Even *I* thought it took forever for someone to open the door, and then I saw him; it was the same burly man in the tight fitting suit from the lounge.

"Yeah," he said, opening the door.

"Let the girls in," someone called from inside.

I let the girl go ahead of me, hoping to keep the room full of men from staring at me. Someone came to escort her to where the bar had been set up, and then, like an idiot, I just stood there. I made a quick scan of the room, and then suddenly the nice-looking man from the nightclub was standing next to me.

Oh, dear.


"You're Charlotte, right?" he asked.

I stood, frozen. Words formed in my mind, but nothing came out. I was still processing what was going on in the room when I managed to say, "Ah, yes."

"I've seen you in the club. You have a beautiful voice."

"Yes," was all I seemed to be able to say.

"Well, I'm Joe," he said.

"Joe!" someone called to him. "Have the housekeeper come over here and clean up this mess."

I looked toward the voice and saw only a bar cart stacked with empty whiskey and wine glasses. Dirty dishes and ashtrays covered the coffee table, and the room reeked of cigars.

Gathering my wits about me, I said, "I need several room service trolleys to get all this cleared. Where's the phone?"

Joe led the way, and I called down for help.

"Someone will be here in a few minutes," I said to no one in particular.

In the meantime, the young woman who came up in the elevator with me was pretending to be interested in two men who were close to manhandling her.

I'd known more gangsters had moved into the hotel, but I'd never seen so many of them in one room. They came in all shapes and sizes, and most of them were either waving cigars in their hands or had them hanging from their mouths. I could hardly breathe.

I answered the door to two other housekeepers, whose eyes widened as they took in the room.

"Close your mouth and get in here," I whispered.

Between the three of us, we had everything loaded up and out the door within a few minutes. I wiped everything down one extra time before I asked if there was anything else they needed.

"Yeah," the voice said. "We need more refills."

"I'm not really sure where to get them," I said, feeling like an idiot. And why would I know anything about that? I wanted to ask.

"Joe, go down with her and get the stuff."

"Got it, boss."

I followed Joe out of the room and he led the way to a large hall closet where the linens were usually stored. But instead of sheets and towels, it was filled with bottles of whiskey, beer and wine, along with clean glasses. He started filling my arms with bottles and as I looked around, I said, "Aren't you afraid someone will see you with all this?"

"Nah," Joe said. "We have the entire floor."

We made several trips, getting everything set up, and I said, "You should have a cart up here. It'll make moving all this a lot easier."

"Great idea, Charlotte."

"I'll call down for an extra trolley," I said with more confidence than I felt.

The elevator chimed, announcing its arrival, and another young woman stood there, unsure where to go until she saw the open door of the suite.

I didn't like being around these men, and the women who came to the suite couldn't possibly be coming up because they found these slime balls attractive. Someone had to be forcing them, but I had to remind myself it was none of my business. And with any luck, I wouldn't have to see any of them again.

"Will that be all?" I asked the voice.

"That should do us for now. I like the way you work," he said.

I later learned that he was the boss. His name was Paulie DeGrazia, but they called him "Knuckles" because he had a reputation for resorting to violence to resolve problems.

# CHAPTER ELEVEN

I told Miles, Finn and Clara how unsettling being in Suite 1512 was. If these men were as dangerous as I'd heard, I couldn't understand how the hotel would allow them to occupy an entire floor.

"Charlotte," Miles said, as if I couldn't grasp the picture.

"I'm not completely naïve," I answered defensively.

He reached out for my shoulder and took it gently.

"I don't think you're naïve. I just think you don't see the world as it is. These guys are paying a pretty penny to stay here, and honestly, it's a way for the hotel to guarantee income while the economy rights itself. And they're everywhere; trust me, no one is turning them away. Do they like it? No. Is there anything they can do about it? No. Your best bet is to look the other way, and hope they don't want you back."

Miles' pep talk hadn't left me very reassured.

I didn't see Joe for about a week, and I secretly wished he and the others would just disappear. But one night, in he came to the club, tipping his hat to us—to me really—and he sat in his regular booth. During a break, he told the waitress to ask me to join him. I looked at the guys, and they just lifted their eyebrows.

There was something different about Joe. He wasn't like the other men in number 1512. He wasn't as rough, and he didn't seem to try to make himself out to be more than he was. If I didn't know differently, I would have described him as an attractive, mild-mannered man with a job as a salesman or something else innocuous.

"Can I buy you a soda?" he asked.

"Sure," I said, just biding time until we started another set.

"You handled yourself pretty well the other night," he said.

"It's what I was trained to do. Has the extra trolley helped?"

"In fact, it has."

Neither of us spoke for a few minutes, and then Joe asked, "Would you want to go out for coffee one night after you close up?"

Was he asking me on a date? I wasn't sure what to say. If I said yes, what would he expect of me? And if I said no, would he have me killed? I hated the thought of being around those men. Except for the terrible stories I read in the newspaper, I had no idea what they were truly capable of.

After a few sips of my cola, I said, "I really shouldn't be here sitting with a customer. I'll get into trouble."

The lights dimmed, which was the perfect time to leave him, and I didn't look back as I got back onto the stage.

Keeping my expression neutral, I said, "He's asked me out for coffee!"

Joe left before we finished playing, and I was both disappointed and relieved. When I told Clara about it that night, she shook her head and said, "Don't get involved with those guys. They're trouble."

I did go have coffee with him. Joe Calderone said his family immigrated to the states from Italy before the First World War and lived in San Pedro, California, where his father worked in the fishing industry. I hadn't heard of the town, but when he explained it was to the west of Long Beach, I had a vague idea.

"My pop went out on the boats all day, and my ma opened a bakery," he said, with a slight smile.

Knowing that, I wondered how someone could get into the kind of work he did, and when I asked him, he said, "Well, one of my uncles moved to Los Angeles and took up with a group of guys who were looking for men. The pay was good, and while he'd never tell me exactly what they did, I had a feeling it wasn't always on the up and up. I knew I didn't want to be a fisherman, so he told me to come to L.A. He was sure he could get me on. And as they say, the rest is history."

"How do you feel about it now?" I asked.

"Being in the mob wasn't what I thought I would end up doing, but my uncle was coming up in the ranks, and I followed him. I'm mostly a driver and I run errands. I don't really do any bad stuff, but I admit I witness it."

"Why don't you leave and do something better?" I asked boldly. "There have to be so many other things you can do."

"The problem with these guys is, once you're in, it's almost impossible to get out."

Joe shrugged his shoulders then. I was definitely attracted to him, but I thought he had so much more going for himself. We were in the twenty-four-hour diner. It was around two in the morning and I was exhausted from a long day and night and I yawned.

"Am I boring you?" he said, with a tweak of a smile.

"I'm sorry," I said. "I'm just tired."

"What were *your* plans growing up?"

I leaned back in the booth and hoped I hid the tears that welled up in my eyes. I still believed showing my emotions, especially to someone I didn't know, was a sign of weakness.

Joe saw the tears and reached across the table for my hand.

"I'm sorry," he said. "I didn't mean to make you unhappy."

"No, it's just that sometimes I get a little homesick and then it settles in. Just when I think I have it under control, I don't. I never know when it's going to hit me."

"If you don't want to talk about it, it's okay."

"No, I'm fine. I'm from a small town in Texas," I started. I told him about my mother dying and how after the tornado and dealing with Jasper Cook, the whackadoodle, I made the decision to come to Los Angeles. "My mother always wanted us to open a diner, but she never got the chance. So here I am, a housekeeper by day, and a nightclub singer by night."

Joe hadn't let go of my hand, and I hadn't pulled it away from him. I liked the feeling of my hand in his; I'd never let a man touch me before.

Unless Joe had to drive for his boss, he started coming in to the club regularly, and after we closed, we'd go to the diner and eat or just have coffee. He was always a gentleman, never pushing himself on me, and never suggesting we go somewhere to be alone. After Clara's failed romance, two things crossed my mind; one was that Joe was married like Clara's beau had been, and the shocking one was that I began wanting to have a place where we could go and be alone. I wasn't sure how it felt, but I thought I was falling in love.

In June, Mr. Ellsworth, the head housekeeper, told me Mr. Green, the hotel manager, wanted to see me in his office. My stomach sank as I thought of all the reasons he'd want to talk to me, and I thought for sure I was going to be let go for dating one of the guests. Management had a way of finding things like that out, and other girls had been let go for far less offenses. I began perspiring on the way to his office, and thinking that was to be the case, I tried to come up with ways I could defend my actions.

"Come in, Miss Hayes," he said as I stood in his doorway.

He took his time looking through a folder, and then he closed it.

"I see you've had a lot of recommendations in the time you've been with us," he said pleasantly. "Please come in. I didn't mean to be rude and have you stand there. Sit. Please."

As I sat, I casually wiped my upper lip, hoping he hadn't noticed.

"It looks like you're going to lose a few full-time guests."

"Are they leaving, sir?"

"Oh, no. You're being promoted. The gentlemen on the fifteenth floor have requested you to be their suite attendant, which is another way of saying you'll be responsible for not only their housekeeping duties, with assistants, of course. But you'll ensure their overall comfort, and you're already aware your sensitivity and discretion are a given, of course. You'll keep your head and eyes down. Do you understand what this means?" he asked with a smile that set my pulse racing.

I was certain I gulped.

"Yes, sir. I understand," I said.

'*I think I do,*' is more like what went through my mind. My stomach clenched when I thought about the nightclub. "Will I still be able to sing in the club?"

"Yes, the group recognizes the hotel also needs you in a different capacity, and it's what we need you to do, so yes. We might have to cut your performing hours so you can be available, but your compensation will be adequate. And the trio will just have to live without you a few nights a week. You'll have new uniforms, and you must do something with your nails," he said, looking at my hands. "Your assistants will do the actual cleaning, so the job won't be as hard on your hands."

I steadied myself on the arm of the chair as I got up to leave, and for a few seconds, I wondered if my legs were going to hold me. Somehow I made it out of Mr. Green's office, and then I stood there leaning against the hallway wall until my heart quit racing.

That evening, my first night in my new role, I knocked, and then I waited while someone came to the door and looked out the peephole. The door unlocked and the big guy who answered, unceremoniously opened the door and let me in.

About a week later, Mrs. Rochester passed away. We'd become close, or as close as a housekeeper and guest would be. She'd continued to leave me the newspapers, and sometimes if I didn't have time to glance through them while I was in her suite, I'd tuck them into my apron pocket and read them during my breaks. I felt guilty now that I hadn't made more time to spend with her, but the men in 1512 were dominating my waking hours.

Only a few days after her death, Mr. Ellsworth called me into his office again and buried under some paperwork, he found a small package for me. I looked at him and he just shrugged. It was Mrs. Rochester's love letters with a folded note tucked under the ribbon that tied them together.

"Oh," Mr. Ellsworth said, shrugging again. "And then there was this with your name on it," he said, handing me a small carved box with my name taped to it.

I knew he'd be interested in knowing what was inside it, but I took everything to the lunchroom, where I knew I'd have some privacy. I made my way to a table in the corner and rested my head on my arms in front of me. After a minute, I sat back up and took the note from her letters and read it.

*"Dearest Charlotte.*

*I can't begin to tell you how much I've appreciated the time you spent with me while I was here in the hotel. You so remind me of myself when I was young. Never let go of your dreams and never settle for less than you deserve!*

*With heartfelt thanks,*
*Adele."*

I set the letter aside, then looked at the box. An intricately carved butterfly perched on a leaf covered vine was on the top, and the vines continued to trail down the front and sides. The box was unlocked, and I wondered if Mr. Ellsworth had looked inside. I immediately saw the locket she wore every day, plus a hundred dollars, and the deed and key to a property in the town of Valley of Enchantment in California. I had no idea where that was, but I tucked the papers into one of my pockets. A little overwhelmed, I unlocked my locker and set everything inside for safekeeping.

I knew getting involved with someone like Joe Calderone could lead to disaster, but I found I thought about him every day. I felt butterflies in my stomach each time I saw him, and every time he looked at me, I thought for sure he could see inside my soul. Everything was so natural between us, and I knew I didn't want the feelings I had for him to stop. Despite my lack of worldly experience, I could tell he cared about me because he was so kind and sweet. He wasn't at all like the men he worked for. He held my hand as we walked to the diner in the wee hours of the morning, and we'd sit across the table from each other with our fingers touching. Sometimes if the wind blew my hair, he'd stop walking and tuck a loose strand behind my ear the way Moira did the last time I saw her. When he did that, the way he looked at me, I thought for certain he'd kiss me. But he didn't. It was as though he was two different men. I'd never seen what I'd assumed could be a rough side of him, just the normal, regular Joe side.

The first time I saw his 1927 LaSalle, I figured he made good money working as a gangster. Sometimes he'd drive us to Venice Beach, where we'd sit under an umbrella in the sand. Or we'd walk the pier in Santa Monica, eating food from the local food carts. After one such afternoon at the pier, Joe took my hand while we drove home, but instead of driving me back to my apartment, he took a detour. I knew what was going to come next, and the anticipation made my heart race. I knew this was what I wanted, and yet I was filled with excitement and the fear of the unknown.

"Are you okay?" Joe asked.

"Yes," I said, squeezing his hand.

His apartment building was in a nice neighborhood, and when we pulled up, I waited in the car while he came around to open my door. I took his hand and stepped up onto the curb, taking a deep breath of the warm summer air.

'I can do this,' I said to myself.

His apartment was not as bad as I'd expected for a bachelor, and one advantage was that he didn't have to share it with roommates like I did. I waited in the doorway while he gathered stacks of papers and put them and other folders into a desk drawer. A crocheted afghan rested on the back of his couch.

"Is someone a needle worker?"

Joe looked up at me and then toward the couch.

"Oh. . . yes, my grandmother. She makes one for everyone." He seemed a little flustered as he cleaned off his kitchen counter.

"I didn't plan this, as you can see. Otherwise, I would have had the maid come in."

I laughed nervously.

"Okay, you may now enter," he said, waving me into the front room. "Coke or water?"

"I'm fine. Can we leave the door open to air out the room?"

"Sure. I'll even open the windows."

I set my things down on a side chair and watched as he wrestled with a stuck window, and I was glad he was a little nervous, too.

Once he settled down, he turned the radio on, and we sat for a few minutes just listening to Bing Crosby singing *After You've Gone*. I hummed along with it and Joe pulled me to my feet.

"Dance with me," he said, holding me tight against him.

I thought for sure he could feel my heart racing as we swayed to the music. When the music stopped, he held my chin in his with his fingers, and gently kissed me. I thought I'd died and gone to heaven. We danced to one more tune, and then he led me to the bedroom. It smelled of his aftershave, and I smiled.

I was curious and yet self-conscious as he undressed me. I felt exposed but at the same time, eager to have him hold me in his arms. He'd obviously been with other women, for he knew what to do, and the outside world seemed to fade as every touch deepened the connection between us. I saw tenderness as our eyes locked and as our kisses lingered, his caresses took me to a place I'd never imagined.

Afterward, we lay in each other's arms and eventually I heard the evenness of Joe's breathing as he slept. Had I just given myself to the devil's cunning, sinister partner?

# CHAPTER TWELVE

Had Clara been there when Joe dropped me back off at our apartment, I knew what we'd done would have been written all over my face. But mercifully, she wasn't home. I took a shower and then got ready for the afternoon shift on the fifteenth floor. As it had turned out, they'd now wanted me on Friday and Saturday nights, so I'd had to accept the fact Miles and Finn found another singer for those days. We made the most money on the weekends, but there wasn't anything I could do about it for now. I had to remind myself I was making a lot more money in tips from the gangsters, but it was the music I missed.

I'd met the new singer, and I wanted to hate her. She was blonde and slender, and she had a lovely voice. Miles & Finn promised me they'd let me back in if things ever changed with my schedule. I knew in my heart there was more for me than being the steward of Suite 1512. The gangsters couldn't stay there forever.

Saturday evenings were the most demanding, and for the next month, it seemed all I did was order food, ice, and clean tablecloths. My girls took away dirty glasses, brought in clean ones, and emptied ashtrays throughout the evening. They replaced the empty bottles of whisky, beer and wine, and gave me an accounting of what was left in the closet so I could order more. We did what we were told, always keeping our eyes and heads down. We were *nobodies*; ghosts in a room filled with rowdy men. When they wanted female companionship, I called downstairs to the bellboy and told him what they were looking for. "I need a blonde," I'd say, or "I need two girls that look young." I was disgusted.

Joe and I kept our distance when we were anywhere at the same time, yet every minute we had before or after work, we spent at his apartment. We made a pact to never discuss what he did or what I saw—it was as if we had secret lives tucked away and out of sight.

I eventually told Clara about us, and she did her best to not criticize me for being so careless with my heart. I told Miles and Finn too; I could tell they also disapproved, by the way they looked at me. Somehow, our little foursome had tilted on its axis, but I wasn't willing to stop seeing Joe.

It seemed like all I did was work. Even with my crazy schedule, I was still called on to fill in when one of the other housekeepers was sick. I was making really good money, but I was suffering from not enough sleep and the stress of not knowing what was going to happen next in Suite 1512. At any given time, fights broke out, and when things escalated, battered bodies were hauled from the room. I'd even had one of my assistants take a girl away to get medical help; apparently she wasn't doing what one of the thugs wanted, and he hauled off and slugged her. She was terrified, and I was disgusted and frightened out of my wits.

"How do you stand for this?" I'd asked Joe.

"I hate it too," he admitted, "but there's nothing I can do."

"You can get out of there," I said bitterly.

"Sad to say, I can't," he sighed. "You can't just walk away."

I took his arm and made him look at me.

"Tell me why you can't leave and have a happy, healthy life."

His shoulders slumped and his eyes remained downcast; he wouldn't even look at me.

They'd gone too far again and yet I agreed with Joe; there really wasn't much we could do. Whether I'd meant to be involved or not, I was. Even though I kept my head down, they knew I'd seen and heard things I shouldn't have, and I knew they watched.

I hated what I was doing, but until I could find another job, I was stuck. I'd have to bide my time, and I knew eventually I'd figure something out. In the meantime, I continued being the ghost in the room, and I kept my eyes down, but my ears open.

One day, Mr. Ellsworth said he needed me to fill in for one of the girls who didn't show up for work. He sent me to clean a room and deliver food to a smaller suite on the fifth floor.

They'd ordered lunch, and when it was ready, I took the trolley up. I knocked and said "Room Service" and a young woman wearing a maid's uniform answered the door.

"With all this food, you must be hungry," I said, lightly.

I removed the pewter cloches and stacked them to the side as I set the table with hamburgers, French fries, and chocolate milkshakes.

"I'm starving," a young boy said, deciding which plate was his.

"They're all alike," the older of the girls impatiently said. "Just take one."

"Where are you all from?" I asked, as I turned to leave.

"Seattle, Washington," the older girl said.

"We're here visiting my aunt," the youngest girl said.

I waited a moment, wondering if they knew to leave a tip, and then said, "Well, enjoy your lunch."

Rich people didn't necessarily have good parenting skills. They should have told the children to have some cash on hand for necessities. There went twenty-five cents. And where were the parents? The girl who answered the door looked old enough to be on her own, but what about the other three?

At dinnertime, I had another order to deliver, and I hoped they'd figured the tip situation out.

I got to the room and called, "Room Service" and the same young woman answered. This time, she appeared to be by herself. There was only one plate, and when I set it out and uncovered it, I was surprised it was a turkey sandwich, cut fruit and a root beer.

"Are you on your own?" I asked, trying to be friendly. "I'm Charlotte."

"I'm Ruth Ann, but everyone calls me Ruthie. Yes. The children—well, they're not really children—have gone down to have dinner with their parents. It's my place to stay here in the room."

"Do you wear your uniform all the time?"

"Yes, that's expected," she said, smoothing out her apron.

"Hmm," I said. "Of course, I have to wear mine when I work, but I have time off every day."

"So do I, but I live in the house with the family, so I'm always on call if there's an emergency."

"That must be hard."

"I'm used to it. I've been working there since I was ten."

"Ten? Good grief. How old are you now?"

"I'll be seventeen in a month. I've heard some girls eventually leave their families to marry, but I don't have any prospects. And my mother has worked for them for ages."

"What's the family like?" I asked, now curious.

"Well," she thought for a minute. "I mostly have the children to care for; the missus is okay, I suppose, but she keeps an eye on me. The mister. . . ," and there she stopped.

"Oh, my gosh!" I said. "You've turned absolutely red!" I went to her and touched her arm—something I would never have done to a guest. "Are you all right?"

Suddenly, she couldn't control herself, and she burst into tears.

"I don't know what's come over me," Ruth cried. "I really don't."

It only took me a few moments to figure it out.

"Well, I do. Does anyone know this? Your mother? Anyone in the household?"

"No. And I can't do anything about it or I'll certainly be let go."

"My god, Ruth. This is not good at all."

I hugged her, and she cried harder.

"We've got to do something about this, before it's too late," I then said. "Let me put my thinking cap on. Will you still be here tomorrow?"

"Yes, we're here for a few more days."

"Here," I said, handing her a napkin. "Blow your nose and splash cold water on your face so you won't look like you've been crying when they get back. In the meantime, try to eat your dinner. It could be your last one here."

At noon the next day, there was another order for Ruth's room. She burst into tears the minute she opened the door.

"Talk to me," I said, sitting her down on one of the beds.

"I should have come forward when he first came to me, but I misunderstood the emotions I felt. And I couldn't risk my mother and me losing our jobs. Even worse, no one would have believed me."

Ruth was sobbing, and I went to the bathroom to wet a washcloth. Ruth put it to her forehead.

"I was ashamed, and I still am. If I'd been honest with myself, I wouldn't have been such a coward. But he came to me last night when he thought the children were out and it was awful. I told him it had to stop."

"How did he take *that?*"

"Not too well. He threw me against the wall and I fell to the floor. I was just getting up when the children came back. He told them he'd brought me money for room service tips and that I'd dropped it. I confirmed I was just bending down to pick it up when I lost my balance. In my heart, I knew I was heading towards a dead end, but I wasn't sure how I was going to find any answer to my dilemma."

Ruthie had been trapped in that house for years. She covered her face and began crying again. I didn't know what to do. Eventually, she stopped and wiped her face.

And then she said, "I'm going to have to think of something. I can't go back."

I didn't have my plan completely formed yet, but I said, "Then come with me. I have an idea."

She had nothing else but her uniform to wear, so we put her undergarments, toothbrush and hair brush into a pillowcase. I put the food back on to the trolley and we pushed it to the elevator. On the ground floor, she followed me down the hall to the kitchen.

"Stay here," I said. "No one will say anything, and as soon as I'm off, we'll leave."

Her mind must have been racing, because mine was. What if the children came back, and she wasn't in the room? Her extra uniforms were still in the closet, but everything else of hers was gone. They would most likely say something to their parents later when they went down for dinner. Would they just think she'd be there when they got back to the room?

Ruth said they weren't due to leave for Seattle for a few more days, but we'd be long gone by then.

"Should I have left a note?"Ruth asked when I came back to get her.

"Are you crazy? And what would you have said?"

"I'm worried about my mother," she said, the beginning of tears welling up in her eyes. "There's no way I can contact her without the staff knowing where I am."

I had no idea what would happen to her mother when the family returned home without her, but I couldn't tell Ruth that. So I said, "Everything will work out fine. Mothers have instincts and hers will tell her you're all right."

I hoped I was right.

"I have no money," she said as we left the hotel.

"I just got my check, and tomorrow I'll cash it before we leave. We'll be okay. I've packed us something for dinner," I said. "We're going to my apartment for tonight. Then, tomorrow we're going on a trip."

"I have nothing to wear."

"You'll be fine. I have plenty of things you can try on."

"Ruthie is coming with us," I announced when Clara came home. "She's a real servant, and she's run away from her master."

Clara's eyes widened, and I cringed.

"I hope you don't mind," I said awkwardly.

Brushing away her surprise, and seeing the tray of food, Clara said warm-heartedly, "You know, any friend of yours is a friend of mine. What did you bring for dinner? I'm starving."

And then it was settled.

# CHAPTER THIRTEEN

We unpacked roast beef, mashed potatoes, vegetables, and some chocolate cake and served ourselves at our small kitchen table. Afterward, we listened to The Lone Ranger and Guy Lombardo's band on the radio, while Ruth tried on several dresses I handed her. At first, she hovered near the Cheval mirror, hesitant. But then as she started trying on dresses, her eyes caught her own reflection and I tried not to laugh aloud as a giggle escaped and I realized Ruth never expected to feel this good.

She touched the fabrics and said, "I haven't worn anything but my uniform for almost eight years. Putting on a soft dress like this feels like silk."

Clara went through her jewelry box and found a pair of drop earrings and then handed Ruth one of her hats.

"Here, try this on," she said.

It suited Ruth perfectly.

"You should cut your hair," Clara suggested.

Instinctively, she reached to touch her hair, which she wore in a bun at the back of her neck..

"It would certainly change my look, wouldn't it?" she said, turning her head in their mirror.

"We can see if there's a shop that can do it when we get there," I said.

"And that reminds me, where exactly are we going?" Ruth asked.

"You'll see. You'll love it," I answered. "Try these shoes on. They look like they'll fit."

They were black T-Bars, with straps that traveled up to meet her ankles, and they fit perfectly. She turned every which way, and I could tell she liked what she saw. Even if the family saw her leaving, they'd never recognize her.

"And to finish it off, here's a pearl necklace," I said.

"These aren't real, are they?" she asked, surprised.

"Of course not, silly," Clara said.

"Well, I don't know about you two, but I'm tired. And we need to get up early to be ready for the guys," I said, handing Ruth a set of sheets and a blanket for the couch. "Our roommates won't mind if we have an overnight guest."

In the morning, we packed a basket with sandwiches, and before we went downstairs, I found a long coat for Ruth to wear. She put it on and looked at herself in the mirror again; it was obvious she loved the luxury of all her new clothes, even if they might just be temporary. We waited outside a few minutes, and when Finn and Miles drove up in Finn's car, the three of us girls crammed into the back seat like canned sardines.

"I need to stop and cash my check," I said to Finn.

After stopping at the bank, we drove for two hours before we turned on to Waterman Canyon, a narrow winding road leading up a mountainside. Immediately we saw, on the mountainside, contrasting vegetation that framed what was a near perfect arrowhead that looked like it had been carved into the mountain.

"It's pointing to the hot springs," I said.

"Where are we?" Ruth finally asked.

"You'll see."

We pulled into a turnout that overlooked the valley below and parked the car. Finn and Miles got out first and stretched, then they opened our doors and took the picnic basket to a table. Finn got thermoses and mason jars from the chest on the fold down luggage rack, while Clara and I set out our lunch.

"French 75 anyone?" Finn asked, pouring a gin and champagne mixture into our drink jars.

Once we finished lunch, we packed everything back up and continued to our destination. A little over two miles up the hill, Finn turned onto a dirt road and we created quite a bit of dust. I was glad we weren't in an open car, or I would have been sneezing my head off. We came up to the twenty-five foot wide arched entry built of granite boulders to the sign that said "Arrow Head." A statue of an Indian pointed the way.

Up ahead stood the magnificent white hotel, and as we drove closer, we could see cars waiting in line to let their passengers off. As before, uniformed bellhops greeted them and took their luggage up the steps to the lobby. We weren't planning on staying at the hotel, so we bypassed the parking attendants and found a spot in the shade not too far from the entrance.

"We'll go in acting like we belong here," Miles said, leading the way. He took Clara's arm, and they walked ahead of us.

To the left, guests waited at the reservation station, and to our right, more guests sat in clusters of sofas and chairs deep in conversation.

"Have you been here before?" Ruth asked.

"Oh yes," I said. "We've come here and had drinks on the outdoor patio. It's fun to pretend we have the money to stay here, and no one even bothers to question us."

Miles pulled chairs out so we could sit around a table with a large umbrella coming up from the center. No sooner had we sat, then an attendant, complete with a white bar towel draped over his arm, stood awaiting our order.

"We'll all have French 75s," he said confidently.

"Certainly, sir."

"We'll have one drink, and then we can walk to the hot springs," I said. "You'll be amazed at how warm the water is."

We sat and watched guests come and go, and once we headed towards the springs, a smell of rotten eggs filled the air.

"*What is that?*" Ruth asked, plugging her nose.

"It's the hot springs," Miles said. "It's the minerals."

"Phew," she said. "I wouldn't want to soak in something that smells so bad."

But there were people in various stages of either getting in or out of the water, or sitting in it waist deep.

Done with our tour, I pulled Ruth aside and said, "You know, this might be a perfect place for you to get a job. I've heard famous actors like Charlie Chaplin, Buster Keaton, and even Marion Davies and William Randolph Hearst come to stay. We should ask the manager to speak with someone."

"Oh, I don't know. . ." she started.

"Well, you can't go back now," I reminded her.

I grabbed Ruth's hand and literally pulled her toward the patio entrance to the lobby.

"Let me find out who you can talk to."

A few minutes later, we were standing in front of the head housekeeper, Mrs. Schmidt.

"Well, you look presentable enough," she said, tilting her head. "And your friend says you've been a maidservant for eight years? You must have started when you were a baby."

"Yes ma'am," Ruth said. "I mean, no ma'am. I was ten."

"And why aren't you serving the family now?" she asked, I thought warily.

"Well," Ruth began.

"They no longer needed her to be in charge of the children. They've all grown up," I said quickly.

"I see."

"We're on our way up to Lake Arrowhead right now to answer an ad for help."

"I see," Mrs. Schmidt said again. "Well, let me look in my book to see what we have available." With this, she sat back down at her desk and opened a record book. With one finger, she went line by line, before she looked up.

"I think we might have something for you, then. Do you have a place to stay?"

"Not yet, ma'am. I'm just newly from Seattle," Ruth said.

"Hmm," she said thoughtfully. "I believe we have a shared room that's available. Can you get along with a fellow member of the staff?"

"I'm sure I can, ma'am."

Mrs. Schmidt's mouth twisted in thought.

"If you'd like, we can check back in after we make it up to Arrowhead. Ruth will know then where she'd rather work," I said.

"There's not another place like this up here, so I know she'll do better here."

I worried I'd pushed too hard and then Ruth said, "It was very nice to meet you, Mrs. Schmidt." She extended her hand, but Mrs. Schmidt didn't take it.

"You can have the job, then. The pay is fifty cents an hour, minus five dollars a month for your room. And you can start the day after tomorrow."

Ruth just about floated out of there.

We found the others outside by the car. Miles had just lit a cigarette and wanted to finish it before we took off.

"How'd it go?" he asked.

"I got the job!" Ruth blurted. "Or, rather, Charlotte got me the job!"

"Well, she had to have liked you or no matter what I said, she wouldn't have hired you," said.

"Still," Ruth said, hugging me. "I don't know how I can ever thank you."

"Buy me an ice cream when we get to Lake Arrowhead."

"It's a deal."

As we continued to climb the winding road up the mountain, I could hear the strain of Finn's engine.

"I hope we don't get stranded up here somewhere," Ruth whispered. "Thankfully, there aren't a lot of cars on the road, going either up or down the narrow road, but I still worry we'll end up going over the side of the road and tumbling down to our deaths."

"You're a worry wort," I said.

Then I could see it in her face—the reeling from side to side when Finn didn't anticipate the bends in the road were making Ruth look sickly.

"I don't know if it was the alcohol I drank or the heat, but I know if we don't stop the car, I'm going to throw up," she said.

"Finn, can you pull over at the next stop?" I asked. "Ruth is feeling queasy from the drive."

"Hell's bells," Finn said. "Hang on there."

"Breathe deeply," I said.

We came to a turnout and pulled over. Clara opened her door, and it wasn't too soon. Before Ruth got all the way out, she threw up.

"Yowza!" Finn said.

I got out and got some napkins from the picnic basket and went to Ruth.

"Are you all right?"

"I think I am now. I've never drank before, or driven on such a winding road. And I do feel better. I'm so sorry." Embarrassment replaced the greenish hue on her face.

"I brought a jug of water in case I needed it for the radiator," Finn called out from the front seat. "It's in the chest if you want some."

"That would be wonderful."

For the rest of the trip, we let Ruth sit by the window, and in no time, she drifted off to sleep.

I'd forgotten how the highway scenery evolved as the elevation changed, and soon, more and more pine trees towered above us. All I could see on the mountain slope, though, were white cottony clouds that hid the valley below.

"Look at that," I said to no one in particular.

We passed several turn offs before we turned left towards Lake Arrowhead. We'd seen a sign along the road that said "Cabins for Rent" and headed in that direction. I was hoping they were the same ones we rented when we'd come up before. Ruth woke as we pulled into the gravel drive to the identical series of log cabins built among the trees. We were all ready to stretch our legs, and the fresh air invigorated me. The shade of the early afternoon cooled the air, and I took in a deep breath and closed my eyes. I could feel *and* hear the wind blowing in the trees, and then I heard a slight crunching sound. When I opened my eyes and looked up, I saw the cutest squirrel looking down on me, casually munching on something he held between his two front paws.

And then an overly enthusiastic dog bounded up to greet us.

"Mabel," her owner called from the cabin office. He took his hat off and scratched his head. "Get back here."

But the dog only barked and jumped, hoping to get a look at the squirrel in the tree.

"It isn't as though she's never seen critters before. Get back here."

"She's a happy girl," I said.

Mabel tilted her head at the sound of my voice.

"C'mere," I said.

She ran back towards me and almost knocked me down.

"That's a good girl," I said, patting her back.

Miles and Clara followed the owner into the office to make arrangements for our stay. Finn, Ruth, and I waited outside. It wasn't long before they came back out, and Miles said, "The guys get one cabin, and the girls get the other."

The air had turned even chillier, and I remembered my coat was still in the car.

"Does anyone need anything?" I called before got it and closed the car door.

"Bring my coat too," Ruth said.


Our cabins oozed with the mountain charm I remembered from before. The walls were made of logs, and the fireplace took up one wall.

There was one bed, which Clara and I would share, and Miles brought in a cot for Ruth. He put some logs on the grate, then got a fire started.

"You girls will have to make sure the fire is lit during the night, so you don't freeze," he said. "I'll bring in more wood from the porch."

We'd finished putting our things away, and when it started getting dark, I wondered about dinner. I was hungry and relieved when Finn soon knocked on our door.

"Is anyone else hungry?"

"I am," Clara said.

We found a small diner down the road and ordered two roast beef meals for the five of us to share. Our waitress barely hid her disdain when we asked for another basket of bread and butter to help fill us up.

"Will you be having dessert, then?" she asked as she took away our plates.

"I'm full," Miles said. "What about you girls?"

"I'm good," we all said at once.

When she left, Finn said, "There's a corner store across the street. What say we stop in there and get some cookies and sodas?"

When we got back to the cabins, Miles and Finn pulled Adirondack chairs into a circle around the fire pit. Clara and I went into our cabin and brought out blankets.

"These are like the chairs we saw at that hotel," I said. "They look clunky, but the way they slant back makes them comfortable, even if they're made of wood."

The boys gathered wood and lit the fire, and we all sat as close as we could so we could keep each other warm. In the dark, our faces glowed red and Miles said, "Why don't we tell ghost stories?"

I hated the idea, but Miles started. As he spoke, I could hear the tree branches move, and I swore I heard a rustling in the bushes in front of us. I knew it wasn't ladylike, but I pulled my knees up to my chest and wrapped myself tighter in my coat and blanket.

"Something's out there," I whispered.

Miles stopped talking and looked from side to side. Then he howled like a dog, and we all jumped. He and Finn cracked up. But when the bushes rustled again, they stopped laughing. We all watched in silence, and then we cried out as a dog came running out to where we were.

"Mabel," the cabin owner yelled. "Git over here! You liked to scare these kids half to death!" He gently grabbed the dog by the collar and pulled her towards him. "Sorry about that. She's out for her evening constitutional. Now don't you kids forget to put dirt over the fire when you're ready to hit the sack. We don't want no forest fires tonight."

The next morning, Miles and Finn borrowed a couple of fishing poles from Mr. Maynard. He told them about a campground where there were plenty of fish, but they promised to take us to the village first. They patiently waited outside for us while we made our way through all the stores. First on the list was the Candyland Candy Store, and it was filled with more types of candy than I'd ever imagined. When I told Ruth I'd treat her to a piece, she had a difficult time deciding what to buy.

We all went into the haberdashery called Brooks Brothers, and the guys looked at clothing they'd never wear: button-down shirts, silk ties and suits. A store filled with preserves and cheeses smelled absolutely delicious when we walked in, but their prices were outrageous. There was a tea store, and after we saw the price tags in a lady's clothing store, decided they catered to more wealthy clients.

Ruth cried, "I think I've died and gone to heaven," when we stepped into the bookshop called Books & Co. I watched as she ran her fingertips over rows and rows of new books, and then she found the used books, where their woody smell filled the air. She closed her eyes and took in a deep breath. And then she saw a copy of *The Swiss Family Robinson* and pulled it to her chest. I thought she was going to cry.

"May I help you?" asked a stout older man who must have been the bookseller.

"Oh," she started. "I can't believe I've found this. I lost my copy. . ."

"How much is it?" I asked as I came to stand beside her.

"It's one dollar," he said. "It's a classic, you know."

"I'll get it for you," I said, looking through my purse.

"I can't let you do that. I don't know how I'll ever pay you back for everything you've done for me already."

"It's my treat," I said. "And you'll figure out a way."

She didn't know what to say, so she just stood there, holding on to that book, like it was the most valuable thing she'd ever owned.

We drove around the lake until we found the beach on the north shore. Miles and Finn unloaded the basket filled with the sandwiches we'd made, and then they headed for the wooden dock, where they started setting up their fishing gear. The three of us girls set up our lunch on the picnic table opposite the dock. When we were ready, we called the guys, and we ate like we'd been starving.

"I swear it's the mountain air," Miles said.

After lunch, the guys went back to fishing, and about an hour later, they came back with four fish, and Ruth asked, "How will you keep them from smelling? We don't have a way to cook them, and I don't even like fish."

"We'll give them to Mr. Maynard. He'll find a use for them," Miles said.

By the time we'd finished our lunch, I could feel my skin growing tender and pink, and I was ready to leave. Once we packed everything up, we kept driving the road around the lake until we made our way back to the cabins. Mr. Maynard was delighted to get the fish, and once Mabel sniffed the bucket and determined she wasn't interested, she followed him into the office.

"I'll have it tonight," Mr. Maynard said, turning to face us. But then he turned to Ruth. "Did you ladies have a good day?"

She turned beet red, and I answered, "We did."

Once inside our cabin, I said, "I think he has eyes for you."

"Oh, don't be silly. He's older than Mr. Fletcher, who is old enough to be my father."

The next morning, after a quick breakfast of peanut butter and jelly sandwiches, we checked out and made our way back down the hill. Ruth hadn't bothered applying at the hotel on the lake, deciding instead on the big white hotel instead. She'd start work the next morning, and was looking forward to getting settled in.

"I had a wonderful time," she said as we drew closer.

"That was the plan," I said, squeezing her hand. "You deserve a much better life than what you had, and I think you'll find it here."

"How will I get the dress back to you? And how will I repay you for the book?"

"Consider them my gifts to you. If a friend can't help another friend, then what are they good for?"

"I hope we see each other again," she said, and tears filled her eyes.

"You'll be fine. Here's my address," I said, writing it on a piece of paper. "Let me know how you're doing, and assuming you can get mail, I'll let you know if we plan another trip up. How does that sound?"

"I can't thank you enough, Charlotte," she said. Then she turned to Clara, Miles and Finn and said, "You guys too."

We eventually pulled into the driveway of the hotel, and Miles pulled in under the canopy to let her off. When a bellman came to open my door, Miles got out and said, "We've got it."

She gave him a quick hug and said, "Thank you for bringing me along."

"I'm glad you had a good time."

He honked as we drove away.

# CHAPTER FOURTEEN

Curiosity got the better of me when I came back to work that next afternoon, and I asked around until I found the housekeeper who regularly cleaned Ruth's suite.

"I was off a couple of days," I said casually. "How's the family?"

"Oh my," the girl said. "You wouldn't believe this, but their maid disappeared! Either someone kidnapped her or she just up and left."

"You're kidding me." I said, feigning surprise. "Were you there? Did they say anything?"

"I never saw the parents, but the children were quite upset. They've gone home now. But isn't that the strangest thing?"

"Wow," I said. As an afterthought asked, "I don't suppose they left a tip?"

"You'd have thought they would have, being it wasn't our fault and all. But no, they didn't."

"Well, in all the uproar, they just probably forgot," I said. I turned to leave and then said, "Have a good day."

Almost two months later, I received a letter from Ruth.

She said working at the hot springs was demanding; the guests were snobby, and they didn't tip well. She told me she'd discovered she was pregnant only a week after she started working, and how she'd been let go from her job when the head housekeeper confronted her about it.

*"Knowing my days were numbered, once I understood why I hadn't been feeling well, I befriended a young man who regularly made deliveries up to the hotel in Lake Arrowhead. I couldn't stay at the hot springs, and I knew he liked me. He was crestfallen when he realized why I'd been interested in him, and I felt dreadful when I persuaded him to let me hide in his truck and help me find Mr. Maynard's cabins where we stayed that night. I had a hard time remembering which road we were on, and yet, once I recognized the turn in the road, we figured out where they were.*

*"The minute I got out of the truck, I realized Mr. Maynard might turn me away since I was by myself, but when Mabel barked and came running up to me, I knew I'd be welcomed. And when Mr. Maynard came out to see what the ruckus was all about, I could tell by the smile on his face he recognized me. He said I could stay as long as I wanted."*

She'd quickly found a housekeeping job working for Vivian Hayes, an actress who lived in the mountains when she wasn't filming. About a month after she started, Ms. Hayes told her she had to go back to Los Angeles for a new film. By then, Ruth's pregnancy was obvious, but the actress reassured her she wasn't being fired because of it. Once the film was finished, she hoped that Ruth would be able to come back to work.

*"I was so distraught when her driver, Patrick, saw me crying. He told me he knew a place that would probably hire me, even if I was going to have a baby. He took me to a remote area with very few houses, and then when we rounded the bend, this large English-style building appeared. He left me in the car while he went inside to talk with someone, and then he came to get me. He told me they'll take me on. I was so relieved, I started to cry again.*

*"When I told Mr. Maynard, he exploded. He told me that the place was a speakeasy and that they ran a gin mill up there. How was I to know? I*

*had suspicions by then he'd figured out I was pregnant, and he asked me
if the boys did this to me, obviously referring to Miles and Finn. Feeling
like I owed him the truth, I told him everything about Mr. Fletcher and
meeting you, and you bringing me up to the mountains in the first place.
"He told me for now to just settle in and eventually everything would
work out for me. Honestly, Charlotte, I'm not sure how it will, but I'll do
what Mr. Maynard suggests and see what happens.*

*"With Love, Ruth Landry"*

Suite 1512 was quiet that next week, and I finally had a chance to
catch a breath. I figured they'd gone somewhere else to cause trouble.
I still had to check the room twice a day, and I should have told Mr.
Ellsworth I had some extra time if anyone needed me, but I didn't.

Clara had already told me about her newest full-time guest, Vivica
Alden, a well-known actress who was recovering from an accident. She'd
been filming when part of the set lighting fell, hitting her in the face,
causing her to fall and break her arm. Her injuries had healed enough
for her to be released from the hospital, but she refused to go into a
rehab facility. Instead, she checked into the hotel and all her doctors
visited her there.

Ms. Alden was insistent that no one could see her without her veil
to cover the scar on her face, but I was dying to meet a real actress, so
I asked Clara if I could go with her to clean the suite. Although they'd
developed a rapport, she told me she'd have to ask first. When Clara told
Ms. Alden she could use the extra help, the actress had agreed.

I was almost as nervous about meeting her as I was working around
the gangsters, and when I knocked on her door, I wasn't surprised it was
Clara who answered. When I saw it was her, just her smile put me more
at ease.

Vivica Alden was a trim woman, and although I couldn't see her
face, I remembered it from watching her movies. Her soft looking hands
went to her veil, and her slender manicured nails told me immediately
she hadn't done a load of laundry or cleaned sinks in years.

"Clara, can you order us some tea?" Ms. Alden asked.

"Certainly," Clara said, calling down for room service.

When the trolley arrived, Ms. Alden said, "Why don't you girls sit with me for a minute before you get to work?"

I looked at Clara, and she nodded.

"So, Charlotte, I understand there are gangsters in the hotel and that you service their rooms," she said matter-of-factly.

I hadn't seen that one coming.

"Ah, yes," I said, obviously surprised. "They're off on adventures this week, and I had some free time. I knew Clara could always use an extra hand, so I offered to help her out."

"Well, I *am* a lot of work, aren't I Clara?" Ms. Alden asked pleasantly.

"Not at all," Clara said. "You're one of my favorite guests."

"See, that's the actress in me. I don't let you, or anyone but my doctors, know how I really feel being cooped up here."

Without thinking, I asked, "Why don't you get out and get some sunshine? It's a beautiful day."

"I'm guessing Clara hasn't told you I don't seem to be able to leave my room lately. Absolutely no one can see my face and the terrible scar I have. Sometimes I don't even let my doctors see me. Of course, they know what I look like."

I wasn't sure what to say, so I said nothing.

"You'll like my doctors. One comes for physical therapy, and the other comes to try to heal my mind. To talk me into doing things I don't want to do."

I loved her spunk.

"I think Dr. Howard has a crush on our Clara."

Seeing Clara's blush, I hoped to change the subject. I said, "Well, where do we start?"

Clara gathered our cups and set them back on the trolley. I opened the door so she could leave it outside the door. Then we went into the bedroom to change the sheets and straighten up the bathroom.

When we came out with the sheets and linens, Ms. Alden was sitting in a chair by the window. She seemed to be lost in her own world. I couldn't imagine being her. Here she was, a famous actress—she couldn't leave the hotel room, and now she'd probably never act again.

We were rearranging newspapers and other reading materials when there was a knock at the door. Clara looked through the peephole, then unlocked the door to let a man in.

"Ah, here's Dr. Howard now," Ms. Alden said. "Trying more brainwashing today."

Dr. Howard looked at Clara, and it was so obvious he was taken by her.

"This is my friend Charlotte," Clara said.

He reached for my hand and shook it.

"Pleased to meet you," he said.

"Well," Clara said, "that's our cue to leave."

"Oh, Clara," the doctor asked, "can I have a word before you go?"

"Certainly," Clara said.

They went outside into the hallway for a few minutes, and when she returned, her face was flushed.

"Dr. Howard," Ms. Alden said to him, "and here I thought you were here to see me."

To me, she said "The next time we meet, maybe you can tell me more about the gangsters. I find them quite fascinating."

"Say it ain't so," I said as we left the suite.

"Well, a man's entitled to some personal life, and I kind of like him."

"Oh, my god! Why haven't you said anything?"

"I didn't want you feeling bad after Joe and all."

"Come on. I think I haven't seen the last of Joe. We're just taking a break."

"He asked me to meet him tonight after work. It'll be our first date."

"Oh, Clara. I'm really happy for you!"

"Well, don't jinx it. We haven't even kissed yet."

"And thanks for letting me meet Ms. Alden. She got quite a personality."

When Clara got home from her date that night, she was practically walking on air. She was radiant, almost glowing, and she smiled to herself as she told me about the evening.

"We went to a Chinese restaurant in Chinatown, and I tried to eat with chopsticks. I made a mess of it, but Dr. Howard, I mean Robert, just laughed at me, which made me laugh, which made it even harder to eat. He's wonderful Charlotte. I'm trying not to read too much into it, since it was our first date and all, but I can tell he likes me."

"Well, it's obvious how you feel about him," I said, caught up in some of her excitement.

"He doesn't make me feel I'm beneath him because I'm a housekeeper, and he respects my opinions when he asks me about Ms. Alden. He's so handsome, and now I'm nervous to see him when he comes to visit again."

Suddenly, her face dropped, and she flopped down on the couch.

"What is it?" I asked frantically. She'd done such an about face, my heart skipped a beat. "Are you all right?" I sat next to her and took her hand.

"Where can this possibly go? How could a doctor marry a housekeeper?"

I thought Clara was going to burst into tears.

"Oh, Clara," I said, now understanding what she was thinking. "Doctors are just people too, and he's already told you he respects your thoughts and opinions. He won't stop feeling that way. You just have to make sure he keeps making appointments to see Ms. Alden," I said, trying to lighten the mood.

She looked at me, and I could see a flood of relief on her face.

"I can certainly do that!"

"Then you have nothing to worry about. Did he tell you he wanted to see you again?"

"Yes, and he gave me a sweet goodnight kiss when he dropped me back off."

"There, then. You have it. It'll all work out. You just might get your knight in shining armor, after all."

The next morning, there was still no activity in 1512 when I checked in, so I went to Ms. Alden's suite again. Clara checked through the peephole, and as I walked in I said, "I've already ordered tea."

"Wonderful," Ms. Alden said. "Now do your chores so you can tell me about those gangsters. I've only seen them in movies."

"What do I tell her?" I asked Clara when we were in the master bedroom.

"Some truth, and some fiction. You can tell her how you feel about them."

By the time tea arrived, we'd finished the bedroom and bathroom, and took a break.

"Now," Ms. Alden said. "What are they like?"

"Of course I can't talk about them specifically, but I can tell you things I've seen. In my opinion, they're mostly thugs. They wear flashy suits and shined shoes, and they're always drinking and smoking those terrible cigars. Sometimes they fight amongst themselves, or I've seen them bring someone in that crossed them, and they punched him around. I've seen girls who have no business being there, stuck with those men, and god knows what goes on. There," I said. "I guess I sound pretty saintly. And that, I'm not. I just think they cheat and make lots of money doing it."

"Well, then, I'd better never tell you some of the things I've done," Ms. Alden said, laughing.

I looked at her, surprised. Not that I expected her to be perfect, but I couldn't imagine her doing anything inappropriate.

"Let's see," she started. "When I was just a young thing, I had no idea how to get ahead in Hollywood, until one day, a so-called movie producer told me he'd show me the way, if you get the gist. I learned from that experience, and I've never forgotten how I felt. And then I had an affair with a married man. That was exciting until his wife found out."

Clara and I just looked at each other.

"Oh, and yes, I've never had children, and I once married a man for his money and connections. So you see, most of us, if we've lived long enough, have done plenty of things that could turn people against us.

"Now I don't agree with what those men do either, especially when it comes to beating up or killing people. And I'm not saying these gangsters must have some good in them. But they probably love their mothers, or their wives and children. And like you, it doesn't excuse the fact they are not model citizens.

"I can see I've shocked you," she said. "And I'm telling you this because if you hate working around them, you only have two choices. Stick it out and try to figure out something good about each one of them, or find a way out. Whether or not you think so, you have a choice."

Turning towards Clara, she said, "I'll have some more tea, if you don't mind. And how was your date with the good doctor?"

It appeared I'd been dismissed.

I couldn't make Ms. Alden out, and I wasn't sure what point she was trying to make. She must be suffering terribly, but she seemed to be taking her fate in stride. I would have been a mess, figuring I'd lost my career. And now, not being able to leave her room? Anxiety must have been eating away inside her, but I supposed the actress in her would never show that side of her.

I checked back in to Suite 1512 and dusted a few tables, just to say I'd been there. My mind was reeling with what Ms. Alden had said. Both about the things she'd done, and then about the gangsters. I knew if I wanted to get out of there, I could. I just didn't know where to go. What I did know was I'd lost my zest for knowing more about Clara's guest.

Instead of telling Clara how I felt, I told her I needed to spend more time in 1512, and that I wouldn't be stopping by to see her again. I was certain she knew why, but I didn't want to talk about it.

"You know, Charlotte," she said, "she puts on a tough front, but inside, she's got to be dying the way her life has turned out. One day, I hope Robert can convince her to have a life."

Indeed, when I checked in on Suite 1512 that next day, I saw remnants of a previous wild night. Cigars filled ashtrays, drink glasses cluttered table tops, and a bloodied towel was lying on the bathroom floor. I couldn't bring it down to the laundry, so I folded it up in another towel and shoved it into a pillowcase, then disposed of it in the trash bin outside.

I'd seen plenty of disgusting personal things after a wild night in the suite, but I'd never seen blood. I found no indications of a brawl anywhere else in the suite, so at least that was encouraging. That night, though, Joe showed up with the rest of the guys, and when I could take him aside, I asked about the blood.

"Oh, that. Ralphie got into a barroom fight last night and crashed here. No one's been killed," he said, trying to lighten my mood. "Hey, I've missed you," he said, taking my hand.

I hated to admit it, but I'd missed him, too. We went to his apartment that night and had no problem picking up where we left off, spending the rest of the night in each other's arms.

I didn't have a knight in shining armor, but I had someone who cared about me, just as I cared about him.

# CHAPTER FIFTEEN

Christmas at the hotel in 1930 wasn't much different from the previous year when the stock market crashed. In fact, it was more lavish. It took almost a week to decorate an even taller tree than the year before with hundreds of lit colored bulbs, and a pianist played Christmas music every day from mid morning into the late evening. Again, garlands draped the stairways and the dining rooms and ballrooms, and while not as ornately decorated, they were still sights to behold.

The hotel made sure even their lesser affluent guests welcomed the holidays with flair. Even I was caught up in the magic of it, believing everything was going to be all right, until I saw in one of the newspapers that more and more people were losing their jobs and their homes. Makeshift shantytowns with shacks built from cardboard, metal, and wood were popping up across the country. They called them Hoovervilles, after President Herbert Hoover. A lot of Americans blamed him for the country's economic crisis and for supporting prohibition.

One afternoon, I asked Joe to take me to the one here in Los Angeles. I couldn't imagine people having to live that way, and I wanted to see it for myself. But Joe said no.

"I've been by there already, and I felt like a gawker, especially in my fancy car. It was terrible, and I don't think you should see it. Men, women and children were crowded into crude shelters, and some of them looked like boxes and sheds. Trust me, it was like being in a war zone, and once you've seen it, you'd have a hell of a time getting those images out of your mind."

I hadn't been singing a lot with the guys lately, and I really missed it. They made sure to tell me their latest singer—the replacement for the girl who took my place—was good enough, but that no one could fill my shoes. Now, over the holidays, there were a few evenings when I wasn't needed in Suite 1512 and, after begging, they let me join them. I was in seventh heaven being back on the stage and I could tell Miles and Finn felt like it was the good old times again.

Joe and Doc, as we called Clara's beau, joined us for an early Christmas Eve dinner and we decided this year to forgo exchanging gifts. No one knew what to get anyone, and I had the kitchen bake and wrap bags of Christmas cookies for each of us. We each put five dollars into a can, then drew a number and Joe ended up the winning pot.

He had to work Christmas Eve, and so did I. I'd hoped this year the gangsters would celebrate Christmas with their families, but it wasn't to be. They played cards, drank and smoked their awful cigars well into the early hours of the morning. Finally, they found beds, chairs or the couch and one by one they crashed. When I went in the next morning, I peeked into the rooms before I left to make sure there'd been no foul play, and found a girl sitting on one bed, crying. I helped her up and got her out of there.

"Do something else with your life," I said as I sent her down with the bellboy.

I began a thorough cleaning. Joe and another housekeeper helped clear everything out of the suite, and get it all downstairs where it could be washed and packed back up.

I'd hoped to spend New Year's Eve with the gang, but when Mr. Ellsworth told me I'd be needed in the private ballroom, I wasn't surprised—just exhausted and angry. I held back my tears until I left his office, then I felt foolish for not having enough control over myself to hold it together. I nearly laughed. Not only did I feel I was somehow being demoted, I resented having to entertain people I detested. To remove any doubt of what was expected of me, before the guests started arriving, Mr. DeGrazia took me aside and reminded me I'd be there to take care of *his* party, not the room.

"Let these other buffoons take care of their own people. You know us, and we like having you around."

Whenever he talked directly to me, I wondered if he'd use force on me if I didn't do what he wanted. I'd mentioned it to Joe, and he constantly assured me I was fine, and that there was no way he'd ever let any of the guys touch me. That would temporarily appease me, until later, one of them would say something to me. I still kept my head and eyes down, and I reminded myself that when I worked, I was barely there. It was going to be a little harder in the ballroom where I actually had to serve only Mr. DeGrazia's tables, but Joe would be there too, and that gave me some sense of security.

Around seven-thirty, guests started arriving. Beautiful women— most likely not wives—in gorgeous black gowns held the arms of the men escorting them. I couldn't help but think the women competed with each other with their stylish dresses and fancy hairstyles, and the men did the same, in their minds, proving to the other men they could still attract beautiful women.

I needed help for the evening, and I purposely didn't ask Clara. Even though she'd earn a nice sum of money, I didn't want her getting involved. Instead, I asked one of the room service boys named Johnnie. He'd always been the one who helped me with cleanups and restocking the suite when there'd been a lot of activity, and I knew he could be discreet.

Champagne flowed freely, and Johnnie helped keep the bottles chilled as I poured. Everyone was drinking and dancing, and as the evening wore on, some of the men were getting a little rambunctious. One in particular, who was not a regular, touched my arm as I was pouring him a fresh glass of bubbly. I politely pulled my arm away, and when he reached out to touch me again, I looked up, and suddenly Joe was standing there.

"How're you doing, Ralphie? Looks like you're having a great time there. Oh, excuse me, miss," he said to me, holding up a glass for me to fill.

Ralphie got the hint and turned his attention to a woman at the table.

"Thanks," I said later to Joe.

"My pleasure."

By the time it was close to midnight, my feet were killing me, and I was more than ready to get out of there. Eventually, the countdown began, and as everyone stood, Joe found me and took my hand.

"Three.....two.....one!" everyone called out.

Joe kissed me, and for a moment, I forgot I was so miserable.

"Joe. What if Mr. DeGrazia sees us?"

"Don't worry. He doesn't miss a thing, and he knows you're my girl."

At two, the doors re-opened, and the guests began leaving. Other waiters and waitresses came in and helped clear the room. By three, I was ready to climb into bed, but Joe and I went to the all-night diner and had burgers. I thought I was going to fall asleep in my food, but I managed to keep my head up long enough to get in his LaSalle first, where I then proceeded to nod off.

I couldn't get out of my uniform fast enough when we got back to his apartment. . . I was only thinking about getting some sleep when I crawled into his bed. But Joe had other ideas, and as soon as he started kissing my neck, I knew sleep would have to wait.

In January, I got another letter from Ruth. I'd been thinking about her, hoping everything had worked out for her. She said she loved being up in the mountains and planned to live in Lake Arrowhead forever if she could. She and Mr. Maynard had gotten married, and she'd had a baby girl; they named her Dorothy after her mother and Rose after Jack Maynard's mother.

"Oh, my god!" I said aloud. "Good for you Ruth."

*"I'll never forget what you did for me, Charlotte, and one day, I'd love to have you come visit us. I think you'd love it up here if you stayed a week. As you saw, green trees are everywhere, the air is fresh, and I seem to have naturally taken to life up here.*

*"Again, I can't thank you enough for everything you did for me. If you can ever think of a way I can repay you, all you have to do is write me."*

*"Ruth Landry Maynard."*

"I'm so happy for you," I said again, as if she were there to hear me. "You deserve everything wonderful in life."

I refolded the letter and tucked it back into the envelope. I could hardly wait to tell Clara and the guys. They'd be just as happy for her as I was.

The next time Joe and I were together, I talked about Ruth, and how I admired her strength and resiliency to embrace the challenges she'd been dealt with. I talked about the mountains, and I thought back to when we all drove Ruth up, knowing the change of scenery would do her good. Ultimately, I'd hoped she'd be able to find a job and start her life over. Although it hadn't happened as she'd planned, everything was working out for her and her new life sounded almost perfect—at least compared to being here.

# CHAPTER SIXTEEN

In March, Clara's actress, Vivian Hayes, sold her home in Beverly Hills, and made plans to move permanently into the hotel. Clara continued to care for her while the hotel remodeled the floor above to accommodate her and her new Yorkshire Terriers, Rascal and Darla. When her accommodations were finally completed, she had four bedrooms, a library, a lavish living room and dining room, and a full kitchen. Her personal assistant, full-time housekeeper and her chef lived in smaller rooms several floors below her.

Although she still retained her doctors, Doc Howard said she'd come to accept her new life and was going to write a memoir. Clara stayed on with her as the manager of her suite, but she only checked in twice a day now. This freed her to begin working for another permanent resident, an eccentric screenwriter that the studio brought in to finish a script. He made it clear only Clara was allowed to clean around his scattered sheets of written pages and empty bottles of whiskey.

"His suite smells like a cigarette factory," she told me.

One night, Miles, Finn, and I were already at the all-night diner, and we were just waiting for Clara to get there before we ordered. The moment she walked through the door, we could tell something was up. Her feet barely touched the ground as she bounced in, and she was literally glowing. I thought the heat had gotten to her. And even though we all asked her what was going on, she fidgeted in her seat until we ordered.

"I know it doesn't seem like we've been together very long," she started. "But Robert and I are madly in love, and neither of us can come up with a reason to wait to get married. *Soo. . .,*" she said, "we're engaged!"

When she held up her left hand, sure enough, there was an enormous diamond ring on her third finger, and she wiggled it to show us in case we hadn't already seen it. We all looked at each other, then broke out in cheers.

"So happy for you."

"Great news!"

And I said, "Oh, my god, Clara. That's wonderful news."

I reached over and gave her a big side hug. I said it, but my heart sank a little, thinking she'd gotten there before me; and even better for her, it was with a guy who wasn't involved with organized crime. As quickly as I thought about those things, I was ashamed of myself for being so selfish, and I looked at her to see if she'd seen the traitor in me. She was still glowing.

"When's the big day?" I asked quickly. "I can't believe it."

"Me either." She reached for my hand and said, "I'm sorry I couldn't tell you, Charlotte. I promised Robert I wouldn't say anything until I had the ring."

Ouch. That stung too. They'd planned it, and I'd had no idea. We were great friends, and I tried to get my brain to work right. It just proved you can still be good friends with someone, but we all have personal lives to live. I hadn't shared any private intimate details about Joe with her either, so why did I feel a little slighted?

Because I was a tad bit jealous? "Grow up," I told myself.

It took a moment for it all to sink in, and then I realized, Clara was probably going to quit the hotel!

"Will you still work?" I asked fearfully. How would I survive without her?

Miles and Finn looked over at me for my reaction.

"Well," she hesitated. "I'll work until we get married. Then, Robert wants to buy a house, and I'd be busy getting it all set up. He's even talking about me working in his office, so I get some other work experience and it would save us a little money every month."

"When's the big day?" Miles finally asked.

"November. That'll give me just enough time to plan everything. It won't be a big wedding—just my aunt if she can make the trip out. And, of course, Robert's parents. It would mean so much to me if you played and sang, but I want you to come as guests, not to work. Maybe you could do a few songs?"

"How can we say no to that?" Finn asked.

"Great," Clara said, as our food arrived. "I'm starved. And I'm glad it's all out in the open. I can relax about telling you all and save the stress for planning the wedding. There's one more thing, though. I don't have anyone to walk me down the aisle. I love both you guys, and I wouldn't be able to choose just one of you. Would you draw straws or something to see who'll do it? I mean, that's if you want to."

Miles and Finn looked at each other and shrugged. I took two straws from the table and tore them in to different lengths. I then held them up for one of them to pick. Miles went first, and waited for Finn, who dragged the game on by not showing his straw.

"I'm it!" Finn called out. "Dessert's on me."

Although we had months to go, Clara was anxious to shop for a dress. It turned out Robert's parents, siblings, aunts and uncles would be coming out from Pennsylvania, so there went the plan to keep the wedding small. Plus, when Robert told his Presbyterian parents about the upcoming marriage, his mother asked if they could be married in the church. At first, Clara, who had no particular religious background, worried that his parents would be disappointed in her, but she eventually agreed to forgo a chapel for a church wedding.

Because Clara wasn't Presbyterian, they had to send a letter to the Clerk of the Session requesting approval. They'd also had to meet with the minister for a series of pre-marital counseling sessions. Clara and

Robert had originally thought they'd be married in November, but it turned out the church calendar was booked until January.

Clara's disappointment was evident after they spoke with the minister.

"I can hardly wait to get out of the hotel and be married," she said. "The guests and their problems are getting to me, and I'm finding I'm having a hard time being pleasant. I am to their face, but the minute I close the door to their suite, I want to scream."

"You're not the only one, at least you have an out. You can see the end of the tunnel," I said, sympathizing with her. "It really isn't that far off, and in no time, you'll be Mrs. Doc Howard."

"If I cover my eyes, like young children do, maybe I won't notice the world around me," she said.

"Just be grateful you don't have to deal with the creeps I have to."

I didn't feel that I could talk to Joe about how lonely I felt. When I originally told him about Clara's engagement, I saw something in his expression. I could tell he was happy for her, but I had a hard time putting my finger on what else was going on in his mind. We'd never talked about marriage, although I knew he loved me. I wasn't even sure I wanted to marry someone who could be beaten up or, worse, killed. He'd told me what he did wasn't that dangerous; he mostly kept an eye on the guys for Mr. DeGrazia. He also said he was more of a "fixer" than a strong arm, working with local police officers and city officials who provided protection to the organization. I wondered if there was more to what he was sharing, and then when I thought about it; it was probably for the best I didn't know anything more. I assumed it was safer for me that way.

Clara had long gotten over her bout of disappointment about the wedding plans, and in October, she and I earnestly shopped for dresses. Even though it was going to be a smaller church wedding, she surprisingly chose a floor length satin dress with long sleeves and a high neckline resembling those that the Hollywood actresses were wearing.

She wanted me, as her maid of honor, to wear a similar dress. Knowing I'd never wear something like that again, I tried to discourage her, but since Doc Howard was paying for it all, I couldn't object.

"A niece is going to be a flower girl, so I need to send a photo of what we decide on so her mother can find something coordinating. Little girls in white frilly dresses always look so cute," Clara said, happy as a clam.

She hadn't said anything about the upcoming wedding to Mr. Ellsworth, for fear she'd lose her job. She didn't take into consideration the services she provided for the hotel, and the unlikelihood of her being dismissed, and yet I understood. So when she was assigned to another resident, she didn't say a word. Between the actress, the screenwriter, and now a self proclaimed real estate magnate, it wasn't unusual for her to work twelve-hour days, and sometimes more.

Lewis Joseph Carrington had come to California when he read about Los Angeles' sudden growth. While the recession had wrecked havoc with so many industries, the movie studios were providing much needed entertainment and the first time he came out from New Jersey, he realized the climate and land offered opportunities to make a fortune.

The hotel remodeled Mr. Carrington's suite to allow for an office, a presentation room, a studio, plus two bedrooms, a posh living room and dining room, and a full kitchen like Ms. Alden's. In no time, he'd begun buying land, finding investors and working with architects and property management firms.

"He's quite eccentric," Clara said shortly after meeting him. "He's a perfectionist and everything has its place. He smokes like a chimney and he loves his Old Fashions. Every day, I restock his bourbon, sugar cubes, bitters, and orange peels. The hotel's even had to find a source for maraschino cherries."

"What does he do exactly?" I asked.

"He has construction drawings everywhere—and the buildings are so tall, he calls them skyscrapers. When he meets with investors, I have to make sure everything is ready, and that includes appetizers and liquor.

Sometimes I stay while they get warmed up, but once they start looking at building plans, they act like everything is top secret, and I'm excused."

Not that I had an interest in building, but I was curious about what the drawings looked like. I asked if I could see them.

"Can you come in late tomorrow morning? He's usually gone by then, and you can help me clean up the morning mess in case he comes back and wonders why you're there."

The next morning, I took Clara up on her offer. I knocked instead of using a master key, in case Mr. Carrington was in, and it was Clara who opened the door.

"Check it out," she said, letting me in. "Look like you're doing something in case he comes back."

In his studio, there were stacks of sketches of all kinds; exteriors of buildings, interiors, lobbies. Rolls and rolls of blueprints were standing up in tall cardboard boxes, and leather weights held several sets open on two separate work surfaces. I didn't understand the terminology, but I found the drawings intriguing and somewhat self explanatory.

"These are incredible," I said to Clara when she came into the room.

"Whatever you do, don't move anything thinking you're straightening the room up. He'll kill me. Just pick up the ashtrays and drink glasses."

Just then, the door to the room opened, and we froze. It wasn't as though we were doing anything wrong, but I quickly picked up an empty bottle and a few glasses.

"And who do we have here?" he asked, standing in the doorway to the studio.

"Good morning, sir. This is one of the housekeepers, Charlotte. I asked her to give me a hand this morning."

"Very well. Continue working. Finish this room first, as I need to get back to the drawing board, as they say." He chuckled at his pun.

As soon as I loaded up a trolley, I excused myself.

"Thanks, Charlotte," Clara said nonchalantly. "I really do appreciate your help."

That night I told Joe about the drawings, and I tried to quickly sketch out what the plans looked like.

"Of course I couldn't read them, but one set showed the finished building, and the other pages showed more details, like where the plumbing and electricity would go. They were pretty amazing. We had to pretend we were cleaning up, so if Mr. Carrington came back, he wouldn't be surprised to see us in the room."

"I've seen a few sets of plans before," Joe said. "They are pretty incredible."

"Where?"

"Oh," Joe said, looking surprised I'd ask. "Ah, at the building department, when Mr. DeGrazia asks me to look into something for him. One time, someone had their plans lying out on the counter."

"If those buildings get built, it sounds like Mr. Carrington is going to make a lot of money," I said, imagining what it would be like to be wealthy.

# CHAPTER SEVENTEEN

It felt like Thanksgiving came out of nowhere. No holiday celebrations were planned in Suite 1512, so I had the day off. Joe had to work, though; Mr. DeGrazia wanted him to handle something, but Joe couldn't go into details. I found it cryptic, and I was rightfully disappointed we wouldn't be able to spend the day with Miles, Finn, Clara, and Doc. We could have eaten in the staff kitchen, but Miles found a pleasant restaurant that was cooking Thanksgiving dinner, and we filled ourselves to the point of being stuffed with turkey, mashed potatoes, gravy, and pumpkin pie.

The only good that came of it was that evening, I filled in for the gal who'd been singing with the guys. She wanted the night off.

Joe didn't return for two days, and I was growing uncomfortable. I was beginning to worry about him, but when I saw him, he looked none the worse for it, so I gave a sigh of relief. I not only hated the gangsters, but I hated that I worried about him getting hurt. Or worse, killed.

It seemed that Suite 1512 celebrated every night between Thanksgiving and Christmas. Didn't these creeps have families to go home to? We spent Christmas morning at Joe's apartment, and he gave me a necklace with a diamond heart. I hadn't planned on such extravagance and I felt I had to apologize for just giving him a money clip to replace the one he'd lost. Again, he had to work Christmas day, so I spent the afternoon with Miles and Finn. Clara and Doc wanted to spend the day together, and I didn't blame them. We ended up at our usual place, the diner, and we toasted root beers. I gladly took them up on their offer to sing with them that night, and although the lounge wasn't very busy, and the tips were sparse, it felt great to be with them.

New Year's Eve was a repeat of Christmas. I had to work the gangster ball as I now called it, but at least I got to see Joe. Clara and Doc spent the evening at some fancy party, and Miles and Finn played in the lounge.

I was hoping I could at least listen to the guys for a bit, but after the gala, Joe told me Mr. DeGrazia wanted to take the party up to the suite, so I was stuck. It turned out to be a small group; it seemed some of the men had the common sense to either go home to bed, or go somewhere else.

Thankfully, I'd been able to clean the suite before heading down to the ballroom, but I hadn't expected to come back and set up more drinks. I called downstairs for trays of caviar, shrimp cocktail, and cheese and crackers. When I went to the hallway closet, I began loading a trolley with a couple of bottles of everything alcohol, along with glasses and cocktail napkins. I was almost finished when I heard several voices in the hallway outside the suite's doors, but I didn't recognize them.

One man said, "Mr. DeGrazia said Vince has been talking too much, and we need to send him a message. I'll take care of it when he leaves tonight."

Another man said, "He told me Tony'd better have the money next week or I'll have to pay him another visit."

"The sheriff's been paid off," another said, "so we don't have to worry about that. But Joe needs to tell the councilman to take care of the zoning. We want that deal to go through with that real estate guy."

Over the months, I'd picked up bits and pieces of conversations between Mr. DeGrazia and the men, but never as much as I'd just heard. I held my breath, thinking they might realize the door to the closet was open and figure out I was in there. I had to think quickly. If someone approached me, I'd just have to pretend I'd never overheard anything.

"Let's see," I'd say. Or, "What else do I need?" and start humming like I was in my own little world. I'd act surprised to see someone standing there. For good measure, I'd add, "Oh, I didn't hear you there," hoping that would satisfy them.

But they didn't notice me and eventually the door to the suite opened and closed again behind them.

I took a few minutes to compose myself before I tapped on the suite's door. They'd mentioned Joe, and I wrestled with myself whether or not I should tell him. I was certain he was the one they were referring to, since that was the kind of thing he told me he took care of. And were they talking about Clara's recent resident, Mr. Carrington? They might have discovered what he was doing with all his big plans, and it made sense they'd want a part of the action.

Once I organized the drinks, the appetizers arrived, and gratefully, Mr. DeGrazia said, "You can take off now, Charlotte. We should be good. You'll have a mess in the morning."

I looked around to find Joe, but he wasn't in the room.

"Thank you, sir. Happy New Year," I said as I made a hasty exit.

I waited for Joe at his apartment and then I told him what had happened.

"Jesus, Charlotte. You can't be around when the guys talk like that. What were you doing in the hallway?"

"I was loading the trolley."

I'd been close to being discovered, and now I was ready to burst into tears.

"I came up with something to say if they saw me," I added, hoping to satisfy him.

"Jesus," he said again, running his hand through his hair.

Joe pulled me to him and hugged me tightly. And when he did that, I cried.

# CHAPTER EIGHTEEN

Little did I know, 1932 would be a year that remained forever etched in my mind. Los Angeles would host the Summer Olympics and the already crowded streets of Los Angeles would grow even more congested. For the first time in two years, availability in the hotel was non-existent, and the staff scrambled to handle the additional guests. Franklin D. Roosevelt would be elected president, Amelia Earhart would become the first female aviator to fly solo across the Atlantic Ocean, Clara would get married, and I would see my second dead body.

Thankfully, Clara was spending more time with Doc, though she'd never spend the night in his apartment. I spent most nights at Joe's. I didn't want to be alone. If I *was* in our apartment, by the time she'd get home, if I wasn't already asleep, I'd pretend I was. If I didn't have to talk to her, I could possibly keep from telling her about the men I overheard. And that was something I could never do. I'd promised Joe, and even if I hadn't, I knew what had to be done. I knew the rules if I wanted to stay safe.

Clara's wedding was not far off, and while I could never tell her, my heart just wasn't in it. All I could think about was those men in the hall, and what would have happened if they would have discovered me? I felt as though I was becoming more transparent every time I went into

Suite 1512 and Mr. DeGrazia was there. I kept my head down, but I was certain he was noticing a change in me. Then I began worrying what he would do if he thought I wasn't able to handle working the suite. Would he tell the men to dispose of me, too?

One morning when Clara and I crossed paths, she stopped me and asked if everything was all right.

"Of course it's not!" I wanted to shout. How could I get dressed up and pretend everything was fine? "It's my time of the month," I said, instead. "I'm just feeling weepy."

"Okay. I just wanted to make sure you're okay." She went on like everything was normal. "I'm getting so nervous. What if Robert's family doesn't like me?"

I wanted to say, "They'll love you, and if they don't, tell them to drop dead." Of course, I didn't say that. I only said, "Stop worrying. They'll love you because Doc loves you."

The rehearsal dinner was at the hotel, and Doc's family seemed nice enough, although I sensed they couldn't understand how their son might meet a housekeeper and fall in love. I was certain they'd heard the story.

Clara's aunt Doris took the train out and Finn drove Clara and me to pick her up at the station.

"Aunt Doris!" Clara called out when she saw her. "Oh dear," she said to me, seeing the older woman dressed in shades of brown. "I hope she has something nice to wear to the wedding."

"She looks fine. Stop worrying about everything." I said. "At least she's here."

At the rehearsal dinner, she wore all browns again. Her mesh stockings, dark shoes, and dark brown floral dress blended in with her light brown wool coat. I sat next to her at the dinner and with her short permed hair and out-of-date attire, she looked older than her fifty-five years.

"I should have bought something new to wear," she said sheepishly.

I thought she might burst into tears.

"You're just fine the way you are," I said, patting her hand. "It's Doc's parents that make us all feel beneath them. You're here, and that's all that's important to Clara. Maybe tomorrow you can go with us to get our hair and nails done."

"It'd be interesting to see what they could do with this hair," she whispered.

Joe was a little late, but he made it to the dinner, and when the time came, he toasted the bride and groom to be, and said that now that he knew Doc, if anything ever happened to him, that's who he'd call. Everyone laughed, but I didn't think it was funny.

Miles and Finn toasted the couple too, and I could tell Clara was touched.

The next morning, Clara, her aunt and I had our nails and hair done. She'd extended the invitation to her future mother-in-law, but Mrs. Howard declined, saying she'd just had everything done before the trip out.

"This is nice," Clara said to her aunt. "We have some time by ourselves, before the madness, and it gives us a time to catch up.

The wedding was at four, and we were dressed and waiting to be called. I should have said something to Clara when we were deciding on dresses, but I didn't want to hurt her feelings. I took one look at myself in the mirror, and the pale pink color of my dress washed my complexion out. Blush and lipstick didn't seem to help. Of course, my mood didn't help either.

Unlike me, Clara looked beautiful in her dress, as she should have. Her mother-in-law, Alberta, came in while we were waiting and brought something borrowed. I'd already given Clara a blue garter and my fake pearl earrings, but Alberta brought her real pearls. When she put them on, she looked lovely.

"You can return them after the reception, dear," Alberta said, not unkindly, but in my mind, cheapening the thought.

Clara just smiled. I could tell she was dying inside.

"What a bitch," I said to her after Alberta left.

Miles and Finn both rented tuxedos and top hats, although only Finn was actually in the wedding. Doc's father also wore a tux, but one that he brought with him, and his mother wore a stylish coat with a fur collar. Doc's niece was the flower girl, and as Clara had predicted, she was darling, dressed up in her frilly white dress.

When the organ began playing, we knew it was our cue. Clara's dear aunt looked so forlorn, being the only one besides Miles and Joe on the bride's side of the church. I saw her glance at the groom's family across the aisle and it broke my heart.

Doc stood at the altar with me and his brother, waiting for the flower girl, and then there Clara was, standing in the opening to the church, her arm in Finns. A hush fell over the church before the organist began playing the wedding march. Her hair was pinned back with a pearl comb and even under her soft veil, her eyes glistened like mine did; although her tears were for her love for Doc. She was so beautiful, and when I looked over at Doc, I realized I'd never seen a man so much in love. I couldn't imagine a dry eye in the church, and I discreetly drew the handkerchief from my dress's bodice and gently dabbed my eyes.

The ceremony was brief, and of course I cried a little more at the thought of two people in love just waiting to start their life together. In no time, the minister pronounced them husband and wife, and they quickly kissed, then walked down the aisle.

"Wait!" Doc's mother called to them as they stepped out of the church. "We have to throw rice!"

Everyone stood at the bottom of the steps and began showering Doc and Clara, and then Clara's foot slid on the rice. Her eyes widened in panic, and I thought for sure she was going to fall, but Doc quickly steadied her and averted disaster. They made their way to the Cadillac Phaeton awaiting them, and a chauffeur opened the back door for them to climb in. As they took off for the reception, tin cans and shoes rattled behind them.

We all followed them to the Brown Derby restaurant, where Doc's parents had arranged for a private room. Just after we were seated, knowing others could hear, Doc's mother whispered loudly to Clara, "You know, Gloria Swanson's former husband, and a man named Cobb, started The Brown Derby. The story is that he introduced the Cobb Salad and we're having that with our dinner."

Once everyone was settled and the doors closed and locked, champagne flowed, and Doc's father toasted the bride and groom.

"To our son and new daughter-in-law. May they be blessed with a happy life and many children."

"Here, here," everyone said, raising their glasses.

"To my best friend," I said, getting teary-eyed. "I wish you every bit of happiness, and ten children."

Everyone laughed.

Since he escorted Clara down the aisle, Finn said, "To my new daughter." And there were more laughs. "I also wish you a long and healthy life together."

Doc's father clinked his champagne glass with a fork so he could be heard above conversations, he said, "To my son. As our gift, we've bought you a new house not far from the hotel and your practice. May you two be as happy as your mother and I have been."

Doc was taken aback, and Clara choked on her champagne.

They honeymooned in Santa Barbara, at a quaint hotel near the ocean, in a cottage nestled in amongst a copse of trees. When they returned, Clara was both radiant and beside herself with joy. As much as I tried not to, I envied her in her new life, and yet the biggest part of me wished her nothing but happiness. She talked about going by the house Doc's parents bought them, and even though they both agreed it was a little presumptuous of them to give them something so expensive, they both loved it.

"Now Robert feels beholden to them," she shared when we had a minute to catch up. "Although he's admitted it's nicer than he'd have been able to afford on his own."

But then she was off onto other thoughts. "We'll have it painted and put in new carpets, and then we'll start looking for furniture. I've never bought furniture before, and it makes me a little nervous I'll make a lot of mistakes. But Robert said I could buy whatever I liked," Clara said, somewhat embarrassed. Of course, she knew I'd never bought furniture either. "Will you come with me?"

She looked so lost in her new role, I couldn't refuse her. If I could get past my own yearning for a new life, I was sure it could be fun.

Clara assumed the hotel would let her go immediately when she gave them notice, which was the custom when someone wanted to leave, but they pleaded with her to stay until they could find someone to take her place. I kept my fingers crossed it would be me, but I wasn't the one Mr. Ellsworth chose.

"You're too valuable where you are," he said, recognizing my disappointment. "You didn't hear it from me, but I think you're the only one who can tough it out with those guys. While it sometimes doesn't seem likely, hopefully one day, and soon, they'll move on to another hotel. I'm really sorry, Charlotte. I'm hoping it's not taking its toll on you." Although Mr. Ellsworth never made me feel my position was beneath him, he'd never taken me into his confidence before and talked to me so candidly—I appreciated that.


The next day we had off, Clara and I went shopping at Barker Brothers and neither of us expected to see such a wonderful assortment of furnishings for the home. There were nine floors of carpets, lamps, bedding, beds and mattresses, living room furniture, and even refrigerators and washing machines! And just as exciting, a uniformed elevator operator announced what was on each floor as she opened the doors to let customers out.

"Sixth floor, dining room furniture. And don't forget the Mary Louise Tea Room on the eleventh floor," she said cheerfully.

I waited until we got off the elevator before I asked Clara, "What's a tearoom?"

"How would I know?"

After looking at the dining room furniture, I asked the operator to take us up there. Of course, the moment the doors opened, our jaws dropped. With its plush carpet, oriental rugs and velvet drapes, we could tell this was a place that was way beyond our means. We didn't get out, but thanked her, and asked to go back down to look at living room furniture.

"I know I don't have an unlimited budget," Clara said, "so what if I pick some things out and you write them down and when Robert gets home, I can ask him what he'd like me to do."

"That sounds perfect."

"We'll need a couch, tables and lamps to start . . . and we can look at bedroom furniture next."

"I'm just following you," I said.

If I was completely honest with myself, I was really enjoying the day.

It was strange not having Clara in the apartment, and I was hoping Mr. Ellsworth wouldn't rush to find a new roommate. I hated the thought of getting to know another girl. When I saw Clara the next day in the staff kitchen, I was anxious to hear what Doc had said about buying the furniture—she said he told her to order the bedroom and the living room now.

"Oh, my gosh," I said, flabbergasted. He must have been saving up for quite a while.

# CHAPTER NINETEEN

Clara's new house was indeed wonderful. She'd wanted to meet me there before the furniture was delivered so I could help her select paint colors for the walls. The workmen were due to be there the next day, and she was frantic. Doc had been no help.

"Pick any colors you like. I'm sure you'll do a good job," he'd said when she showed him paint swatches she'd found at the hardware store.

Joe offered to drop me off and pick me up, and just driving through her neighborhood, I felt elevated to another level. Everyone had green lawns and flower beds filled with flowers in all shades of yellows, reds, and pinks. Two women with baby carriages stopped to talk to each other, and when one of them picked up her baby, the other woman touched the child on the cheek. Even from my vantage point, I could see the child's mother beaming with pride. Joe reached over and took my hand.

"It's nice here, isn't it?"

He pulled up in front of Clara's house, and she opened the front door before I could even get out of the car.

"The hardware store mixed some colors and gave me little containers so I could test them on the walls. Come see what they look like."

I took my hat off and set it on a card table in the middle of the living room, and I couldn't miss the splotches of sea foam green, a muted gold, and a pale blue painted next to each other on one wall. I'd never thought of Clara being so colorful and it surprised me; I would have chosen white or off-white.

"These are lovely," I said honestly.

"Oh, here are samples of the fabrics," she said, handing them to me.

"I'm afraid I'm no help. I like them all," I said.

"Well, that's not going to do. You need to pick one color."

All three would have worked, but I sighed and decided a scientific approach to this would work best. I told Clara to go into another room for a minute, and then I pointed to the colors and said eeny, meeny, miny, moe. Sea foam green was the winner.

"I picked one!" I called out.

"Really?"

I smiled smugly.

"I love it. Charlotte, you're the best. Thanks! "

Clara held the fabrics up to the wall and agreed.

"Now we need to do the master bedroom."

This time, it was easier. I preferred the pale blue to the gold.

"This one," I said quickly.

"I love it."

She'd made some iced tea, and we sat in the living room on two mismatched chairs, sipping it.

"You look really happy," I said.

"I am. And you look stressed."

"The whole situation in 1512 is getting to me. Joe says it won't be forever, and I'm trying to believe him, but sometimes they really frighten me. I overhear them talking about taking care of business, moving merchandise and making sure someone keeps quiet. I'm hoping for a miracle. I think Joe and I could have a chance at a good life if he could get out of there, but he says he can't yet. I'm not sure what that means, but that's what he keeps telling me. In the meantime, I just keep to myself, and keep my head and eyes down like I'm not even in the room."

Then I remembered Clara's real estate developer and asked about him. I couldn't tell her I'd overhead them say something about real estate and zoning.

"Oh, he seems okay. I heard him talking to someone important about forming a partnership on some large projects. I was surprised he wasn't very happy since that's what he's here for; finding partners and all that. Why do you ask?"

"Oh, nothing. I was just curious how he was doing," I lied. "Well, I guess I should get back. I see Joe has pulled up. I have to work tonight, and I wanted to spend a few hours with Joe."

"Give him my best," Clara said, hugging me and kissing me on the cheek.

"And you also, to Doc," I said.

# CHAPTER TWENTY

About a month later, I was doing what I did best for Suite 1512; I was setting up for the evening. Mr. DeGrazia had mentioned they were going to have an important meeting, and he wanted the best hors d'oeuvres sent up. He also wanted to add a few bottles of champagne and two blondes.

It always turned my stomach when I had to call down and ask for women, but the hotel insisted on turning a blind eye and there was nothing I could do about it. My only hope was that the girls wouldn't be mistreated, as I'd seen in the past.

I was almost finished putting out the plates and napkins when Johnnie knocked and called out, "Room Service." He had trays of food and two blondes with him. About ten minutes later there was another knock on the door, and when I opened it, to say I was surprised was putting it mildly. There stood Clara's real estate tycoon, Mr. Carrington, tugging at his vest and tie.

I didn't think he even recognized me from the day I was with Clara, and if he did, he didn't let on. I didn't acknowledge him either, and I could tell he was uncomfortable just being there.

"C'mon in," Mr. DeGrazia bellowed in his big voice. "Welcome to the meeting!"

Mr. Carrington glanced around the room before he came in, and I didn't blame him for being cautious. I wouldn't want to be at one of these meetings either.

"C'mon," Mr. DeGrazia said again, this time coming up to Mr. Carrington and shaking his hand. "You're right on time. Councilman Cochran should be here any minute, and I think you'll appreciate getting to know him. I've already told you, he can do a lot for you, and us, when it comes to getting our zoning approved for all the projects we're planning. C'mon and grab a drink. We have champagne or whiskey."

Mr. DeGrazia stopped for a second and said, "That's right, you're an Old Fashion guy I hear. Charlotte, can you make sure we have everything Mr. Carrington needs?"

I nodded and called downstairs again. Before Johnnie could get back up, someone I'd never seen before stood at the door when I opened it.

"Congressman Cochran!" Mr. DeGrazia called loudly.

All eyes were on the congressman and it was obvious he, too, was uncomfortable being there. Joe came from behind Mr. DeGrazia and reached out to shake the congressman's hand. I sensed reluctance, but he shook Joe's hand. Joe didn't flinch, and he kept his eyes focused.

Johnnie was next at the door and he brought in the tray of bitters, syrup and orange peels and set it on the counter. I knew how to make Mr. Carrington's drink, and when I handed it to him, I could see a slight sheen of perspiration on his face. I handed him a cocktail napkin, and after a quick cough, he casually wiped his lip.

"Thank you," he said.

"Councilman Cochran, this is Mr. Carrington, the developer we've talked about. We have a lot of projects on the table, and we sure could use your help. I know we can count on you, right?"

Mr. Cochran didn't immediately answer, and I took this moment to finish bringing in the whiskey. Excusing myself, I quietly backed out of the room. To my surprise, when I went to the laundry closet, I found it fully restocked. Someone had been busy. I pulled the trolley over, and just as I finished loading it, I heard what I was sure was a gunshot from within. A second later, I heard the thud of a body landing on the floor.

"Oh, god. Was it Joe?"

I was frantic.

I left the trolley and ran into the suite. I stood there for a few seconds while my brain caught up to what my eyes were seeing. My hand flew up to my mouth, and somehow I didn't scream, although that was my first instinct. The gunshot wound was graphic. I was still processing what I'd seen when Joe grabbed me by the arm and pulled me away.

"Get the hell out of here, Charlotte!" he yelled.

I couldn't turn away. Councilman Cochran was lying on the floor, covered in blood. He'd been shot in the chest and blood soaked his shirt. I could tell my heart was racing, and I began to tremble. I still couldn't say anything and poor Mr. Carrington, the real estate developer, just stood there in shock. Men were talking around me, some even shouting, but by this time my brain muffled their voices. I couldn't have said who was saying what.

"Leave," Joe said again, pulling me into the hallway. He checked to see if anyone else had heard the gunshot and come up from below. Men were rushing around inside the suite and Joe tried to shield me from seeing inside.

"Get her outta here," Mr. DeGrazia yelled as Joe rushed me from the room. "Is she going to be a problem?"

"No," Joe said.

I didn't want to, but once Joe closed the door behind us and held me, I began sobbing.

"You're all right," he repeated, trying to comfort me. "You're all right."

"But I'm not," I said.

"Yes, you are. This didn't happen and we'll clean it all up. When you come back tomorrow, there won't be a trace of anything, not even the party."

"I can't go back," I cried.

"Yes, you can, and you will. You need to show them there will not be a problem."

I was shaking uncontrollably as Joe gripped me firmly. He was trying to remain calm for both our sakes, but his face had turned purple. I closed my eyes trying to take deep breaths, but it wasn't working. I slid to the floor, crying.

"You have to show them you're all right," he said again. "Then there won't be any trouble. If you break down, then I don't know what. But you're not going to do that, are you?"

Somehow, I stopped crying.

"Let me go in and tell Mr. DeGrazia I'm going to take you home. We'll stay at my place tonight."

"I guess they won't be needing the trolley?"

"Stay here. Promise me you won't go anywhere."

He was only gone for a few minutes, but it seemed like hours before he came back out.

"We're good. I told him you were all right, and that everything was going to be fine."

Joe took me by the arm and pulled me down the hall, then pushed the buzzer for the elevator. I must have looked a fright, for when Freddie the operator opened the gate, he stepped back in surprise.

"You all right, Charlotte?" he asked, stunned.

"She's good," Joe said quickly.

"I'm fine, Freddie," I said, getting into the elevator car.

We rode in silence down to the basement, and before we got off, I said, "Please don't worry and I'm fine. Please keep this to yourself."

"Sure thing, Charlotte," he said. I could tell he wasn't convinced, but I knew he would keep his mouth shut.

I waited out in the back while Joe brought his car around. Although the evening was pleasant, I was shivering and by the time I got into the front seat and my teeth were chattering. Joe looked at me and just shook his head. He grabbed a blanket from the back seat.

"This was never supposed to happen," he said, looking in his rearview mirror. "Mr. DeGrazia is really pissed."

"What happened?"

Joe waited until we were halfway to his place before he answered.

"They're getting into buying property. The real estate guy in the hotel, Mr. Carrington, is being forced to partner with us. You told me you met him one day with Clara?"

"Yes. But I didn't think he was working with the likes of the mob. I had no idea who his clients were, but I don't think anyone in his right mind would willingly get involved."

Joe turned the heater up.

"Well, he's not exactly jumping for joy about it. And now that the councilman has been shot, I'm sure he'd run if he could. Mr. DeGrazia never planned on eliminating either of them. I've been working with the councilman, trying to get him to see things our way, but he told Mr. DeGrazia he'd made up his mind; he wasn't going to be intimidated into doing anything he didn't feel comfortable with. Jeez."

"So who shot him?"

"Lenny did. He's a new soldier, and I'm sure this will be the last we see of him. Jeez," he said again, slamming the steering wheel.

I was still shivering when he got to Joe's apartment and he tucked me in bed, clothes and all.

"Here are a few more blankets until you warm up," he said, tucking me in on both sides like I was in a cocoon. "Try to sleep if you can."

"I don't think *that's* going to happen anytime soon. Will you stay with me?"

"Yeah, let me get a drink first."

I tossed and turned all night, and by morning, I was totally drained. When I reached over for Joe, I panicked. He wasn't there. He'd left a note on the nightstand, letting me know he'd gone to get bagels and coffee. I dragged myself out of bed and jumped into the shower, hoping the hot water would wash away the cobwebs in my brain.

I was surprised I was hungry, and the bagels were just what I needed.

"What now?" I asked.

"We go back to being normal."

"What is that?"

# CHAPTER TWENTY ONE

I stayed with Joe for the next few days—he was the only one I could talk to about that night. I didn't go in to work until Joe assured me everything was back to normal. He'd notified housekeeping that one of the tubs overflowed, and the damaged carpet had been cut out. If it didn't make sense that the bathroom was on one end of the suite and the living room—where the bloodstains were—was on the other, the hotel said nothing. The next day, the suite was re-carpeted, and the day after that, everything was back as it was the night of the meeting.

I was a bundle of nerves when I filled in my time card, and I did my best to hide the fact my stomach churned as I knocked, then unlocked the door to the suite. I would have sworn I heard men's voices and that awful sound of the gunshot, and I stopped to take a deep breath and reassure myself it was just sounds my brain was remembering.

Carpet dust from the installation was everywhere, and fortunately, no one was there as I quickly dusted and vacuumed. I gathered the few empty bottles and glasses and set them outside until I was ready to leave. The sooner I got out of there, the better.

When I came back that evening, the room went silent as I stood in the doorway, not certain I was going to be able to enter. But once the men realized it was just me, they went back to their conversations. No one spoke of the other night, and that was fine by me. I kept my head and eyes down, and continued to be a ghost as I went about my job.

One time, though, I did catch Mr. DeGrazia's eye, and he waited for me to waver, but I didn't. I looked him straight in the eye, and I asked, "Can I get you anything?"

"I'm fine, Charlotte. And you?"

"I'm fine too, Mr. DeGrazia," I answered with a forced smile.

Suddenly, a sense of dread turned my stomach cold, and the hairs on my neck stood up like a warning. I realized I could have been done away with at any time.

"Unless you need me, I'll see you later when I come back to clean up," I added, hoping he couldn't sense my fear. I'd read stories where wild animals could smell the fear, and I prayed this wasn't the case with me.

I knew I needed to leave. I wasn't going to be a problem for them, but Mr. DeGrazia didn't know that, and he might not continue to feel that way. And my gut instinct was that his mood could change at any time and no one would know where I ended up. I needed to talk to Joe without telling him too many details.

That night, when I went back to finish cleaning up the suite, the party was winding down and there were only a few men there. I knew Joe wasn't going to be there, and I almost panicked as I got off the elevator; he would be my only protection if Mr. DeGrazia tried to do anything. If I didn't show up, they'd be suspicious. If I did, then I was going to have to put on a hell of a show.

I tried to act as I usually did, just doing my job and keeping my head down. But when Mr. DeGrazia came up behind me in the kitchen, he caught me by surprise and I jumped.

"Oh, you startled me," I said, attempting to regain my composure.

"I didn't mean to, Charlotte," he said in a quiet voice. He handed me a dirty ashtray. "Are you okay?"

I turned and looked him straight in the eye. "I'm fine, really. And I'm here for you as I've always been. Please rest assured." I tried to spread it on thick enough to put him at ease, but not overdo it.

"Good," was all he said as he turned to leave, then handed me a hundred-dollar bill.

I'd given a lot of thought to just disappearing, but I loved Joe and I wanted to talk to him first. I waited at his place and tried to calm my nerves by taking a warm shower and having a couple of glasses of wine. By the time he got home, I was feeling better. I knew I needed to talk to him, and I was afraid he would not understand.

"We need to talk," I started, point blank.

He flinched.

"I need to know how you feel about me."

"Wow. I think you know. I love you."

"I love you too, which is why we need to talk."

"Okay..."

"I've told Mr. Degrazia I'm fine. He came up behind me in the kitchen and scared the hell out of me. I told him I was there for him as I've always been. And he gave me a hundred dollars. But I'm not sure he's going to believe me forever. I'm too nervous."

"Charlotte," Joe started, taking me in his arms. "I think he's fine. I've told him you're okay, just a little shaken. But I understand how you feel." I could hear it in his voice, that he meant it when he said, "I wish I could take you away from here, but I can't right now."

"Why do you keep saying 'right now'? What does that mean?"

"The only thing I can tell you is there is an end in sight, and then I'll be out of there. It's not the life I want for me, or for you. And I want to be with you. Do you want to be with me?" His eyes caught and held mine.

"Of course I do!" I said impatiently. "I just don't think I can go on with this charade of acting like everything is okay when it isn't."

"Let's go to bed. I'm here for you, and you know that."

He showered, then came to bed. I knew he wanted to prove how much he loved me by making love, but my heart just wasn't in it. I tried to hide my feelings, and although he didn't say anything, I knew he understood I just couldn't respond the way I usually did. He cuddled with me, and eventually we both slept. In the morning, when I turned to face him, he was just looking at me.

"No matter what you decide to do, I'll find you," he whispered.

# CHAPTER TWENTY TWO

In the back of my mind, I knew my leaving would be inevitable. Weeks ago, I'd asked Finn to drive me to the hardware store to buy a footlocker. We dragged it up into the apartment, and I told anyone who asked that it was for additional storage. I slowly began packing my entire life into it. The warmer weather meant I hadn't needed my blankets, and I found them in my closet. I carefully wrapped the framed photos of myself and my mother, then collected all the letters from Moira, Ruth, and Mrs. Rochester, and tied them with a string. I couldn't leave anything behind in case they came to look for me; no one could know where I'd come from or where I was likely to go.

On my next night off, as planned, Finn's car was waiting for me outside the back entrance to the apartments. Clouds partially hid the moon and while there was no forecast for rain, I insisted on at least trying to disguise my identity under an umbrella, in the event anyone was keeping track of my comings and goings. Poor Miles ended up carrying the bulk of the weight as I struggled with my purse and the umbrella.

"Was all this necessary?" he whispered hoarsely.

Miles shoved me onto the floor in the back seat, and he quickly covered me with a heavy woolen blanket that instantly scratched my skin. I was certain no one would suspect me of being in the car.

"Are we good?" I called out.

"Shh." Finn said. "We're good. There's no one here."

"Ah, shit," Miles said as we came around the corner. "I can't see who it is, but it looks like someone's poking around in front."

"We're out of here," Finn said, turning out onto the street.

"Can I take this blanket off yet? It's claustrophobic, and it itches."

"Hang in there. You should be fine in a few minutes." Miles said.

That night, I stayed with Miles, because he didn't want to make the trip in the dark, and I agreed. I didn't want to get this far and die when the car ran off the road and tumbled down the mountain.

In the morning, Finn showed up bright and early, and both Miles and I checked over our shoulders several times before I climbed back in to the backseat of the car.

"This blanket itches," I complained as he tucked me in.

We hadn't thought to make something for breakfast, so about a half an hour in, we stopped at a coffee shop and had a big breakfast.

"This'll have to last us until we get there," Finn said.

"I miss them already," I whined.

I'd had to tell the guys what had happened in order to convince them to become accomplices in my escape plan. Once we were out of town, we stopped at a diner and had something to eat. Again, we made sure no one suspicious was lurking about when we left and we all agreed I was safe to sit in the back seat without being covered up.

"This could be a movie where we escape, and I check my rear-view mirror and discover someone's been following us," Finn said, chuckling.

Miles looked at him as if to say, 'are you crazy?' And I reached over and hit him on the back of his head. I could picture what he was saying, but it wasn't funny.

It had been a few years since we'd made the trek up to the mountains, but Finn remembered how to get us to the highway where the exciting part of our trip was about to take place. As we began the climb, the motor went into overdrive like it had done when we drove Ruth up, and I could see why she'd been concerned.

"Are we going to make it?" I asked.

"We sure are," Finn said. "I just need to keep it in low gear."

We passed the arrow head etched into the mountain and then to the right, we saw the big white hotel tucked in between the trees and hills. I recalled us stopping for drinks and pretending to be rich and famous. Like Ruth, I hated the smell of the hot springs, so I understood how she must have found working around them nauseating, especially knowing now that she was already pregnant.

Finn ground his gears a few times as he navigated the twists and turns of the mountain road, and soon there were hundreds of pine trees to our left, and the steep mountainside on our right. This morning, I could see the valley below, and I preferred the beautiful clouds that often hid it to the barren land below. A few times, I grabbed the armrest to keep from being tossed from one side of the back seat to the other, and again, I thought of Ruth getting queasy. But there was something about the mountains that was welcoming me home.

We passed the lumber yard in Rim Forest, then the white diner where we'd grabbed a bite to eat when we came up before. We didn't recognize the turnoff to Lake Arrowhead, where Ruth and Mr. Maynard had their cabins. Finn took the next left and while the road didn't look familiar, he assured us he'd figure out how to get there. After a few more turns, we began to recognize some of the familiar landmarks; the denser forest road dotted with cabins and the stone walls where, so many years ago, the mountain had been carved away to make way for the highway. And then we all saw it at the same time; the carved wood sign said Cabins for Rent and we knew we'd arrived.

# CHAPTER TWENTY THREE

The minute I climbed out of the car, the sound of gravel crunching under my shoes brought me back to the first time we'd come here. The moment we drove in, Mr. Maynard and his dog Mable had greeted us. Mabel took immediately took to Ruth, standing almost as tall as her and licking her face.

"Mabel," I remembered Mr. Maynard calling out to her, his face turning red as he did. I could tell then he immediately took a liking to Ruth.

Even before Finn turned the engine off and climbed out, I could tell Mabel heard us. I stood there stretching, almost willing Ruth to have heard us too. She'd most likely be curious who it was. Then it struck me she might not have a cabin available, so I waited a few moments before having the guys get my trunk out of the car. Mabel barked again, and came running to us the minute the front door to the office opened. I could hear Ruth call to her, "Mabel, behave," just like Mr. Maynard used to say.

Her hand shielded her eyes from the bright sun, and I could tell she didn't recognize the car or me. Of course, she wouldn't have. It'd been over two years, but I was still disappointed. Then she looked back towards me again, and her face lit up like a neon sign.

"Oh, my god. Charlotte! Is that you?"

Mabel stood and put her paws on my shoulders like she'd done with Ruth, and I hugged her. Apparently, she took this as a sign that it was okay to greet me like a long-lost friend. Her wet kisses covered my face.

"Mabel!"

All the ruckus brought Mr. Maynard out, and I could tell he was trying to figure out who we were. The guys came around to the side of the car so he could see them too, and then I could see recognition in his eyes and his smile broadened.

"Well, I'll be," he said.

"You all remember Jack." Ruth said, and to me, she said, "I can't believe you're all here! You should have written."

I made a slight face, and then she stood back and held me by my shoulders.

"Are you all right?"

"I will be," I said lightly. "Do you have a place I can stay?"

Without hesitation, she said, "Absolutely. Are you all staying?"

"Nah," Miles said. "We'd love to, but we have to play tonight."

"Well, come in anyway. We need to see if we have an opening," Ruth said, winking. "Plus, the baby is inside. Well, she's not exactly a baby anymore. Listen to me, I'm just running off the mouth!"

We followed her, Mr. Maynard and Mabel inside and there, standing in her playpen, was her baby Dorothy.

"Look who's come to visit," Ruth said, picking her up.

"She's just beautiful," I said. "Can I hold her?"

"Here you go, auntie," Ruth said, handing Dorothy over.

The way the baby looked back at Ruth, I thought for certain she was going to burst into tears. Coddling a baby didn't come naturally to me, and I hoped she couldn't sense my inexperience. Dorothy looked back at me and figured I was all right, for she began playing with my necklace. I pulled her close and kissed her soft cheek.

"I could just gobble you up!"

"Can I get you guys anything to drink?" Ruth asked. "I could make sandwiches."

Miles said, "I could use your bathroom, then we should probably get going. We just wanted to make sure Charlotte made it up here."

I could hear Jack pop the tops off two bottles, and he came back with two Cokes.

"Here you go, for on the way back down," he said, handing them to Finn. He turned to me and asked, "And for you, too?"

"Actually, that sounds great. Thanks."

Ruth found the key to a cabin and said, "Follow me."

The guys got my trunk out of the car and set it on the bed for me.

"This is the cabin I stayed in when I came back up," Ruth said. "Hopefully, it'll bring you good luck, like it did for me."

"Well, we better hit the road," Miles said. "It was great seeing you again, Ruth, and nice to see you too, Mr. Maynard."

"You need to call me Jack. After all, we're family now. And that includes you too, missy," he said to me.

To Miles and Finn, I said, "I'm not sure where I'll end up, but I'm sure you can write to me here."

Ruth wrote their address on a notepad and handed it to Miles.

"Tell Clara I'll write when I can, but make sure she knows I'm all right. I know it was the chicken way out, but I left her and Joe a note." I hugged them fiercely. "I can't thank you enough for being my friends, and if Joe asks about me, tell him I'm safe. That's all he needs to know for now."

"You can always leave a message for either of us at the hotel, and I'll expect to hear from you once you get settled in. You know, you're the best singer we've had," Miles said.

"No one can take your place. You always have a spot with us if you decide to come back."

"Okay," I said, wiping tears from my eyes. "You're getting all sentimental on me."

Jack took Dorothy back inside and Ruth and I watched Finn turn around in the drive. They both waved as they pulled out, and part of me wanted to go back home with them, but I knew I was where I needed to be right then.

Ruth took my hand in hers and said, "So, after you're all settled, you'll have to tell me what's happening. Come get me and we can talk before dinner if you want to. Jack has errands to run, so he won't be back home until later. "

"Thanks," was all I could say.

I watched Ruth walk back to the cabin before I went inside and opened my trunk. I knew I'd be staying for a while, so I started unpacking. The closet smelled pleasantly like cedar and there were plenty of hangers to hang my dresses, and when I opened the drawers in the dresser, I picked up the scent of lilac. I wondered what I'd smell like in the morning.

Just as I'd remembered, my cabin was at the same time, rustic yet charming. New plaid curtains stirred in the breeze from the open window, and the cool air felt good. Once I finished putting my clothes away, I set my photos on the dresser. Suddenly I longed for the past, for the time I was younger and had no idea what cards life was going to deal me. My mother and I looked so young then. I was no more than eleven, which would have made her twenty-six or twenty-seven.

I washed my face and ran a brush through my hair, then headed over to the office. The moment I stepped outside, I felt it. A slight breeze rustled through the tall trees all around the property, and a profound sense of calm and peacefulness that I hadn't felt in a long time surrounded me. I took in a deep breath and just absorbed the forest's earthy scent and its vibrant hues of color. It wasn't anything like Los Angeles or Texas. It was the mountains and the rugged environment. And it tugged at me.

I could see why Ruth stayed.


The door to the office was open and I could smell a roast, or something equally delicious, in the oven as I made my way to the office. I hadn't realized I was hungry until then, and when I poked my head in I asked, "What's for dinner?"

"Just a roast and potatoes like Jack likes. He's my meat and potatoes guy. Plus, when I cook a roast, we usually have leftovers which make great sandwiches the next day. Are you hungry?"

"Actually, I am. I was so nervous this morning, I didn't eat much."

"Well, help yourself to some carrots and I have cheese in the icebox and crackers in the cupboard. It'll be a while before we're ready to eat."

I sat at the kitchen table and munched while Ruth was busy cutting vegetables. Dorothy was sleeping in her crib, and it reminded me of how precious and innocent children were. While my near future didn't necessarily include children, I was hoping to return to a calmer, more relaxed state.

"So," I started. I knew Ruth was happy to see me, but she also wanted to know why I suddenly appeared. "The bright side is that Clara has married a doctor, no less."

I explained how the hotel had taken in more permanent guests, and one of them was the actress.

"He adores her, and his parents bought them a beautiful house. I didn't tell her I was leaving because I didn't want her to know where I was in case the gangsters asked her."

I could tell she hadn't comprehended what I was saying.

I told her about Joe and Mr. DeGrazia, and how I witnessed the councilman's dead body. "I began to wonder if they'd do away with me too, because I knew so much. Joe assured me they wouldn't, but I was a constant jumble of nerves. And I hated them being there, so I planned my escape."

Ruth took it all in, then looked around the room as if someone could be listening.

"You know," she whispered, "we have our own gangsters up here."

"You've got to be kidding me!" I drew back in the chair, too stunned to speak.

"Oh, they're there, but they don't bother anyone. In fact, they want to remain as inconspicuous as they can. I wrote to you about them when I stopped working for the Actress. I'd totally forgotten. They have women, gambling and alcohol, and they even make their own gin. I hear the place is full of Hollywood types, too. You've heard of Bugsy Siegel, right? Well, he's involved in the operation."

I was flustered, and I said, "You mean if I stay up here, I've just traded one group of gangsters for another?"

"We have them in a remote kind of way. Like I said, they're here, but mostly the people who come up there are trying to keep to themselves. Nothing like what you said about the men in Los Angeles."

I was having trouble processing this, and suddenly, I started to cry.

"How can life up here be no different from what I just left?"

Ruth rushed to my side and hugged me.

"It's not like that. Most people don't even know they're here. They have a speakeasy, and Hollywood types come up to gamble and drink. It won't be like living in Los Angeles at all. It's beautiful up here and them being here hasn't made a bit of difference. Trust me."

I sighed.

"Jack should be home anytime and then we can eat. You'll feel better, I promise. It's heaven here, even when we have to shovel snow," she said, leaning into me. "I hope you decide to stay."

Just then, I heard Jack's tires on the gravel, and Mable ran outside to greet him.

I knew I looked like hell, but I was hungry, and I figured Ruth could fill Jack in on what I'd told her. Dorothy woke up and Jack picked her up.

"Daddy's home, and it's time for dinner," he said, giving her a kiss. He put her in a high chair, then said, "I'll go wash up. I'm hungry."

Although it was still spring, the temperature dropped, and Jack lit a fire. We listened to Jack Benny on the Ed Sullivan Show while watching Dorothy try to raise herself up on to the couch. The first time she lost her balance and fell, the impact of her rear end on the floor startled her, and the look on her face was priceless. Determined to get back up again, she finally made it to a standing position, and Jack picked her up. She must have been exhausted from the day, for in no time, she fell asleep in his arms and he carried her into their room and put her in her crib.

I'd known when I saw him again this afternoon, and now his gentleness with Dorothy proved it; he was a good man for Ruth to have in her life.

I was getting tired too, and after making sure the dinner dishes were washed and put away, I made my way to my cabin. The evening sky had begun to darken, and through the treetops, the sky had turned several shades of red and orange. In a way, it reminded me a little of the early evenings in Texas, and then I realized lately I hadn't given much thought to my home.

I don't know how, but I slept like a log that night.

# CHAPTER TWENTY FOUR

Rustling in the bushes outside my window jolted me awake that next morning. I lay there frozen, thinking maybe I'd just been dreaming, when I heard it again. My heart raced as my brain conjured up images of Mr. DeGrazia finding me. But then I realized how unlikely that was. When the rustling stopped, I recalled Jack and Ruth warning me that bears and coyotes roamed the forest. They'd also assured me that wild animals usually stayed away from humans unless they've been provoked.

When the rustling started again, I rolled out of bed and crept along the wall of the cabin. When it was quiet gain, I let my breath out. Suddenly there was scratching at my door, and I jumped backwards. Whatever it was, it was persistent, and I was certain I was going to die my first day in the mountains.

Like it was going to protect me, I grabbed a wooden hanger and made my way back to the door; and then the scratching stopped. Maybe whatever it was had given up and moved on. I moved over to the front window, building up my courage to actually peek outside, when I heard a bark. And then another.

I pulled the curtain away and looked down. When she saw me, Mabel was sitting at my door, happy as a dog could be, and she barked again.

"Mabel, you're the devil himself!" I yelled, but she just barked again.

I looked out again, just to make sure nothing else was out there, and then opened the door to let her in.

"You liked to scare me to death," I said to her, but she jumped up and licked me.

"Mabel?" Ruth called out.

"She's here with me," I answered, poking my head out the door. "She was my wake up call."

"Mabel!" Ruth scolded.

But Mabel was content where she was, just watching me, probably knowing she'd scared me silly.

I asked her if she wanted to go back out, but when she didn't move, I closed my door and then showered. She continued to wait until I'd finished dressing and doing my hair, and then we both made our way to the office. I was hoping Ruth was cooking up something wonderful for breakfast.

"I thought I'd show you around town this morning, if you're up to it," Ruth said as she flipped pancakes.

"I'd love it," I said.

"I've been wanting to go to the bookstore." She turned to look at me, then continued. "Do you remember the one—where you bought me *The Swiss Family Robinson*?"

"Of course I do," I said, recalling how, when Ruth found it, her fingers touched the scuffed leather cover.

"Clyde still owns the shop, and he always lets me know when something new has come in."

"Is the candy store still there?" I asked.

"It is, and no trip to the Village would be complete without a stop there. We can stop and buy some duck food so we can feed the ducks, and then we need to stop at the grocer to find something to cook for dinner. By that time, Dorothy will be ready for a nice long nap, and we can continue where we left off."

"Just let me know when you're ready," I said.

I didn't expect Clyde at the bookstore to remember me when Ruth introduced me, but he said he hadn't forgotten me buying her that book.

"*Swiss Family Robinson*, I believe. I'm glad you've come back up. Do you read?" he asked.

"Not as much as I should. But I'll have plenty of time on my hands for a while, so now's as good a time as any to find something good to read."

"Ruth knows the inventory as well as I do, so I'm sure she'll help you find something," Clyde said, when another customer came in.

I remembered how she'd loved the smell of old books, and it appeared she still did when I saw her move to the used book section. She ran her hands across the spines like she had when I was there with her years ago.

"I love their fragrance," she said to me as I watched her.

She selected a few books and said that once I was finished reading them, she'd add them to her collection since she hadn't read them yet, either.

Dorothy seemed to be as enchanted with the books as Ruth was, for she wanted to touch them all, too.

"Not with your messy hands," Ruth said sweetly. "We'll get something for you to read too. Or I should say, something mommy can read to you."

The next stop was the candy shop, and my mouth started watering the minute we walked in the door. I loaded up on dark chocolate-covered almonds and some peanut brittle. I hadn't had either in years.

I said, "Let me buy something for Jack. What would he like?"

"He loves peanut brittle too, so he can share yours. That is, if you'll share."

"I'll get him his own bag. I'm not planning on sharing any of mine," I said with a quick laugh.

I stopped short. I didn't remember when the last time was that I'd laughed.

We finished the morning at the Village by feeding the ducks, and Dorothy was so cute when she tried to throw food into the lake. When the ducks rushed to where their food had dropped into the water, she jumped and squealed with delight.

"I forgot. Jack wanted me to get something at the hardware store, so we'll stop there next if you're okay."

"I have nowhere else to be, and it feels good to get out in the fresh air and do something different than clean up after people."

The aisles inside the store were so narrow, I stayed outside with Dorothy while Ruth ran in and picked up whatever it was Jack needed.

The last stop was the grocer, and he had everything we needed to make meatloaf and mashed potatoes. At this rate, I was going to get fat, but when I thought about it, I didn't mind.

I helped with dinner, and when Jack got home, we were all hungry enough to eat. It was a repeat of the night before; we ate, cleaned up the kitchen, then listened to the radio as we watched Dorothy, still determined to climb up onto the couch.

When she fell asleep in Jack's arms again, it was my time to leave.

"I can't believe how nice everyone is up here," I said. "It's nothing like the hustle and bustle of Los Angeles, where people are dodging cars and delivery trucks. It's all quite different."

"Do you think you could get used to it?"

"The thought has crossed my mind."

# CHAPTER TWENTY FIVE

That night, I couldn't sleep. I was tired but my mind wouldn't shut down. I kept seeing the councilman's bloody body on the floor of Suite 1512, and I couldn't stop thinking about Clara, Miles and Finn, no matter how hard I tried. And then I couldn't stop thinking about Joe. Although he knew I'd probably leave, I'd never said goodbye. I worried about him and hoped against hope there hadn't been any fallout with Mr. DeGrazia when he tried to explain my sudden departure. I knew he would be worried about me, and I wondered if he missed me as much as I missed him.

It was the first time I'd ever fallen in love, and I'd never been so lonely. I knew I hadn't been in control of anything that had happened, but I still felt like I was a failure. While it had only been a few nights, I realized nighttime was going to be the worst for me. And that night, I woke every hour, checking the clock on my dresser, and I watched the hours drag on. It seemed the more I tossed and turned, trying to find a comfortable spot, the more restless I became. At one point I was so twisted in my sheet and blanket, I had to get up and remake the bed. I longed for the times Joe and I spent the night together, waking to each other in the morning, and I envied Ruth and Clara for the lives they were living together with their men.

It didn't feel like it right then, but I still knew I'd made the right decision. There was no way I could have stayed in L.A. even if I'd found a new place to live and work. I'd forever be looking over my shoulder to see if anyone was following me, afraid I'd talk.

Just before dawn, I finally slept.

Over the Memorial Day weekend, the Arrowhead Women's Club held their annual membership drive and rummage sale in the parking lot at the Village. All the funds raised would go towards improving the town's park and buying new books for the school libraries. Most of the residents donated clothing and household items they no longer wanted, and according to Ruth, the club members spent weeks pricing everything and getting ready.

It had become a tradition for some people who wanted to take advantage of the weekend celebrations to set things out in their yards, hoping to attract people coming to the sale. You'd see them along the road on your way in to the Village. We stopped at a few and I held the baby while Ruth and Jack picked through treasures. Jack found a pocket knife and Ruth bought some clothes for Dorothy.

"There are plenty of kitchen things if you're interested," Ruth said when she got back into the car. "I'm not rushing you out, but if you're thinking about finding a place of your own, you might see if there's something you could use."

"Hmm. Good thought. Are you okay if I look?"

"Take your time."

I ended up filling a box of pots and pans, cooking utensils, and a hand painted vase of all things.

"When you're ready, you can usually find everything you'll need at the secondhand store in town. I've found more things there, haven't I, Jack?"

"Indeed you have," he said, chuckling.

On Memorial Day itself, we went to The Village, and families had already started setting out their blankets and picnics on the lawn in the square. Somehow, we found a spot under a tree and began unpacking the dinner Ruth and I had packed. Later in the afternoon, a band set up on the stage and I was looking forward to hearing live music. Once they got started, children danced and chased each other until the adults came up to dance and shooed them away. Baby Dorothy held on to Jack's finger as she tried to dance too, and when she finally went to sleep, I kept an eye on her when they got up to dance. Watching them, I had to admit, Ruth looked truly happy, and I could tell Jack adored them both.

I found I loved the charm of the mountains more every day. Ruth warned me I hadn't experienced winter yet, but I could only imagine it would be chilly and white with snow. I'd need to buy a winter wardrobe and boots, but I also kept thinking about finding a place of my own. I needed a job, and so far, I hadn't seen anything promising in the Village or in the small shops in town. I'd also have to start thinking about getting a car—continually relying on Ruth would eventually get tiresome for her, and I felt guilty taking her time.

Beginning with the local newspaper, I began checking out the help wanted and cars for sale ads. Jack did jobs for people in town, and I asked him to keep an eye out for a good running, inexpensive used car.

He looked at me and, with a quick laugh, said, "Well, you might find one or the other, but probably not both of them." And then he winked. "I'll let you know if I come across anything."

Less than two weeks later, he came home with a name and phone number scribbled onto a sheet of paper.

"This here lady has a car for sale that might just be perfect for you. I looked at it and the engine sounds good. It's only a Model A 2 door, and only a couple of years old. She's asking two hundred dollars, and if you don't have it all, I know her pretty well. I'm sure she'd take a couple of payments on it. She just wants to get rid of it. Her husband doesn't drive anymore, and it's just sitting there taking up space in their driveway."

"If you saw it, then I'm sure it'll be perfect. And I have the cash to pay for it," I said. "When can I go look at it?"

"I'll see her again tomorrow, and then we can go look at it."

"Thanks, Jack. You're really very kind."

"Anything for a friend of my girl," he said affectionately.

Two days later, I had a new car, and I celebrated my freedom by driving down to The Village to feed the ducks and buy some candy.

# CHAPTER TWENTY SIX

I ate two chocolate-covered almonds before I made my way to the lake and when I got there, I was more than a little disappointed that a young family was already there in my favorite spot. Without a word, I sat on one of the wooden benches and watched as the father held a young boy up on the railing as they tossed bread crumbs into the water. I wanted to resent their intrusion into my morning, as I had a glimpse of what my life could have been with Joe if we'd been free to be together. I was also hoping the peacefulness of the lake would take me to a place I needed to be to figure out what I wanted to do next, but that was not to be.

Their laughter and the child's delight at seeing the ducks was so pure it almost took my breath away. My attention turned toward the woman standing to their side, swaying slightly, her arms snugly cradling a baby in a pink blanket. Her smile spread as the baby reached up and reached for her hair. When she turned her head away, she saw me sitting there, and said, "Oh, are we in your way?"

"No," I managed to say, "Honestly, I don't know what I've enjoyed more. Watching you and your family or enjoying the view of the lake."

I gave her my duck food and headed back to the cabins. Everyone, including Mabel, was gone, and I relished the time I had to sit out at the fire ring by myself. As the warmth of the afternoon sun touched my skin, the heat seeped into my muscles, reminding me of life's simple pleasures. I welcomed the warmth. I wasn't sure how long I dozed. I was jolted awake by the sound of car doors slamming shut. Thankfully, the trees surrounding the property had filtered my exposure to the sun, but my skin still felt warm to the touch.

Ruth called out to me, "Can you come get Dorothy while I unload the groceries?"

Once everything was brought in and put away, we started a stew and Ruth put the baby down for her nap. I cleaned and cut vegetables and filled a bowl of water for the potatoes, and set them aside on the counter for when Ruth wanted to add them. I'd learned from my mother that every cook had a method, and I didn't want to disrupt hers.

"Let me know when you need me," I said.

"I wouldn't mind reading for a half hour," Ruth said, pulling out a book that she'd already started. "I have a new one if you want to read as well."

One thing I'd picked up from Ruth since I'd been up in the mountains was that I'd enjoyed reading. I perused her bookcase and found something that looked interesting and, with that, we sat in comfortable silence at the kitchen table.

That night, there was a full moon, and I wanted to fall asleep by its light, so I left my curtains pulled open. The night was warm, so I tossed aside my blanket and pulled up only my sheet. From my bed, I could see the moon as it rose in the sky, and as it disappeared, I said aloud, "Please let me figure out what to do."

By the time it was out of sight, I'd turned over and somehow fallen asleep.

The next morning, I awoke to the glare of the rising sun on my face and my first response was to roll away from it. But as I lay there, I gradually let my eyes adjust to the brightness of the new day. Alternating between shielding my eyes and soaking up the warmth, I couldn't help but wonder if the light was promising me a new beginning.

Suddenly, I was eager to go outside and take in the fresh morning air. I grabbed my robe and the minute I opened the door to my cabin, Mabel came running as if she'd been waiting for me. She stood and put her paws on my shoulders, and I couldn't help but hug her back. She eventually went back down to all fours, and I scratched behind her ear. Typical of Mabel, she quickly lost interest when she heard a noise in the bushes and ran to investigate. I couldn't help but smile as I wondered if the forest critters taunted her on purpose.

Mabel quickly lost interest in the bushes when Jack called to her, and as I watched her run towards him, everything felt different. It was if a door to my future opened and I realized if I wanted to, I could make a new life up here. I loved Joe, and I knew that my life going forward did not include him. And if anything was going to change in my life, I would have to go out on my own.

The next thing I needed to do was to get a job.

# CHAPTER TWENTY SEVEN

I started my search in the help wanted ads in the weekly newspaper. There was a clerical position available at a real estate company, and the woman's clothing store in The Village was looking for a clerk, but neither sounded like something I'd be good at. It felt like déjà vu when I stopped at the hotel; I knew I could be a maid again, and they might have a nightclub where I could apply. After speaking with housekeeping though, my hopes were dashed; they had enough maids and there was no lounge. The candy store and bookstore weren't looking for help either, and on the way back into town, I decided to wallow in my misery and grab something to eat at Lu's Diner.

An older woman greeted me and said, "Sit anywhere you'd like."

When she came to my table, she handed me a menu and asked, "Are you new in town?"

"I am, actually. I'm looking for a job, and so far I'm not having much luck."

"Hmm," she said. "Do you have any experience serving food? One of my girls is moving back down the hill and I'll be needing someone to fill her space."

"Indeed, I do," I said.

Without giving it a second thought, she said, "Then let's give it a try. Lucille's the name. But most people call me Lu."

"Charlotte," I said, reaching out to shake her hand.

"You can start the day after tomorrow."

"Dinner's on me tonight," I said to Ruth when I stopped in the office. "I got a job at the diner."

She initially protested, but then her face lit up. "Really? I can't remember the last time we ate out."

Her face fell when she said, "I don't have anyone to watch Dorothy."

"She's invited too. Decide where you want to go," I said, turning to leave. "Let me know when Jack gets home. Oh, and I assume it's okay if I rent the cabin for a while longer?"

"Absolutely. And we'll come get you when we're ready."

As I left, Mabel ran ahead of me and once I got to my cabin, I said, "Go back home, girl."

I wouldn't start training at the diner for another day, but I went in the next morning for breakfast. I wanted a chance to look at the menu and familiarize myself with it. I splurged on French toast and bacon, and loaded it up with powdered sugar. Just like the diner back home, I was sure I would quickly tire of the food, but that morning, everything sounded delicious.

A girl named Ramona waited on me.

"Where you up from?" she asked, setting down my food.

"Los Angeles. I'm staying with Ruth and Jack Maynard over at their cabins," I said, thinking she'd know them.

"I don't think I've seen them in here," she said. "It's such a small town, usually everyone knows everyone. But I've only been up here a year."

"I don't think they go out to eat much. They stay pretty busy, and they have a little one."

"I hear you're starting tomorrow. I'll be here too. I'll show you the ropes. Well, I hope you enjoy your breakfast," she said, leaving me to it.

I went back to studying the menu while I ate, and I'm sure it was because I was hungry almost everything sounded delicious except the Tuesday Nite Special, Liver n' Onions. I hoped no one ever asked me if it was good, as customers often did when they couldn't decide what to eat, because I'd have to tell them it was probably the only thing I wouldn't eat no matter where I was.

As I enjoyed my breakfast, I observed how the owner, Lucille, greeted almost everyone by their first name, and when most of them left, they made sure to say goodbye. Just like back home, people wanted their recognition. I watched as Ramona checked in on her tables, and when she got to me, I told her everything was good.

Over the next few days, I shadowed her and it all came back to me. How to write an order, what to tell the kitchen when there was a special request, and how to balance plates as I brought them out to the tables. When the bus boy didn't come in, we cleared our own tables and reset them for the next customers. During quiet times, we wrapped silverware in napkins and filled salt and pepper shakers.

I gradually learned who the regulars were and what they liked. Mr. and Mrs. Davidson liked their hot coffee brought out right away, and they always ordered the same thing; pancakes for Mr. Davidson and poached eggs for his wife. Elizabeth, the realtor from across the street, came in every day at lunch and ordered iced tea with lots of ice and lemon and a half turkey sandwich with fresh fruit. Sometimes she'd take the fruit back to the office for an afternoon snack. Quite a few men came in by themselves for both breakfast and lunch, and at least once a week, a group of them in matching work clothes sat at the back table and made a lot of noise.

It took about three weeks for everyone to get to know me; they asked the same basic questions—like where I was from, what brought me up to the mountains, did I like it, did I have snow boots for winter— and both men and women casually glanced at my left hand to see if I wore a ring. Everyone was friendly, tips were decent and if any of the men got out of line, Lu was there, quick as a jackrabbit to put them in their place.

My shift was sometimes split: I worked breakfast until around one, then I was back in for dinner from five to nine when we closed. It wasn't surprising, mostly it was single men on their way to work for breakfast and couples for dinner.

One morning, I saw a new face. When he came through the door, Lucille called out, "Hey Abe. We haven't seen you around for a while. Everything going okay?"

"Yeah, I'm good," he said, holding up a bandaged hand and sliding into a booth. "Just cut my hand at the lumberyard and was off. I'm back to work today though, thank god. Being home with two teenagers is enough to drive a man crazy. I don't know how you women do it."

"We do it because we're wired different," Lucille snapped.

"Whoa," Abe said, holding his hands up in surrender. "I was just trying to be funny."

"Right," Ramona said, plunking his breakfast down.

"Geez," Abe said, turning ten shades of red. "Sorry."

I watched from afar as he quickly finished his breakfast, and as he stood to leave, I caught his eye. He said, "I gotta get to work."

Ramona cleared his dishes and smiled when she saw her tip.

Abe didn't come in for the next few days and we all assumed his comment embarrassed him, but the next Monday, he was back.

"Got my hand unstitched," he said, holding it up for us to see.

"Good for you," Ramona said.

Abe looked around towards the back of the restaurant where my station was and made his way back there. I wasn't sure if he did that because he'd seen me the other day, or if he just wanted to escape Ramona. Either way, he sat at one of the tables, and when I handed him a menu, he took it, but said, "I don't need one. I already know what I want. I'll take the pancakes and bacon."

I wrote his order down, then dropped my pen. Abe reached down and picked it up, and when he handed it to me, I shoved it and my order pad into my pocket. I knew I was beet red and quickly turned before I realized he still had the menu. When I turned again to take it back, he held it for a few seconds until I looked at him. I wasn't sure it was possible, but I could feel myself turn even redder. I was burning up.

When his breakfast was ready, I casually set it down on the table and tried not to look at him. I figured Abe was in his late thirties, with light brown hair, green eyes, and any girl would have killed for his thick, long lashes. He was clean shaven, which I thought was interesting, especially since most guys I'd seen who worked at the lumberyard were on the scruffy side. I also noticed he didn't have a wedding ring on.

"How'd you hurt your hand?" I asked.

"I was working with a beam and it slipped. The boys had to load me up in the truck and take me to the emergency room. I was lucky the beam didn't do me any more damage."

He raised his hand and turned it back and forth to show me he was okay.

"You're new here, aren't you?" he asked, slightly raising one eyebrow.

He was young, but his face bore the marks of an outdoor life— deeply tanned and a few perfectly placed freckles. His hair fell onto his forehead, and he raked his fingers through it. The ease of his smile should have warmed me, but instead, it made me see myself through his eyes. Should I have taken more time to do my hair this morning? Were there food stains on my apron? I'd started picking at my cuticles and the skin on my hands was rough and dry. I hated I was so self conscious and I blamed it on everything that had happened in Los Angeles. No one was perfect, and I forced myself to smile back, even if it was weak.

"Well, I'm off to work," he said, pulling out his wallet and leaving me a tip.

Part of me was both relieved to see him leave, and yet another part was a little sorry.

I still had my free meal coming, so I brought home that night's dinner special, stew and mashed potatoes. I figured Ruth could use a break, and it was a small way for me to pay them back for putting up with me. I was tempted to tell Ruth about Abe, but when I realized there really wasn't anything to tell, I kept my thoughts to myself.

That night, though, as I tossed and turned in bed, I thought about Abe, and I was ashamed I'd even been remotely interested in him. I still loved Joe, although I knew I'd never be able to let him know where I was. I'd run away, and if he loved me as he said he did, I'd broken his heart as well as mine.

Yet, the next morning, as I was getting ready for work, I made a point of spending a few more minutes on my hair and even wore a touch of lipstick. I looked for Abe all morning and tried not to watch the minutes tick by. But when he didn't show up for breakfast, I felt what I could only call the sting of rejection. It didn't matter that he'd never come out and said he was interested in me; I could tell he was. So far, our conversations had been harmless, but I couldn't help but fantasize about the beginning of a relationship and I took his absence personally.

What an idiot I was.

That didn't keep me from thinking about him all the next day while I changed my sheets and did my laundry. I took baby Dorothy for a few hours while Ruth went into town to do some shopping, and after bundling her up, we walked the property with Mabel at our side; I looked at everything and nothing at the same time. Dorothy was a sweet baby, smiling and laughing at the simplest of things, and I wondered if I'd been that way as a child as well. I knew how much Ruth loved her daughter, and for the first time, I could see how much my mother had loved me. The thought of living the rest of my life without her brought tears to my eyes. And then I wondered if I would have stayed in Los Angeles, would Joe and I have ever had a chance to make something of our lives together? I was miserable and, to make the melancholy go away, I hugged Dorothy tightly until she squirmed. I had grown to love her, too.

The next morning, just as I was seating a couple, Abe's after shave preceded him as he came through the door. He held his work hat in one hand and ran his hand over his damp hair with the other. His boots were already caked with mud. Hopefully, he left them outside when he came home from work or his floors would have been a dirty mess.

"Well, look what the cat drug in," Ramona said dryly. Then to me she said, "My advice is, don't go there. If you're looking for a man and security, Billy over there is on the lookout for a wife."

Out of curiosity, I checked Billy out and there was nothing I was interested in. He was an older man who chewed with his mouth full, and gray stringy hair hung out from his sweat stained cowboy hat. Instead of using his napkin, he wiped his mouth on his shirtsleeve.

"Who said anything about looking for a husband?" I whispered.

"Just saying," Ramona said.

And then Abe came in and made his way to my section. My heart started hammering in my chest, sending a rush of warmth through my body. I couldn't deny there was a pull, almost like a magnetic draw, to him. It was all I could do to give him enough time to sit in the booth before I brought him a cup of coffee.

"No menu?" I asked, trying to sound casual.

My mind raced with a thousand thoughts. Would he notice I'd done my hair differently? Was he happy to see me, too? Was I betraying Joe? And then, what the hell was I doing?

"Naw," he said, giving me the once over. "You look nice this morning. I'll have the pancakes and eggs. But soft bacon this time."

I wrote down his order, just so I'd have something to do, and Lucille liked having a paper record of what her sales were. My nerves got the better of me practically yelled his order into the window of the kitchen.

I startled Lucille, and she looked up. "I'm not deaf, you know," she called back to me.

I thought I'd die right then and there, and it was worse when Ramona gave me a look. I pretended to go about my business, but I wanted to melt into the floor. Instead, I greeted new customers and since it was Ramona's turn, I lead them to her section. When Abe's order was ready, Lucille yelled, "Charlotte, pancakes and bacon are up!" to make her point.

Knowing I'd drawn their attention, to be obstinate, I chatted a bit more with Abe. He told me he'd been up in the mountains for almost ten years, and he had two young daughters, aged twelve and thirteen.

My breath caught, and I was certain my eyebrows shot up in surprise. I almost said "Oh" out loud. I hadn't expected *children*, and I was at a loss for words. I quickly gave him his bill and went into the bathroom, where I could gather my wits. *Now* what?

When he finally left, I wasn't sure what I was feeling, but it wasn't good. My heart and my mind were being pulled in too many directions. I felt we had a connection, but I also realized I missed Joe, and was possibly clinging to old memories and hoping to make new ones. And I wondered if maybe I was jumping into something I wasn't prepared to deal with—especially if he had children.

Despite my uneasiness, I was drawn to Abe, and the intrigue was troubling.

He didn't come in for the next two days, and more than once I caught myself looking up when the front door opened. Although I was relieved, my actions weren't lost on Ramona.

"You're barking up the wrong tree with that one," she finally said.

"What?" I asked, pretending to not get the gist of what she was saying.

"He's got two kids and a wife," she said matter-of-factly. "I can tell he's interested in you, and vice versa, but everyone knows his story."

*Everyone* didn't include me, and I tried my best to suppress my surprise.

Ramona went on. "Yeah, his wife's in that sanatorium down the hill, and has been for a couple of years. It's for people with TB, but I've heard they keep people with other issues there too."

To anyone watching, they'd think that Ramona and I were just exchanging gossip, and I nonchalantly started drying a new rack of glasses sitting on the back counter. On the surface, I appeared as cool as a cucumber, but beneath the surface, I was dying a thousand deaths. The more she rambled on, the more aggressive I got with my dish rag, but Ramona didn't seem to notice how uncomfortable I was, and for that, I was grateful.

I was glad I hadn't shared any of my fantasies with anyone now that I was going to have to nip our flirting in the bud. As soon as I could, I took a break and made my way to my new favorite place, the bathroom, so I could splash cool water on my face and get a grip.

After my lunch shift, I drove back to my cabin and just sat in my car, trying to think of a way to avoid Abe. I couldn't come right out and tell him I knew about his wife; first of all because I didn't have the courage to, and second, I didn't want the restaurant to lose him as a customer. When Mabel came out to check on me, I knew I'd have to face Ruth somehow, and see if she had any ideas.

"Do you have any of your mother's jewelry?" she asked. "Like a wedding or engagement ring?"

Why hadn't I thought of that? I had both her rings, and right then, the simplest solution was to wear the engagement ring to work every day. I'd make sure he saw it the next time he came in and I waited on him, and unless he was a total lamebrain, he'd get the hint. And then I'd avoid any more idle talk.

And sure enough, that worked. I thought Abe's eyes were going to pop out of his head when he saw my mother's ring, and he turned ten shades of red. I pretended I didn't notice and continued writing down his order. And then a sudden movement caught my eye as he fumbled to conceal the red rose on the seat of the booth. I did my best to pretend I hadn't seen it, but it was too late. His face turned beet red.

"That'll be it then?" I asked. I held a menu to my chest, as if I could hide behind it.

Even though we hadn't gotten any further than just talking in the diner, I felt like I'd broken his heart and dashed his hopes. He must have known everyone was aware of his wife, and that someone was sure to tell me. And yet he was trying to bring a new person into what I thought was an obviously lonely life. It was all I could do not to cry as I walked away from him, but there was no way I could have allowed anything more to happen between us. I resolved to avoid Abe by any means necessary. If he came in and sat in my section, I'd ask Ramona to cover for me, telling her I needed her help, and if he didn't eventually get the hint, I'd ask Lucille to change my schedule so I wasn't working breakfast.

But Abe got the hint; he quit coming in altogether.

# CHAPTER TWENTY EIGHT

Temperatures in October cooled, and after getting caught during a cold spell, I made sure I carried my jacket with me everywhere I went. Other than the pines, the trees had turned vibrant shades of orange, red and gold and most of the trees were bare. Fallen leaves, scattered by sudden gusts of wind, crunched underfoot. I was already looking forward to spring when Ruth told me my favorite trees, the dogwoods, would bloom again.

I loved the smell of wood burning chimneys and the cool, crisp weather in November, and while we hadn't had snow yet, I broke down and bought a pair of boots, a thick scarf and mittens so I'd be prepared for the even colder weather to come.

Ruth never told me she was trying to play matchmaker when she invited a friend of Jack's for Thanksgiving dinner. I'd asked Lucille at the diner to bake my favorite apple and pumpkin pies, and I'd chipped in when Ruth and I did the shopping for everything we needed to make dinner. I cut vegetables and peeled potatoes and left the turkey and stuffing to Ruth. Just as we pulled the turkey out of the oven, I heard a car door slam and Mabel barked, announcing a visitor. Jack went to the door, and he tried to act nonchalant as he invited his friend, Will Cummings, in.

I shot Ruth a look, and she acted surprised.

"You're just in time," she said. "Jack's going to carve the turkey in a few minutes, then we can sit down and eat."

"Charlotte, this is Will, and Will, this is Charlotte," Jack said, avoiding my frown and taking Will's coat.

"Pleased to meet you, Charlotte."

Jack brought the turkey to the table, and I helped Ruth bring everything else out, but not before bumping her.

"So, Charlotte's from Los Angeles," Ruth said. "She's found a new home up here with us."

"It's a far cry from L.A.," Will said, tucking his napkin into his shirt. "If I don't do this, I'll be wearing part of my food before the end of dinner," he said, chuckling. "And what do you think about our mountain? Will it suit you?"

"I love it," I said. "And I think it'll suit me fine."

"Charlotte has a job at the diner," Ruth said.

"So I'll never starve."

Everyone laughed.

"Will owns a car repair service and plows the roads during the snow season. We'd be lost without him," Jack said. "Dinner is delicious, Ruth."

Will and I agreed.

It turned out to be a pleasant evening, and Will was comfortable to be around. It was impossible to tell his age, with the creases around his eyes and his weathered face. His beard was thick, peppered with streaks of silver, and his longer hair was the same. He wore clean jeans, weathered boots and a flannel shirt. Apparently, they hadn't told him there would be an extra guest either, or I was sure he would have worn a nicer pair of boots.

Once Dorothy was put to bed, the four of us sat at the kitchen table and played gin rummy. I hadn't played in years and needed a quick refresher course, but I quickly picked it up. Around nine, we called it a night and Jack walked Will to his truck.

"I'm sorry I didn't tell you," Ruth admitted. "I just thought it would be nice if the two of you became friends."

"Friends, or ..."

"Friends, Charlotte. You need new people in your life."

"I agree," I admitted. "I was just surprised."

"Maybe we could play cards again?" she asked.

"That was nice. And Will seems to be a personable man."

"Did you like him?"

"As a friend, yes."

"Okay, I'll leave it at that."

Fortunately, Will was also just interested in friendship, which spared us potential awkwardness. Ruth told me he'd lost his wife a few years earlier, and I wouldn't have guessed it by the lighthearted conversation and his good nature. When Ruth brought up spending Christmas with them, she asked if I minded if they invited Will to join us again.

"Absolutely," I said. "It's your house, and I enjoyed his company," I said honestly.

"The cabins are full for the holiday, and it's supposed to snow. It's everyone's dream to wake up to a white Christmas, and hopefully they won't be disappointed," she said.

On Christmas day, I provided pies from the diner again, and Ruth cooked a ham. Baby Dorothy loved the mashed potatoes and candied yams, and by the end of dinner, I'd have sworn half her meal made it into her mouth and the other half was smeared all over her face, clothing and high chair. I was dying to wipe her off, but Ruth and Jack just laughed at her, which made her bang her spoon on her plate.

After Jack put her to bed, he brought out the cards and stoked the fire before we gathered at the table. For a few cozy hours, the four of us spent a warm and comfortable evening together. Both Will and Jack could sense the beginning of the snowfall, and after checking outside, Will got up to gather his coat and gloves.

"Well, I'm off," he said as he made his way to the front door. "Duty calls. And thanks for the evening."

We heard the sound of his snow plow start up and then the grinding of gears as he put it in reverse and pulled out of the drive. He seemed more than ready to get out into the snow and plow the roads, even if it was just beginning to snow. We cut the evening short.

The next morning, I woke to the laughter of young children and when I pulled the curtain back from my window, I saw four of them with flushed cheeks, three throwing snowballs through the air and one failing miserably at building a snowman. The morning was alive with their energy and I envied them. I tried to recall winters where we'd had enough snow to play in when I was growing up, and I could not think of one time I was that carefree.

Soon their parents came out with toboggans, snow hats and blankets and called out to them to get into the car. Once they left, I climbed back into bed hoping I'd fall back asleep, but I just laid there thinking about my next move. Suddenly, I sat up with a start and checked the time on my nightstand clock. I'd forgotten I had to go to work. I dressed in layers, knowing I'd be freezing on the drive in, but then when the diner warmed up, I'd get comfortable enough to shed the extra sweater I put on.

Once I got in my car, even my mittens didn't keep my hands and fingers warm, and then when I started to back out of my space, I realized I'd never driven in the snow before. There were only about four inches on the ground, and thankfully the road had been recently plowed. I tried to recall Jack's snow driving tips, and carefully pulled out on to the highway.

I think I only drove about ten miles an hour and I tried not to pay attention to the cars that were lining up behind me. If they didn't like the way I was driving, then tough; I wasn't going to drive any faster than I felt comfortable. When I came to a turnoff, I pulled over to let them drive past me before I got back onto the highway. I parked in my space behind the diner and the crunch of my boots in the snow echoed in the still air as I made my way to the front door. Warm puffs of my breath reminded me just how cold it was, and it felt wonderful to step into the warmth of the restaurant.

On New Year's Day eve, most small businesses closed early if they were open at all, so I was surprised we were busy for breakfast. Ramona and I split the floor as usual and I offered to take the counter; those diners usually ate by themselves and were a quicker turnover than the tables and booths, which also meant smaller but more tips.

I hadn't noticed a new customer and when he cleared his throat, he caught my attention.

"I'm sorry," I said quickly, as I cleared the pervious dishes. "Menu?"

"Yes, please," he answered.

"Coffee?"

"Yes."

His dark hair was slicked back, and his chiseled features and deep-set eyes made me think he belonged on a movie poster. His black suit and fancy shoes made him stand out like a sore thumb.

I left him to the menu and when I came back, I could sense his impatience but he didn't say anything. He ordered a club sandwich, which was an unusual choice for breakfast, although when I thought about it, people ordered all kinds of things to eat in the morning. When he handed me his menu, he met my gaze and I couldn't read him. There was something vaguely familiar about him that made me question if he was the type of man to fear or follow, and I hated to admit I was intrigued.

I made sure to refill his coffee, and when he was close to being finished, I gave him his bill.

"You have something on your face," he said, pointing to my left cheek.

"What?"

He pointed again.

"Oh," I said, reaching for a napkin to wipe my face. "Thanks."

"See you next year," he said as he got up.

"What?" I asked again. I suddenly felt like he wondered if I could hear him.

"Next year? Happy New Year?"

"Oh, right," I said, feeling my face flush. "Happy New Year to you too."

The minute he walked out the door, Ramona was on me. "Who is that?"

"I'm not sure, exactly," I said.

"You'd better watch out for that one. I can tell he's up to no good."

"Sure. I don't think he's interested in me. And there's something about him anyway," I said, clearing his dishes. He'd left me a fifty-cent tip on a fifty cent bill!

I was having New Year's Eve dinner with Ruth and Jack, so I brought home four pieces of chocolate cake in case Will decided to join us. I also made up plates of potato salad and ham for sandwiches. Ruth made baked beans, and we both agreed potato chips would perfectly round out the menu. Will did decide to celebrate with us, and after dinner, we played cards until the countdown on the radio. We all stood and cheered with our sodas, and when it was time to kiss, Will and I awkwardly kissed each other on the cheek.

That night, the sky opened up, and we got a deluge of rain, but the temperature wasn't cold enough to bring more snow. I loved the sound of rain on the roof—the steady rhythm that acted like a lullaby once I snuggled up in my blankets. The diner wasn't open on New Year's Day, so my plan for the next morning was to sleep in.

However, Mother Nature and my cabin had their own ideas. At around seven A.M. I bolted awake to a different rhythmic sound; that of the steady dripping of a leaking roof right into the middle of my bed. Everything was soaked, including me and my pajamas and even though there was still a trace of a fire in the fireplace, I was freezing. I rekindled the fire, then stripped down to my socks and underwear. I remembered seeing more blankets in the closet, so I pulled one out and quickly shook it to make sure there were no spiders hiding in the folds. I then wrapped it around me and went to the bathroom to draw a warm bath.

Once the cabin and I were warm and cozy, I quickly dressed, gathered up my bedding, and headed down to the office.

"My roof is leaking," I said as I came in. I hung my wet coat on the rack by the door and brought my bedding into the laundry area.

Jack came out into the office and asked Ruth to get a bucket. "I'll take this down there. We'll have to move you to another cabin," he said.

"No problem. I'll go back and start packing up my things."

"And I'll start the laundry," Ruth said. "I'm sorry."

"You didn't cause the problem."

"I'm still sorry. I'll come up and help you once I get this in the washer."

Back in my cabin, I helped Jack move the bed to one side so the mattress wouldn't get any wetter, then I pulled out my footlocker and suitcase and started packing up my belongings. Ruth came in a few minutes later and we started emptying the dresser.

"This is lovely," she said when she came across the box Mrs. Rochester left me.

I told her about long-term guests who'd begun staying at the hotel, and how I'd been Adele's maid. I went to the drawer and found the deed she'd left me.

"Look at this," I said, opening it up. "There's a key somewhere,"

"Charlotte, do you have any idea what this is?"

"Of course I do, although I'd forgotten all about it. I've seen the name of the town somewhere, but I'm not sure where it is."

"I have to ask Jack. I think I know, but I'm not certain. He's been up here longer than I have."

"Up *here*?" I wasn't sure I'd heard her correctly.

"Come over for dinner tonight and bring the deed. Jack will know."

I spent the rest of the afternoon packing everything up, then unpacking it all into my new cabin. While all the cabins looked similar on the exterior, the interior of this one was also very charming, decorated with a brown and tan rug, a brown blanket on the bed, brown and green curtains. The wood flooring creaked slightly, which, for some reason, was more comforting than annoying, and two overstuffed chairs faced a bear painting on the fireplace.

Mabel came to check in on me a few times, and I gave her a treat—I'd bought dog biscuits the last time I was at the general store. I'd also bought some squirrel food, but kept forgetting to ask Jack if I could put up a feeder. I left the bag out on the dresser to remind me to ask him that night.

Once I had my photos and my mother's hairbrush set out, I was finished, and I still had an hour or so to kill before dinner. I went down to the office to see if Ruth needed any help and I mostly sat at the kitchen table and entertained Dorothy, which Ruth reminded me was enough help in itself.

While I waited, I looked at the deed again, and the longer I sat there, the more anxious I got. What if there was a cabin on the property? Was it somewhere I could live? Was it somewhere I'd *want* to live? By the time Jack got home and cleaned up, I'd made myself a nervous wreck with all my speculation. I made myself wait until Ruth brought it up, and Jack said he'd look at it after dinner.

Ruth put Dorothy to bed, and I sat with Jack as he unfolded the paper.

"Ah," he said with only a quick glance. "Who did you say gave this to you?"

"One of the permanent guests at the hotel where I worked. She died."

"Well, the Valley of Enchantment is Crestline. Not too far from here. And you say you have a key?"

His words hung in the air for a moment, sinking in as my mind scrambled to catch up.

"Yes."

"That might mean there's a cabin on the property." His expression was warm and teasing, and he watched me, I could tell, waiting for my reaction.

"That would be a little too much to hope for," I said, chewing the inside of my cheek.

"Well, you can always drive out there. I think I might have a map somewhere. I'll dig it out before you go home."

"What did I miss?" Ruth asked.

"You won't believe this," I answered. "The property is up here. In Crestline."

"Now, who would have thought?" she said.

"Will you go with me to find it?"

"That's a dumb question. Of course I will."

# CHAPTER TWENTY NINE

I worked my morning shift in the diner as I always did, and I tried my best to act like I wasn't on pins and needles. When Ramona said, "You've been acting like you have ants in your pants," I forced a casual shrug, but I knew I hadn't done a very good job trying to act like nothing was on my mind. I didn't want to say anything for fear the property I inherited would just turn out to be land with overgrown plants in the forest—or worse, that there really was a habitable cabin on it and people might think I was too good for my britches.

Ruth came by during my break between lunch and dinner, and she drove me over to Crestline.

"I've been there before so I can get us to town, then we can ask someone for directions," she'd said. "There are two ways to get there; one is to go back on to the highway, and the other is to take a road that only the locals know. It's what we take when it's so foggy on the rim we can't see. For some reason, the fog doesn't usually go that far inland."

"I'm a nervous wreck."

I held on to Dorothy as we drove and she cuddled with me, which helped calm me down. There was nothing like cradling something so impossibly precious as a child.

There wasn't much to the town as we drove in and it looked like they were working on building a lake. A general store was on the left, and a filling station was just across the street.

"The Pacific Electric Railway down in L.A. built a camp up here, and people come up to stay, so the town's growing. Once the lake is finished, I imagine a lot more people will be coming up. In the meantime, let's find out where your place is."

We stopped at the filling station, and a young man came out, wiping his hands on a towel.

"Fill 'er up?" he asked.

"We just need some directions," Ruth said, and I could see the disappointment on his face.

He looked at the map and pointed us up the highway, and then said we'd be able to find the turnoff easily enough. We thanked him, and as we pulled out, I wondered if I should have put gas in Ruth's car.

We passed a place that sold caskets, a post office, a real estate office, and what was called The Tavern, although we were still deep into prohibition. At least if I stayed here, there'd be basic essentials. We rounded a corner, and then found the turnoff, and I was pleasantly surprised to see a few cabins. Mine was up ahead, and before we got out of her car, I made sure we were at the right address. I didn't want to get out and have someone shoot us for trespassing. Ruth opened her car door, but I stood there for a few moments, taking in the property. It was impossible for me to tell how large the property was, but my best guess was that it was on over an acre.

As we walked up the path to the cabin, I heard a whistling, then sheck-sheck-sheck sound, and quickly found the source. A blue and gray bird was sitting on an old fallen tree trunk singing. He sensed us and stopped, but not before cocking his head to see who we were. Then, to my dismay, he flew away.

"Did you see the blue bird?" I asked Ruth.

"I didn't, but it's probably a Stellar's blue jay. They're all over up here."

"Listen. I hear something else," I said.

"You're just full of observations. It sounds like a stream. It must be out back."

"We can check it out once we see what shape the place is in."

From the outside, the cabin itself was magical, with a lot more detailed woodwork than Ruth's cabins. It was built out of logs, which seemed to be the rule up there, and red shutters with cutouts of trees adorned the windows. An old rocker sat on the porch, and a bird or squirrel feeder of some type was nailed to one of its posts. Sunlight filtered through the pine trees that shaded the property, and the front of the property was overgrown with ferns and wild shrubs with purple flowers.

"At least it's colorful," I said, making my way to the front porch. I couldn't help but notice that the windows were thick with cobwebs and layers of dust and pollen. "These'll need a good cleaning."

"It's lovely, though," Ruth said.

"Let's see if we can get inside."

I propped the screen door open with my hip and tried the key. I was surprised it unlocked the door with no problem. Still, I gingerly peeked my head inside, not sure I wanted to rush in without any warning of what I might find. I thought Ruth was going to push me in; she was so eager to see inside. When I didn't see anything or anyone lurking about, I stepped inside.

It was freezing inside, and other than smelling a little musty from being closed up, the cabin itself was both rustic and cozy. A captivating painting of a deer coming out of the woods hung in the center of the stone fireplace that dominated one wall. Faded plaid red curtains hung on the windows, and a Navajo type rug covered the wooden floors. Old family photos filled the wall space on either side of a large window. Two red leather oak chairs and two rocking chairs made with twigs and wood slats sat facing the fireplace. A square planked cocktail table was stacked high with books and boxes. In fact, there were boxes everywhere.

The kitchen cupboards were fully stocked with dishes, pots, pans, and silverware, so I wouldn't need much more than what I bought at the Memorial Weekend sales. Two small mismatched chairs sat at the kitchen table, and a wood stove was off to one side. There were two bedrooms; one full of a hodgepodge of stuff, but the other one was decorated with a red and green braided rug, red and green striped curtains, and a red quilt as a bed cover. Adele's clothing and her winter gear still hung in the wardrobe, and although it was a little creepy, I tried on one of her jackets. Surprisingly, it fit.

Framed photos of what I assumed were Adele and her husband sat on her dresser and two kerosene lamps and a small stack of books sat on the nightstands. Curious, I drew close enough to read the spines; *The Great Gatsby* by F. Scott Fitzgerald, *Women in Love* by D.H. Lawrence and *The Age of Innocence* by Pulitzer Prize winner Edith Wharton.

"She certainly loved romance," Ruth offered. "I'd love to read this one," she said, picking up *The Age of Innocence*.

I knew very little about Adele, except she most likely lived in an expensive home in Los Angeles with her husband until he died. He did well enough to leave her enough money to stay in the hotel, and yet she'd never mentioned having a family. Were there children? And if there were, where were they? Who did she leave the rest of her money to?

Down a short hall was what appeared to be an add-on bathroom, for the walls were knotty pine instead of log like the rest of the cabin. There was also a slight step down, which could be dangerous if you had to get up in the middle of the night. The claw-foot tub and a pull chain toilet seemed to be in good shape, although when pulled the chain, there was no running water to test them.

"It doesn't look like it needs much for you to move in," Ruth said. "I could come over and help you get rid of all the dust and cobwebs."

"Other than the thick layer of dust everywhere, I agree. I have to give Adele Rochester credit for the way she decorated."

Before we left, I wanted to see the stream. We made our way through more overgrown bushes to the back of the house, and off to the left, we could hear it. I saw an old tire swing hanging from one of the largest trees, suggesting that children once had played there, or that a previous owner had left it behind. We found the small creek, and I was back to imagining children trying to capture tadpoles or frogs.

The sounds of the rhythmic flow of water and the wind weaving itself through the trees was incredibly soothing.

I closed my eyes and imagined myself living there.

# CHAPTER THIRTY

Low clouds and the trees surrounding the cabin turned the early afternoon dark enough that I searched for candles to add some light to the front room. We weren't going to stay much longer, but I wanted to take another look around and start a list of things I needed to do to get the cabin move-in ready. I'd thought ahead to bring paper and a pen, and went room by room making what turned out to be a daunting checklist. I knew once I got started, I'd find more things I wanted to do, but I had to start somewhere.

About twenty minutes later, we blew the candles out and locked the front door behind us.

Ruth dropped me back off at the diner just in time for the dinner shift, and although I was dying to share my good fortune with Ramona and Lucille, I decided against it. They'd find out eventually, and that was soon enough for me.

Every day between shifts, I made a trip to my cabin with the goal of checking off just one thing on the list. Breaking everything down into small, doable tasks made the process a lot less overwhelming. I swore him to secrecy, then the first thing I did was hire the young man from the diner to help rid all the ceilings of cobwebs and to dust where I couldn't reach. I also showed him what I wanted to clear from the property and he said he could work outside on days I wasn't home.

Ruth tackled the bathroom, and I went through the wardrobe and dresser before she started in the bedroom I'd be sleeping in. Meanwhile, I pulled everything out of the kitchen cupboards and cleaned the shelves. I went nuts when I saw mouse droppings, but then Ruth reassured me that was from the house sitting vacant for so long.

"Plus, every house has mice up here at some point," she said, shrugging her shoulders. "You just learn to keep everything sealed up or in the icebox."

Before I washed everything and put it all back, I decided there were some things I didn't need. I set those aside and Ruth suggested I trade them in at the secondhand store the next time I stopped in there. Certainly there'd be things they had I needed.

We took all the curtains and linens back to Ruth's so we wash everything.

"I need to see how expensive it would be to build on another room for a washer," I said as we loaded my car.

"We can ask Jack," Ruth said, wiping her dirty hands on a wet towel.

"I can't thank you enough for your help," I said, climbing into the car. "It's coming along, isn't it?"

"Yes, it is. It'll be ready for you in no time. And I hate to think about it, because I'll miss you."

"I'll miss you too, and of course, Jack. And Dorothy. And Mabel."

I was in too good a mood to feel wistful, plus it had been less than a week since we'd begun tackling everything on my list, and so far we were almost halfway through it.

I'd all but forgotten about the attractive man with the chiseled movie star jaw until he came back in to the diner on my next morning shift.

"Haven't seen you in a while," He said, taking a menu from me. "I've been really busy," he offered, although I hadn't asked. "My name's Dino."

"I'm Charlotte. Nice to meet you. Coffee?"

"Sure."

When I returned, he said, "I'll just take the club sandwich again."

"Don't you eat breakfast?" I asked, taking the menu back.

"Sometimes, but lately, I haven't been in the mood."

I wasn't sure why I asked him. It wasn't my place to ask him, and I shouldn't have. I could sense Dino studying me as I placed his order, then I waited on other tables. His dark eyes followed me, and it reminded me of when the interplay started with Abe—appearing harmless in the beginning, but growing into something much more complicated.

Again, he was dressed in a suit, which should have sent up a red flag; no one in the mountains wore suits or had polished shoes. He reminded me of the men in room 1512 at the hotel, and yet he wasn't rude or overbearing, like the heavyset man who called me doll. I reminded myself I wasn't looking for love or anything remotely close to it, but I had to admit, he intrigued me.

"Stop for a minute and talk to me," Dino said when I checked in on him.

I looked around to make sure no one was watching me.

"What do you do for entertainment up here?"

I followed his eyes as he searched my hand for a ring, and when Abe quit coming it, I stopped wearing my mother's engagement ring. Now I wished I hadn't.

He looked at me with a slightly raised eyebrow and a knowing smile. I couldn't just walk away, so I said, "There's a dance pavilion in The Village. I've never been, but a lot of people go there."

"Maybe we can grab a bite to eat and go dancing sometime? I like to dance." My silence gave him the confidence he needed to continue, for he said, "I'll be up here quite a bit from now on, and I think we might hit it off."

My stomach did a flip-flop, and I turned again to see if Ramona or Lucille were growing suspicious of me standing there talking.

"I'm really not allowed to go out with customers," I lied.

"*Really?* Now that seems like a silly rule. And I like to break rules, so you think about it and I'll be in tomorrow for breakfast. You can tell me then, deal?"

Dino pulled out his wallet, and I said, "I'm off tomorrow," and then instantly regretted it. "Let me get you your bill."

"That's even better," he said. "We could go tomorrow night."

"I'm in the middle of remodeling my cabin, so that wouldn't work."

He nodded and gave me a smug look that said, "I can wait."

Ramona came up beside me and handed me his bill. "Were you looking for this?" she asked.

"Actually, I was. I thought I lost it," I lied.

"I'll see you sometime next week then," Dino said, bringing out a wallet filled with bills.

The minute he left, Ramona was on me like a moth to a flame.

"I have two questions for you," she said. "First, what's this about a cabin? And second, you're attracting bad boys like there's no tomorrow."

I had no choice but to tell Ramona about the cabin, and she was speechless for the first time since I'd met her. She had a hundred questions, and I answered them all. I figured it was easier than trying to remember what lies I'd told her. But then I had to tell Lucille before Ramona did, so that it didn't look like I was playing favorites.

The first thing Lucille wanted to know once she got over the surprise was if I was planning on leaving, since it would be a little bit of a drive to come to work. I told her I wasn't planning on going anywhere, but then I also hadn't planned on seeing Dino either.

All that next week, he came in every day for breakfast and ordered a club sandwich. He wore me out asking when we could go dancing, so I finally asked Ramona if she'd cover for me that next Friday night. I worked all day on my cabin, and although I could have started staying there, for some reason I just wasn't ready. I'd finished going through all the boxes, which were mostly filled with Adele's old clothing, and I donated most of them to a place in town that took in things for people who needed them. I kept all her old books, including some recipe books I was sure I'd never use, and filled a bookcase that I traded at the secondhand store.

Towards the early afternoon that Friday, I was tired, and I needed a well-deserved bath. I didn't want Ruth and Jack to know I had a date, so I stayed at my cabin and soaked in the tub there and washed my hair. For the occasion, I put on some of my mother's lipstick and rouge, but when I stared back at myself in the mirror, I looked like a floosie with those pink cheeks, so I ultimately wiped some of the rouge off. I could have kicked myself for not doing a better job of looking through Adele's dresses, but it was too late now; everything was gone. Not that I thought I'd have many opportunities to wear dresses in the mountains, I made a mental note to start adding to my wardrobe.

At five on the dot, Dino was at my front door wearing a striped suit, shiny black shoes, and a black hat. He looked quite dashing, but I was going to have to tell him that no one up here wore hats like that unless it was New Year's Eve, and even then, it was a stretch.

"Wow," I said. "You really dressed up."

He must have been reading my mind, for he took the hat off and asked, "Too much?"

I gave him a fake cringe, and he got the hint.

We drove back toward The Village and went to one of the few nice restaurants up in Lake Arrowhead. We must have made quite an impression, for we were immediately taken to a table by the window. Dino ordered chilled shrimp cocktail and bacon wrapped scallops for appetizers—things I'd only seen brought up to Mr. DeGrazia's suite at the hotel. The main meal was filet mignon with broasted potatoes. Dino certainly knew his way around a menu.

He held up his water glass and said, "If we could have wine, I would have toasted. To a wonderful evening with a beautiful woman. I hope this is one of many."

No one had ever said anything that romantic before, and I felt goose bumps all the way to my toes. I couldn't turn away from him, even though my thoughts suddenly turned to Joe. I hadn't thought about him in days, and wondered how that could be. What was he doing now? Had he found someone new? And what was I doing going out with someone who, I hated to admit, looked like a gangster?

"Are you all right?" Dino asked.

I couldn't tell him what I'd been thinking, so I said, "I was just thinking about home."

I told him about Texas and the hotel, leaving out the gory parts about working with men who killed people. Truthfully, I was ready to go back to my cabin, and when I told Dino I was tired, he insisted we still go dancing. I knew it would cheer me up, but if I was honest, I actually wanted to feel sorry for myself. I wanted to remember Joe for a while longer.

It turned out we had a great time. I think we danced every dance, and it felt good to be in someone's arms. Dino was an excellent dancer and quite fancy on the dance floor. When a slow song came up, he pulled me tightly toward him, and I didn't resist. Being up against his body brought back the feeling of making love and having someone there for me. I could feel him breathing into my ear, and then when the next slow dance came, he gently kissed my cheek and before I knew it, his lips were brushing mine. I didn't care if anyone was watching. I just knew I wanted him to continue holding me.

I had my hand on this thigh all the way back to my cabin, and when he pulled my hand up to his lips and kissed it, I knew how the night would end. I hadn't met my neighbors yet, and I didn't care what they would think if I came home with a man.

Once inside, Dino lit the fire to take the chill out of the rooms, and we started gently undressing each other before going into my bedroom. Our lovemaking was awkward at first, and it soon became obvious Dino had been with other women, for it didn't take him long to figure it all out.

The next morning, I woke to him sitting in the bedroom chair, smoking a cigarette. I peered at him through half-closed lids, watching him back. His hair was a mess, and I thought he'd looked much more handsome dressed in his suit. But then I wondered what he'd be thinking about me.

I'd have to tell him I preferred he didn't smoke in the cabin.

# CHAPTER THIRTY ONE

Before Dino left the next morning, we had breakfast at a small cafe in town; I honestly didn't want to go anywhere where anyone knew me. I felt self conscious enough as it was. I would have been lying if I'd said I didn't think about him all day. Both the good and the regret. The good was that I'd found someone I was attracted to, and who was attracted to me. The regret was that I'd actually let myself be intimate with someone other than Joe.

I was glad I had the extra day off. I wanted to finish going through the last of Adele's boxes, and finish cleaning the second bedroom. I wasn't sure what I wanted to do with it yet. It wasn't like I was going to have company, so I couldn't see furnishing it. I decided for the time being to set up the ironing board and use the wardrobe cabinet for the rest of my clothes.

I heated up some soup and made myself a ham sandwich for dinner, then sat in front of the fireplace and listened to programs on the small radio. Since the radio was going to be my main source of entertainment when I was alone, I added buying one to my list. I remembered seeing a Philco at the secondhand store, and after lunch, I drove into Lake Arrowhead to get it.

By the end of the day, I finished my to-do list, but I was exhausted.

In my mind, I was ready to spend my first real night alone in my new cabin, and I put a few extra logs on the fire, hoping it would stay warm enough until morning. But I had a hard time falling asleep. I thought about Dino, and even then, I wondered if he was going to be the right person for me. I really didn't know much about him. He'd said he had no family, and that was one reason he'd been promoted to the job he had. I wasn't really clear what that was exactly. When I asked, he said he did whatever he needed to do for his boss. I let my imagination go a little wild and somehow that added to his mystique. I'd never been attracted to someone who was a little too handsome and showy, but I found those two qualities attracted me to him. That night, when I climbed into bed, the scent of his hair cream lingered on the other pillow, and I couldn't help but think how nice it felt to have a man in my life.

However, that night, every unfamiliar sound jarred me awake, whether it was the walls creaking or the scurrying of critters on the roof. Not that I'd ever needed them, but Ruth and Jack had only been a few hundred feet away if I needed help. So far, I'd only walked past my nearest neighbor's house, and as far as I could tell, there was no one else around.

Turning on the lamp on my nightstand only made the room so bright, I knew I'd never fall asleep, so I blew it out. Just as I dozed, the hoot of an owl woke me, and I pulled my covers over my face.

"I can do this," I repeated until I fell back asleep.

I somehow made it until the next morning and woke to the sunlight shining through my bedroom window and a dusting of snow on the ground. Of course, I'd seen snow, but it had been years since I'd truly seen snow falling and it was magical. It started with flakes that were barely noticeable, melting as they hit the ground. And for the next week, the sky filled with what resembled a steady rain, but was really white in color, layering rooftops, tree branches and our winding mountain roads. I think it was the hushed silence that came with snowfall that mesmerized me the most. Mother nature graced us with perfectly timed intervals, giving us opportunities to shovel walkways and clear the roads so we could all still go about our business.

I didn't see Dino the rest of that week, and after the first few days, I began to feel that I'd made a terrible mistake letting him into my life, even for the night. There was no way for me to contact him, and in fact, I had no idea where he even worked or lived. How could I not know that about a person I'd been intimate with?

When I looked at Ramona and Lucille, I felt shame written all over my face. In my mind, I begged Ramona to not ask about him, for even if it was just in idle conversation, I knew I wouldn't be able to pull anything over on her.

Thankfully, she didn't.

The next week, though, Dino was back, and I felt myself turn ten shades of red when I saw him come in. He sat in my section, and the minute I came to his table, he said, "I'm so sorry, Charlotte. I was called away, and I didn't have a choice. You must think me a cad. Will you forgive me?" He didn't give me a chance to say a word before he continued. "I want to see you tonight. I've done nothing but think about you—about us."

He was about to reach for my hand, but I quickly stepped back. I couldn't let anyone see him touch me.

"I'll think about it," was all I said. "Having the club sandwich?"

"Yes."

I let him eat, and when I brought his bill, I gave him a slip of paper that said I'd be home after nine.

What on earth was I doing?

I wanted to make sure I had a soak in the tub before he got there, mostly to try to relax. If Dino had indeed been thinking about us, I was going to have to decide whether or not to let him into my life. I needed to know more about him, and I was determined to find out. My life was an open book and so far, our relationship wasn't starting off on an even keel.

My stomach was in knots waiting, and it wasn't until almost ten that I heard his knock on the door.

"I'm late. Sorry again," he said, standing there with a somewhat wilted bouquet of flowers.

He was dressed in a suit, but tonight he had on a vest. I wondered if he ever wore anything informal. I found one of Adele's cut glass vases, and after adding water, I cut the bottoms of the stems, arranged the flowers, and set them on the kitchen table.

"These are lovely," I said honestly.

"I've had them with me all day. Sorry," he said sheepishly. Then he added, "I haven't eaten all day."

"I can make you a sandwich."

"That'd be great. Anything."

Dino took off his jacket and hung in on the back of the kitchen chair. There was no way of hiding the shoulder holster with the pistol in it, and watching me, he took that off too and set it on top of the bookcase. He sank into the small chair, and after I handed him a plate with a turkey sandwich on it, I plopped down at the kitchen table and watched him eat. I should have suspected something dark and menacing about him.

I felt no fear, but I knew I didn't want to know what I needed to know.

He let me talk first.

"So," was all I could get out.

"I didn't want to tell you about what I did until you had a chance to get to know me. To see the real me, and not the bad guy you could think I am." A flicker of apprehension crossed his face, and he grimaced.

Even though I'd half expected something like this, his words sent a shockwave through me. His voice remained steady, but the air was heavy and I felt frozen. Dino shifted his weight in the chair, but his eyes never left mine. Finally, he exhaled, waiting for my response.

Images of Mr. DeGrazia and the bloodied body lying on the floor of the penthouse rushed through my mind. I put my head in my hands and sat that way for what seemed like an eternity, but was really only a few seconds.

"Did someone send you?"

My question caught him off guard. His reaction told me he wasn't expecting this, and now he was trying to figure out how to respond.

I told him about Los Angeles—everything except falling in love with Joe.

If I let him stay, I was just trading one awful life for another, and I might as well go back to Los Angeles and take my chances. At least I'd be with Joe.

But then he reached across the table and touched my hands.

"Please let me stay with you tonight."

My common sense, if I had any left, said, why would he ask that if he planned on killing me? My instinct was to tell him to get the hell out. But instead I began crying and ran to my bedroom and slammed the door behind me. If he was going to kill me, then he was going to kill me. I didn't have any way to defend myself.

But not a minute later, Dino knocked gently and when I didn't answer, he slowly opened my door. He came in and lay down beside me, rocking me, trying to calm me down. Eventually, I got up and undressed. It seemed I'd made a decision, even though it went against everything I believed in.

# CHAPTER THIRTY TWO

I never took Ramona into my confidence, but eventually it was obvious Dino and I had become an item when he came into the diner more frequently. Even though we tried to be nonchalant about how we felt about each other, someone would have had to be blind to not see how he touched my arm when I served him, or when they saw the intensity in his eyes when he looked at me. I saw it too—when he smiled, his eyes smiled too, creating little creases that just added to his handsomeness.

Ramona only said something once, but I cut her off.

Ruth now, was another subject. I knew I couldn't share my relationship with Dino with her, especially after knowing why I'd left L.A. and Joe, whom I professed to love. And it was hard not to mention how I felt. Since I'd moved to my own cabin, though, we only saw each other infrequently. I claimed I had to work long hours, and she didn't question it. If Dino had to be out of town, I'd sometimes go to their cabin and we'd have dinner.

I did tell her how uncomfortable I'd been staying there by myself, and one night she recommended I get a dog for companionship.

"You love Mabel. You'll find a dog that needs a home," she'd said.

On my next day off, I went to the pound, and I was hoping to find a dog that immediately came to me, loving me at first sight. But that wasn't how it happened. After looking at each dog twice, I stood in front of a kennel with a handsome German shepherd who didn't rush to greet me but only looked back at me with sad eyes. One of his ears looked like it had been chewed on, and the other one was floppy.

"Tell me about his fellow," I said to the caretaker.

"This guy has a sad story," the man started. "He and his owner were out in the recent snow, and somehow the man lost his footing and fell down the mountainside. We only know that because the dog stayed with him during the night, and in the morning, and soaked and freezing, he went looking for someone to help. The man who lived around there heard the dog barking and whining and followed him to where the body was. He was wearing a collar with a leather tag engraved with the owner's name and address."

"Oh my god," was all I could say. No wonder he was so sad.

With some gentle coaxing, the dog eventually came to me, and when I saw him up close, I could tell he was skinny.

"He hasn't been eating much since he got here." The caretaker said, no doubt seeing the look on my face.

"Well, we'll fix that, won't we boy," I said, scratching his forehead through the wire gate.

I was surprised he jumped into the car without much persuading, and he seemed to love going for a ride. I swore he even looked at me for approval for having a great time. We stopped at the feed store in town and bought a big bag of dog food and treats, and then headed home.

I decided I'd call him Sam.

He made a wonderful bed warmer, and although Dino initially disapproved of a third bed partner, he finally realized he was going to lose the battle. Sam at least had the decency to allow us privacy when we made love, and then afterward, he'd wiggle his way in between us as we all slept. Sam loved Dino, especially when he brought treats with him.

Every now and then, Sam would wake me with twitching and whimpers, and I wondered if he was dreaming about his first owner. It broke my heart when he did that. I would gently touch him, and he would fall back into a peaceful sleep. And before we went to bed, he would lie protectively at my feet as I sat in my chair, reading by the fire.

His good ear would perk up at any sound, even those only he could hear, and when he was sure everything was all right, he'd relax.

Even in the cold of winter, when I let Sam out to wander the property, I'd watch him run up ahead to the stream, where he loved to prance in the water. Growling and biting at the water as if there were something swimming in it, he acted as if he were a great fisherman.

While Dino couldn't tell me much about what he did, over time, I learned he worked at the speakeasy that Ruth told me about. In the beginning, when I started asking about what he did, the silence would stretch between us, sometimes heavy, depending on what he was willing to share. He'd answer my questions without naming names. There was one woman who managed the property, and he did let it slip once that he interacted with Bugsy Siegel regularly. Famous Hollywood stars frequented the club, and just like at the hotel, liquor flowed freely. I even learned they had their own gin distillery, and that wagons filled with barrels of it made regular trips back down the hill to a warehouse in L.A. to be sold and distributed.

I remembered Ruth telling me once they operated in the shadows, avoiding any unwanted attention and blending in with the surroundings. They were on a road not heavily traveled, and if someone unwittingly drove down there, to them, nothing would seem out of the ordinary.

I'd finally written to Clara, letting her know I was settled and doing well. She knew I'd inherited the deed to a property and when I told her it was up in the mountains near Ruth, she couldn't believe my good fortune. I'd told her that if she wrote back, to address the letter to Ruth in case anyone was looking to figure out where I was. I'd also made her promise she wouldn't tell Joe where I was if he asked.

She'd written right back, letting me know, unsurprisingly, she was pregnant. I knew that was what she and Dr. Robert were hoping for, and I was delighted for her. I could picture them raising children in their new house, with his parents providing them with every comfort, even from a distance. Her mother-in-law would most likely want to come out after the baby was born, and I knew without even asking, that Clara would be miserable.

She asked if I'd heard from Joe, and of course I hadn't. He had no idea where I was. Just reading his name brought back memories of the fun times we all spent together. And I couldn't forget—I didn't want to—about how much I cared for him.

I hadn't intended to fall in love with another man. I remember Moira telling me there was always someone else out there for us, if we looked. And I was certain someone could love two people at the same time. I realized that sounded crazy, but it was true. I still loved Joe, and I probably always would.

I wrote back and told her I thought of her often, about how she befriended me when we worked in the laundry, and how she'd been a wonderful friend to me throughout the years. I told her Ruth and Jack were happy and that baby Dorothy, who wasn't really a baby anymore, was absolutely a delight. I also told her it was wonderful to be able to cuddle until she became a handful, then give her back to Ruth when she got cranky.

I decided not to share about Dino—so now there were two dear friends who I chose to keep at arm's length. It was better if neither of them knew anything about him. I hadn't gotten a post office box yet, so I asked her to keep writing to Ruth's address.

"Just know I miss you," I wrote.

I also wrote to Moira. I told her about the cabin, my job at the diner, and about Sam.

I told her I still remembered my mother saying she always wanted us to open a diner, and how I hoped that one day, I'd be able to make that wish come true—although I wasn't sure how I'd ever be able to pull it off, and that I hadn't stopped dreaming.

When the weather started warming up, I went to the feed store and bought a bag of sunflower seeds, a hanging bird feeder and a different type of food for the squirrels. Jack had reminded me it wasn't a good idea to feed wild animals, but I couldn't resist doing my part to make sure they had enough to eat. I found a branch low enough for me to reach and hung the bird feeder, then sat on the porch waiting like a child with a new toy for them to find it. After ten minutes, I lost my patience and took down the old rusted squirrel feeder and nailed the new one up. I didn't know why I'd waited until the end of winter to put these up, when it dawned on me these critters needed to eat all year round.

We hadn't had snow since the beginning of the month, but the air was still crisp and biting in the wind. One afternoon, despite threats of rain, Dino wanted to take me somewhere he'd just learned about, and afterward, he wanted to take me to a new place in town called The Stockade on Lake Drive, Crestline's main street. I'd seen it, but I'd never been there.

Dressed in heavy coats and bringing umbrellas, we packed blankets and Sam into the back seat of his car, and headed to a place called Heart Rock Waterfall. It hadn't rained in a week, so the ground was dry. Our boots crunched in the dirt and gravel and the air smelled of a mixture of pine and campfires from the local campground. As usual, Sam raced ahead of us, checking to see if there was anything that interested him, and from constantly stepping over roots and rocks, I felt the muscles in my legs burn. The walk was refreshing, but I was glad when we got to our destination so we could rest.

A small waterfall marked the end of the trail and to its left, an amazing rock formation was almost perfectly carved into a large heart shape. It reminded me of the marvel of the natural arrowhead rock formation on the mountains going down the hill into San Bernardino.

"If I could have carved this for you, I would have," Dino said, taking a ring from his coat pocket. "Will you marry me?"

# CHAPTER THIRTY THREE

His words hung in the air, almost as if they hadn't just been spoken aloud. I hadn't been prepared for this, and my mind raced to process his proposal. My heart raced, and I felt as though my world had tilted. I searched Dino's face for some kind of hint; there was nothing that explained why I felt so unprepared. I glanced down at the ring he held in front of me, and then up at his expectant face. I tried my best to hide the shock, and I realized I hadn't been successful when I caught just a faint glimmer of doubt cross his face.

I hadn't meant to fall in love with Dino, and I certainly didn't want to be married to someone who was involved with gangsters. It went against everything I believed in, but I'd allowed it to happen, and now it was too late to turn back. Time stretched on, and I could tell he was dying there, waiting for me to say something.

The truth was, I loved Dino, but I still loved Joe.

I couldn't think of any way to rectify this, to destroy his unrealistic expectations of our relationship and still leave him standing. I couldn't think of anything else to say, so I said yes.

He hugged me so hard I couldn't breathe. He'd taken my shock and silence as that of happiness, and I couldn't think of any way of freeing him of that belief. I closed my eyes, thinking I could stop my mind from seeing images of marriage and telling everyone about him. I'd had a chance to change my life, but I'd somehow lost my way.

Throughout dinner, I could only move my food around on my plate. I had no appetite, and yet I told Dino my meal was delicious; that I was just so preoccupied with everything. There was no reason for him to doubt what that *everything* was. He thought it was about being in love and planning a wedding and a life together. I thought it was my punishment for being so stupid. I would have to tell Ruth, but maybe I could lie about what Dino did. I knew she'd see right through me.

I could never tell Clara or Moira, and in the end, they really didn't need to know.

When we got home, I gave Sam my leftovers, and he was as happy as could be.

Dino stayed the night and wanted to celebrate our engagement by making love. For the first time since being with him, I dreaded being intimate. My heart just wasn't in it, and yet I didn't think I could successfully fake it. But I did, and then I hated myself for being so deceptive. I told him my brain was going in too many directions and it seemed to satisfy him.

Sam could sense I had a hard time sleeping that night, and he constantly raised his head, giving me a curious grumble. It was as if he was asking, *what is it?*

Since my mother died, I'd only allowed myself to cry when I was alone. I cried silent tears when I was in my berth on the train to California; I cried when I was alone in the apartment after I got the job in the laundry. I cried after I witnessed the murder in suite 1512, and now I cried the moment Dino left my cabin that next morning.

First with Joe, and now with Dino, I'd used the hope and pray method of birth control. I figured my luck was going to run out one day, and I knew I didn't want a child right now, so I took a day off work and made an appointment with a doctor down in San Bernardino. Being a single woman, I couldn't take any chances the doctor in Lake Arrowhead wouldn't accidentally say something to someone, plus I was extremely embarrassed.

I kept the apparatus hidden in my undergarment drawer, and telling Dino was never in my plan. We hadn't really talked about children, so I knew it wasn't something important to him at the moment, and I figured I'd deal with it if and when the time came.

I wasn't looking forward to setting a wedding date, so I told Dino I wanted to get married in the fall of the next year. I told him I wasn't going to wear my engagement ring to work using the excuse it was unsanitary since I worked with food. It also gave me an excuse for keeping the engagement a secret from Ruth, Ramona, and Lu. From then on, I only wore my engagement ring when we went out, and Dino could introduce me as his fiancé.

We began going to the speakeasy when we wanted a fancy night out. At first I was hesitant, expecting to see a room full of gangsters like the ones in L.A. But I was surprised to see that half of the people who went there were Hollywood types, like Ruth and Dino had said. I tried not to stare when I recognized well-known actors and I even met Bugsy Siegel himself. I soon grew accustomed to seeing these people, and ending up paying them no mind.

Once, when Dino introduced me to a movie producer, he took my hand and drew it to his lips. As he handed me his card, he said, "You're a lovely young lady. If you'd like to be in the movies, give me a call."

"Why thank you," I said, looking at his card.

Of course, I was flattered, but even if he was sincere, I'd never go back down to Los Angeles. When I didn't jump at his offer, he quickly turned to search the crowd for someone else to impress. In the meantime, I hadn't noticed Dino's jaw had tightened, and he gripped my arm tightly. I could see there was a storm brewing beneath his fixed smile, and I wasn't sure what to do about it.

"You're hurting me," I said between my own clenched teeth.

I saw the darkness quickly fade, and he gave me a quiet, almost guilty glance, then released me.

"I'm sorry."

I'd never witnessed what I considered this type of behavior in him, and I was still upset when he brought me to meet Bugsy Siegel. Mr. Siegel also took my hand and brought it to his lips, and I could sense something darker, almost dangerous, about *him*. I'd heard terrible rumors about him, and I was certain they were true. My pulse quickened both because of what I saw in his beautiful blue eyes, and because I knew working for him could be dangerous for Dino. While Mr. Siegel was talking to me, I saw something entirely different from the jealousy happening with Dino. His jaw was still clenched, but only slightly, and he turned his head towards the people on the floor, avoiding any eye contact. There was no gripping of my arm and no aggression. With Mr. Siegel, Dino acted as a submissive dog and I could picture him laying down and rolling over on the floor to show his belly. I totally understood.

For the rest of the evening, Dino was on edge. We had a few more drinks, and then when he wanted to go back to the cabin, he stood in front of me and made it known. That night when we made love, he showed a side of him I'd never seen. His breath was hot against my neck, and his kisses were demanding. His touch was almost desperate, like he was trying to prove I was his.

I didn't like it at all.

Even with the February rain, which tended to freeze the ground at night, we started seeing more signs of spring. As more of the snow melted, hints of green pushed their way through, and bushes that were once totally covered in snow reemerged. In most places, though, gritty mounds of snow still lined the roads and edges of sidewalks. And because it was naturally shaded, there were still numerous patches of it scattered across the ground in the front of my cabin.

One day, what I could only describe as an unexpected gift awaited me as I returned home from an early shift at the diner. As I grabbed bags of groceries out of my car and made my way up my walkway, bright green shoots of what I could only think was some type of wildflower were coming up in clusters. While I had no idea what they were, I took this as a sign that mother nature was giving me a sign that a new season was upon me, and that spring was coming,

My neighbor, Liz, would know.

After putting everything away, I took Sam out for a walk. I hated leaving him cooped up in the cabin all day, but because we had wild animals roaming freely, I couldn't leave him outside to fend for himself. He'd never win if one of them came after him.

Liz was out in her yard, raking snow from her garden, and she, too, had those same green shoots coming up.

"You're supposed to let them bloom by themselves, but I don't know about you, I'm tired of this winter and I want to see spring now," she said when I asked what she was doing. "They're daffodils. They come back every year, just like clockwork. You'll see them along the roads too, where they've self-seeded. They're called voluntary. They sprout from seeds that fell the previous seasons."

"I'm anxious for spring, too. So, should I just let them come up by themselves?"

"Probably. There's something to be said about seeing them bloom out of a cluster of snow, though. If I were you, I'd just let nature take its course. That's always best, isn't it?"

Although it was hard to tell her age, Liz looked to be in her mid-fifties. She'd inherited her cabin too, from her father, who built it before there were any other cabins around. He loved to fish, and he figured he didn't need much in the way of creature comforts. It hadn't had running water, or electricity, when she got it, but she'd managed to bring the plumbing inside so she wouldn't have to go out to the outhouse to "do her business" as she called it. She still used kerosene lanterns, like I did, and once you got used to them, they weren't so bad.

She alternated between staying up here, and in the other house she inherited, down in Redlands. I'd discovered most of the time she came up only during the warmer months, and in a way, I didn't blame her. When she got a divorce, she said she spent a lot of time up here, just to get away from her ex, as she referred to him. She had a cousin who used to come up with her, and she told me they used to go dancing at the pavilion in The Village.

"There were lots of single men up here back then," she said. "Not too many now that don't have a lot of baggage. I'm happy being by myself now, anyway. They say women come with a lot of drama, but men do too. Especially ones that drink. That's what my ex did, and boy, when he drank too much, I had to leave the house or else."

When I left for my afternoon shift, I made myself a mental note to not accidentally pull the daffodils, thinking they were weeds. I could hardly wait to see them in full bloom.

# CHAPTER THIRTY FOUR

At the beginning of March, the daffodils blossomed in full, and they were everywhere; there were random patches across my property, and along the highways, as Liz had predicted. They were even in Lake Arrowhead. Wanting to bring their beauty inside, I cut stems from the farthest point on my land, well past the creek, and set them in a vase on my kitchen table. I loved coming home to color for a change.

While it was improper for an unmarried couple to live together, Dino continued to spend the night when Mr. Siegel didn't need him. When he brought up the subject of the wedding, I reminded him I wanted to get married in the fall, and assured him I had plenty of time to plan it all. I reminded him it would be a small affair on my side; Ruth and Jack, and maybe Ramona and Lucille, who I knew weren't too keen on him. It was his lifestyle, as they said, and I didn't blame them.

By April, I still hadn't told Ruth, and I knew I was going to get caught up in my deceitfulness if I wasn't careful. So I promised myself that by the end of the month, I'd tell her. It was one afternoon between my breakfast and dinner shifts I stopped by the cabins. I brought her some of Jack's favorite cookies, oatmeal raisin, and we each had one as we sat at her kitchen table.

"So," I began.

Ruth's eyebrows lifted slightly, as if to say *anytime now*.

"You see, I've met someone."

She hardly let me get it out before she jumped up from the table and hugged me tightly.

"You might want to sit back down," I said, slowly.

"What is it? You're acting weird."

"Well, do you remember me telling you how I didn't want to be with someone who was involved, in—"

Now she sat back down, and she gave me the biggest frown.

"Well, I've met someone named Dino. And he's involved with the Tudor House speakeasy." I didn't wait for her to ask me any questions, I just kept going. "And I didn't mean to fall in love, but I have. And he really loves me, and Sam, and he wants to get married. There you have it."

I waited for her to say something.

"Let me have a minute," was all she said. "What about Joe? Don't you still love him?"

"What's crazy is I do, but unless I go back down to Los Angeles, he'll never be a part of my life, and I live here now. I can't believe it myself. And the worst part is, I'd rather not get married, but I don't know how to get out of it. His proposal took me by surprise, and I didn't know what else to say."

"Dear god, Charlotte. You, of all people, should have said no. But then, I'm not in any position to tell you what to do or even judge you. I still need to think about this."

We just sat there until Dorothy's cry broke the silence. Ruth got up from the table to get her. She was so precious, rubbing her eyes and then when she saw me, her face lit up, and I thought I would burst out crying myself.

"Auntie Charlotte is here," Ruth said, bringing Dorothy to me.

"Hi, my precious girl," I said, kissing her tear stained cheek. "Did you just wake up?"

Dorothy was the tension breaker we needed, and Ruth sat back down.

"When is the wedding?" she finally asked.

"I told Dino in the fall. I figured that would give me plenty of time to figure out what to do." I grimaced. "I do love him, I just didn't plan on this."

Ruth only sighed.

"Well, you'll figure out how to make the best of it. Have you been to the speakeasy?"

"I've met Mr. Siegel, and everyone has been very pleasant to me. I've not been afraid of anyone, unlike L.A. It's just different."

"Have you decided where you'll get married?"

"No. Will you stand up for me? Will Jack come? I'm sure you'll actually like Dino; he doesn't act at all like a thug. He's romantic and I know he truly loves me."

"Of course we'll be there. You're my friend, Charlotte."

"Thank you. It might even be at the speakeasy. That way, we don't have to go down the hill, and no one in town will need to know."

"What about Ramona and Lucille? Have you told them yet?"

"They only know I'm seeing him. Of course, they've had their opinions too, but I'm trying not to let anyone judge him."

"Well," Ruth finally said, changing the subject. She got up and took Dorothy from me. "I'm sure you need your diaper changed," she said.

The minute I got back in my car, I said to myself, *well, that's done.*

In March, Clara wrote and told me Miles had fallen madly in love with their new singer, and they were planning on getting married. I wrote a separate note wishing him all the best and tucked it in my reply. Clara was finally over her morning sickness and was feeling back to normal, and they'd decorated the baby's bedroom with a circus animals theme. There were no toy shops up in the mountains, so I promised myself that the next time I went down to see the doctor in San Bernardino, I'd shop for something to send her.

I wished I could be there with her, but there was no way it could happen. Dino wouldn't have it and I could never go back to Los Angeles for fear Mr. DeGrazia would somehow find out. And then there was Joe. I couldn't see him now that I'd promised to marry another man.

In April, Lucille broke the news she was going to retire, and that Ramona had offered to buy the diner. Her words hit me like a punch to the stomach. I only stared at her, hoping what she'd said was a mistake, but she assured me the decision was already made and reminded me I always had a job there.

Somehow, I made it through the rest of the week, but I felt like I was chasing a dream that had never really been there. I'd given everything to that place, and now it had slipped through my fingers. I knew I'd have to put in my time until I could figure out something better. I hated the thought of working for Ramona, who had proven she could be quite the witch when she felt like it. And now I feared she'd take her new status out on me.

Most of all, I wondered what would happen to the diner? Would Ramona treat our customers the same as Lucille did? Would the regulars still come in, and would the warmth and atmosphere disappear when she took over?

And the worst part of it all was there was nothing I could do about it.

When I told Dino about it, he just shrugged when he said, "You won't really have to work when we get married. I make enough money to support us."

"But I *want* to work. I need to save enough money to open up my own diner, just like my mother dreamed about doing. Who knows where and how, but it's still something I want to do for her."

"You'll see. Something will come up that'll let you do that," was all he said when he patted my hand as if to appease me. All it did was anger me. Most men didn't understand women also had dreams and aspirations, and no matter what he thought, I was going to pursue mine, no matter what it took.

Not long after the news that Ramona was my new boss, she announced she had a new boyfriend. In fact, he was going to help her run the diner. When I found out he had no restaurant experience, I wanted to tell her she was nuts, but there was no way I could tell her what I really thought.

His name was George, and he came in strutting like he owned the place *and* the world. Insincerity and arrogance oozed from him, with his hard, cold, calculating eyes, like he was watching everything and everyone, sizing them up. The minute I met him, I saw the superficial charm and the sense of superiority. To say I instantly hated him would have been an understatement. It was unusual for me, because people didn't normally get under my skin, but George did.

He greeted customers when they came in, gravitating to the women, and on more than one occasion, I saw the husbands reel back in disapproval. He looked at every order ticket and counted the cash throughout the day, most likely checking to make sure none of the waitresses were stealing. Ramona continued on, now as the head waitress with the best section, and that left me with the back of the diner, where typically there weren't as many full tables.

After that first week working with George, I counted my tips, and I was off by about fifty percent. At that rate, I'd never get out of there.

# CHAPTER THIRTY FIVE

I sensed some hesitation in her voice when, in June, Ruth told me she was pregnant. We were living such opposite lives, but that didn't keep me from being so happy for her and Jack. There were just enough years between Dorothy and the coming baby, she wouldn't be handling two little ones at the same time.

"After the baby is born, I'm going to get in touch with my mother and bring her down here if she'll come," Ruth was saying, and then she looked at me. "Are you all right?"

I was off in my own world, thinking I still wasn't certain I wanted to get married, much less have a baby. Dino hadn't brought up the wedding for a month or so, and I was hoping beyond hope he would forget my idea of getting married in the fall. That wasn't to be the case though, for no sooner had I thought it, he asked me if I'd come up with a date yet. He wanted the wedding to be held at the speakeasy, as I'd thought, and I'd resigned myself to the fact when I accepted his proposal, I'd made my bed and now I had to lie in it. I found my calendar, closed my eyes and picked a date.

Over the fourth of July weekend, visitors flocked to the P & E camp site in town, and a child drowned in Lake Gregory. It was all that the town talked about for days. A family with a baby and a three-year-old were picnicking, and the mother left the child at the lake's edge with his wooden sailboat while she went back to their blanket and unpacked lunch. Both she and her husband hadn't checked on the little boy for a while, and when the mother finally had everything laid out, she turned to call him in and he wasn't there where she'd left him. Frantically, she ran to see if she could find him, and she called out to others to ask if they'd seen him. No one had, and eventually they found his sailboat about twenty feet out from where he'd been, and him floating farther out, face down in the water.

The local newspaper covered the story the next week, and the headlines read

## LAKE GREGORY'S FIRST DROWNING!

It seemed that within days, there were blue signs posted in the sandy ground around the lake, warning visitors to avoid leaving their children near the water unattended, and red buoys were already floating at the most shallow part of the lake for the safety of children

I hadn't wanted to say anything about it to Ruth, especially with Dorothy being around the same age, but it was all over the newspaper. She brought it up the next time I saw her, and she cried when she told me she'd read about it. She said it was a parent's worst nightmare.

It seemed the incident was written up in any newspaper I read, and I thought if they'd just quit writing about it, people could get over it sooner. Unless it was just a coincidence, I swore more and more people came up to the mountains after that, flocking to the lake to see where the child had drowned. Ruth wouldn't drive into town to see me, and months would pass before I could drive past the lake without thinking of that poor child and his family.

A perfect distraction in July was the news that the California Electric Light Company began bringing more electricity up in the mountain. The towns got upgrades first, and then poles started going up outward from there. Later that summer, when they finally finished, the town celebrated with a parade. The twentieth century had finally arrived for us.

That August, just weeks before our wedding, the building next door to The Tavern caught on fire. The volunteer fire department finally put out the blaze, but only after it was was completely destroyed. The Tavern sustained major smoke damage. Frank Thomas, the owner of both buildings, had insurance, but he was injured in the fire and ultimately chose to take the money and retire, leaving the brick building in a sorry state for what would be almost a year.

I'd put off buying a dress, and I needed to see the doctor again, so the week before the wedding, I made the trip down to the department store in San Bernardino and found something that would work. I also found a stuffed elephant for Ruth's new baby in the toy department and had them wrap it in pink and blue paper in case it was a boy or a girl.

When I got back to the cabin, Dino was outside smoking up a storm.

"*Where have you been?*" he asked, clearly annoyed.

"I thought I told you I needed to go down and pick up my dress," I said, clutching it and the birth control to my chest. "I also bought Ruth a gift for the new baby. They're doing the room up with circus animals and I found the cutest elephant—"

I hadn't seen Dino like this since that evening at the speakeasy, and I didn't like the way he spoke to me. I attempted to show him the toy, but he wasn't interested. He'd been moodier lately, and I didn't want to agitate him more.

"Is everything okay?" I asked, trying to keep my voice gentle and even, not knowing where he was coming from.

He did what I hated; he stomped out his cigarette and went inside the cabin. I thought better of saying anything to him about it. Instead, I went into our room and hid the diaphragm, and then I said lightly, "I'm hiding the dress so you won't see it until the wedding. So don't come looking for it unless you want to spoil the surprise."

When I came back into the dining area, he was sitting at the table bouncing his leg. I hated that habit as well. "Something's obviously going on—what is it?"

"They've brought another guy up. Mr. Siegel says things are getting so busy up here, they needed a backup. I couldn't read him when he told me, and I can usually tell when something's wrong. But I don't like it. I don't like sharing with anyone." He lit another cigarette, then looked up at me, almost daring me to say something, before he got up and went outside.

If Dino was having mood swings and temper tantrums in front of Mr. Siegel, no wonder they brought someone else up. Either way, even not knowing the details, it didn't sound very good for Dino. I tried to think rationally, and yet thoughts of him being bumped off filled my mind.

I had the most dreadful thought; maybe I wouldn't have to get married after all.

That wasn't to be the case. That next Saturday afternoon, we got married outside on the patio at the Tudor House. Mr. Siegel was there and seemed genuinely happy for us, and Dino had finally relaxed. Ruth took it all in stride; she got all dressed up, and I kidded her she looked more beautiful than I did. Ruth, along with Dino's best man, stood by us and when we said our vows, they handed us our rings.

Throughout the afternoon, she smiled and confidently mixed in with our guests, but Jack was on edge and really uncomfortable. Throughout the entire ceremony and even during the reception, I caught him vigilantly surveying our surroundings, trying to keep an eye out for any trouble. I felt awful for him, and I was sorry I'd involved them. I knew I'd come down a few notches in his opinion of me and the choices I'd made.

Although I would have to wear my rings, I knew Dino wouldn't wear his after the honeymoon; it just wasn't done by anyone other than the big bosses and I really didn't mind one way or the other.

When the Justice of the Peace pronounced us man and wife, I knew Dino loved me; it was so obvious in the way he looked at me that day. I loved him too in my own way, but when I heard "You may now kiss the bride," all I could think of was that I should have been kissing Joe.

We only took two days off for a honeymoon. We both needed to get back to work, plus I'd asked Ruth to take care of Sam and I didn't want to impose on her more than I already had. I dropped him off the day before the wedding so that he and Mabel could get acquainted, and we were both relieved when they quickly become friends.

We drove to Big Bear, then known as Pine Knot Village. The lake itself and the bridge to get into town had only been completed in the early 1900s, and with two new hotels, the small town had already become quite a tourist attraction.

Even though we'd been living together, Dino thought the idea of a honeymoon was to spend two days in bed. I had other ideas, like sightseeing and shopping at small little shops, and I finally came right out and told him if we didn't do something other than have sex, he was getting cut off. He looked at me like I'd slapped him in the face, but he later asked me where I'd like to go.

"Let's find a nice restaurant for dinner, as a start," I suggested.

Dino found a perfect spot for us to sit and watch the sunset, and when he took my hand, I knew he was trying to make me happy. If he let himself, he could be romantic.

We ended up having a nice time, and Dino took me everywhere I wanted to go. I bought a spoon rest for Ruth so she could have a place to put her cooking spoons while she was preparing dinner, and I found a doll for Dorothy and another stuffed animal for the baby, who was due any day now. And to hopefully make amends with Jack for tolerating me and Dino, I bought a pocket knife. Every man I knew could use a knife.

On our way back home, we picked up Sam and part of me was disappointed Jack wasn't home so I could give him his gift, but the other part was relieved I wouldn't have to see him pretend to be glad to see us. I gave Ruth a big hug and thanked her for watching Sam, who was so excited to see us, he ran to the car and spun in circles until we opened the door for him.

I'd had to tell Ramona about my wedding plans, both so I could get two days off and then to keep her from asking questions when I returned to work. When we got back, I wondered if it was just my imagination, or had something had changed. I felt a touch of coolness in their demeanor, and I couldn't tell if she was envious that I'd gotten married, or that maybe just she and George had just had a spat. He was acting funny too, solicitous, even apprehensive. We suddenly went back to the fairer way of waiting on tables, where we each got an equal chance to get the best tips, and what was really strange was that George started helping both of us clear tables.

Whatever was going on, I wasn't going to let either of them make my life more miserable than it was, so I made sure I was as sweet as I could be. To an outsider, we looked like three best friends, but to me, we were putting on some sort of show.

I learned why they were acting so strange soon enough. Before we left to get married, Dino had paid them a visit and, according to him, 'put the fear of god into them'. Apparently, he'd been paying attention when I complained about the new management hierarchy and it was obvious they realized the error of their ways. Once I understood their new attitude, I actually felt a little bad for them, and I tried to go back to being more friendly.

By the end of September, I was reminded why fall was one of my favorite times of the year. All the trees that weren't evergreen began changing colors, and depending where you were, sometimes you could see indescribable vast expanses of shades of oranges and reds. But when the leaves started falling, those trees reminded me of naked sticks coming out of the ground, the glory of it all faded. It was also the first fall in my cabin, and the grounds on my property were covered in leaves. There was no way I'd be able to rake them all up, and I didn't know the first thing about burning them or turning them into compost. Dino was of no help, so I hired someone to clear them.

That's when I wished instead for the spring regrowth or for snow-laden trees.

It was also towards the end of September when one night, around three in the morning, Dino came home smelling like sweat and mossy dirt. Hearing him come through the front door, I watched him in the shadows as he came into the bedroom and undressed, leaving his dirty clothes in a pile. When he pulled the covers back, I could smell him, and I said, "You're not getting into this bed until you've had a bath."

A half an hour later, he climbed into bed and rolled away from me towards the wall. He was obviously not in a good mood and I wasn't sure if he was more annoyed by what I'd said, or upset by what I imagined he'd just done. Either way, I could eventually hear the slow, even breaths of him sleeping, but I could not fall back asleep.

In the morning, I made a big breakfast and I could see the telltale signs of dirt under his usually manicured fingernails as he drank his coffee.

"Do you need to go into work today?" He asked.

"Yes, in fact I'm going to be late if I don't get out of here. . . are you okay?"

He didn't answer. Sometimes I hated what he did, but I wasn't a coldhearted woman either, and I wasn't sure how to comfort him. He was living a life he'd chosen, and I was forced to live it too. Before I closed the front door, Dino said, "I'll be gone for a few days. You know, if anything ever happens to me, you'll be taken care of."

What was I supposed to say to that?

Even though he'd already told me I didn't have to work, I knew it was the only way I'd be able to save enough money to open my diner. He hadn't been too keen on the idea when I first shared my dream with him, but he'd gotten used to me talking about it over the months we'd been together. Truthfully, I didn't care what he thought—I was going to do it, anyway.

With owning a diner constantly on my mind, when I came home from work that night, I saw a For Sale sign posted on The Tavern building. My heart jumped in my chest as I wrote down the phone number. I was so wound up; I was glad Dino would not be home. I don't know if I would have been able to hide my restlessness. My mind wouldn't slow down, wondering how much damage the fire had caused, and hoping beyond hope that buying it could possibly be within my reach. I tried everything I could do to relax, but my body wouldn't let me.

"Please, please, please, don't let anyone buy it," I said aloud.

We didn't have a phone yet, so I had to wait until I got to work the next morning to make the call from the phone booth outside the diner. I was certain Ramona could see me out there, and that made me even more anxious. She'd probably think I was calling about another job, although since our new arrangement had taken effect, everything was peachy between us.

I nervously asked the operator to connect me, and on the second ring, a man answered. I told him I was calling about The Tavern in Crestline, and he told me to hold on a few minutes while he got the information.

"Let's see now," I could hear papers shuffling in the background. "Ah, yes. We just put that up for sale. You're an anxious one," he said, not unkindly.

"I live in town, and have driven by it ever since the fire."

"Will you and your husband fix it up and open it back up?"

His question didn't surprise me, for it was rare that a woman bought something like that on her own. So I just answered, "Yes."

"Let's see," he said again. "Okay, here it is. The price includes the building and the business, although I know there's not a business there now. But there is still goodwill, that is, customers know it was there, and that's worth something. The interior is pretty smoked up, but with a good cleaning and some repairs, you could get 'er up and running in no time."

*Just tell me the price!* I wanted to shout into the phone.

"So they're asking a thousand dollars for it all."

My breath caught, and I could feel the involuntary recoil of my head at his unexpected reply. There was no way I was going to be able to come up with that kind of money. Since I'd been up there, I'd only been able to save five hundred dollars. And who knew how much it could cost to fix all the damage?

I was glad I hadn't given him my name, for all I could do was hang up the phone. It had felt like someone had pulled the rug out from under me. I just stood there, stunned stupid, like the world had cracked a little and I fell right through.

# CHAPTER THIRTY SIX

There was no way I could hide my disappointment from Ramona; even if we weren't friends, we'd worked together for too long. And when I walked back through the front door, she didn't even give me a minute before she asked if everything was all right. I couldn't tell her the truth, so I lied and said, "My pregnancy test came back negative."

If I'd been a drinker, I would have gotten drunk. All that day and into the night, I could see my dreams go down the drain. I was going to be stuck working with Ramona unless I just quit. But that wouldn't solve my problem. I tried to think what my mother would have said to me if she were here.

"When something doesn't work out the way you hoped, there's always a new opportunity around the corner. When one door closes, another one opens. Just wait."

"Okay, door. I'm ready."

I did believe her, and I tried to remind myself that other opportunities would present themselves to me, but I couldn't get over the disappointment. Even in its existing condition, the location of The Tavern was perfect.

To make matters worse, we weren't going to spend Christmas with Ruth and Jack. I knew they wouldn't invite me and Dino, and I didn't blame them. Plus, she was about ready to pop, and I assumed she was feeling uncomfortable. Instead, we spent Christmas Eve at the speakeasy, and had our photos taken next to a tree that was even taller than the one in the hotel lobby in Los Angeles. Mr. Siegel was there with a woman I didn't know, but then I didn't know many of the women he knew. As usual, he was very cordial, and seemed to have a good time.

We left around nine and the moment we opened the door to the cabin, Dino was undressing himself and me. It appeared I was to be his Christmas Eve gift. Something had changed between us since that night he came home smelling like dirt. He was more aggressive, and I was not as interested in being intimate with him. I couldn't tell if he'd noticed, but it was obvious to me.

We waited until morning to open our gifts. When we finally got up, I made pancakes with bacon for breakfast. We sat in silence across from each other, and then Dino said, "You know I love you, don't you, Charlotte?"

I thought it was an odd thing to say, but I said, "Of course I do. And I love you too."

Dino got me a beautiful diamond necklace to wear when we went to the speakeasy and I got him a new pair of cufflinks with diamonds in them. I knew he'd love them, and he did. And not wanting to forget Sam, I gave him his own pancake.

I needed another doctor's appointment, so I told Dino I was going down to San Bernardino to buy a new dress for New Year's Eve. Naturally, we celebrated at the speakeasy, and I could tell Dino was so proud of me in my new dress and necklace. It was as if he wanted to show me off, and a few times, he made me feel a little awkward. We drank champagne with dinner, and then again until the countdown, finally toasting to a brand new year. He was tipsy when we left to drive home, and a few times I thought for sure he was going to run us off the road into a tree. But we made it home safely, and without even taking off his tux, he plopped on the bed and fell asleep.

In a way, I was relieved. I'd been his Christmas present, and I wasn't really interested in being his New Year's present too.

The diner was closed three days a year. On Christmas, New Year's, and Thanksgiving, so I was glad to have another day off. I started reading a new book, and Sam and I sat in front of the warm fireplace all morning. In the afternoon, it began to rain, and I dozed listening to the calming sound of raindrops on the roof. Dino slept most of the day, and when we both woke, I made ham sandwiches for dinner before he left for work.

Ramona and George broke up and while she cried almost every day, I wanted to jump for joy. A few days after he left, she told me he'd stolen not only the cash from the restaurant, but he also wiped out her savings account. I knew how it felt to have very little to your name, and I tried to show compassion, but I hadn't forgotten how she had been so quick to cut my income when George first arrived on the scene. I never thought I was the type of person to hold a grudge, but apparently, I was. I wanted to say *I told you so,* but I didn't. But it was difficult to look at her in the same way I had before she let that jerk into her life.

Eventually, she stopped crying, and when, a couple of weeks later, a handsome stranger came in to eat, she perked up.

"You new up here?" I heard her ask.

And he said yes, he'd just opened his law office across the street. When she established there was no missus in the picture, she was all over him like flies on honey.

At the end of January, Dino told me he needed to go out of town for a week. He never talked about what they needed him to do, and I never asked. When I spent too much time thinking about it, it only reminded me of Joe and being in Los Angeles. I couldn't help but wonder how he was doing. Had he ever gotten out? If so, where would he have gone? Once you've been involved with the gangsters, what do you do next?

Without much fanfare, one morning Dino left for his trip, and Sam and I stood at the doorway to the cabin and I waved goodbye. I'd forgotten to fill his thermos with hot coffee, but I figured he could stop somewhere and have it filled. I closed the front door and almost sighed in relief. Not that Dino ever really got in my way, but I relished having a week to myself. I still had to go to work, but I had one less person to take care of.

Once I realized the time, I let Sam out for a minute and quickly dressed into my uniform. When he came back in, I kissed him on the head and said, "Have a good day. I'll be back as soon as I can." I left the fireplace going if it was cold out and I waited until he curled up in front of it in his bed. He was a good dog, and hadn't regretted getting him.

I turned left instead of right on Lake Drive so I could drive by The Tavern. It had only been a short time since I'd called on it, but I wanted to make sure there was no Sold sign up on the wall. Ramona and I were now getting along, but I would have bought that place in a heartbeat if I could. I turned around at the end of the block and headed toward work.

The first night Dino was away, I shared a tuna sandwich with Sam. One thing about him, he would eat just about anything. After dinner, we listened to the radio until the programs went off the air, then I opened my book to where I'd left off. Before I knew it, I'd fallen asleep in my chair, and only woke when Sam nudged me with his nose, letting me know he wanted to go out. Even though it was cold outside, I waited on the porch for him to do his business. I never felt comfortable leaving him outside for long. Eventually he came back in and when we crawled into bed, he snuggled close to me. Before he laid his head down, he turned to look up at me, and I wondered what he was thinking. Did he like it better when it was just me with him in bed? Or was he just letting me know he'd checked to make sure I was okay before he went to sleep?

The next day was like any other. When Ramona asked me if I could close for her, I guessed correctly; she hadn't let any grass grow under her feet. She had a date with the new lawyer. Naturally, I told her I'd cover for her, knowing she'd owe me one if and when I ever asked for the same. After she left, I made up a plate of roast beef, Sam's favorite, to take home for our dinner.

I hated to admit that after a few more days of being by myself, I started missing Dino's presence. If nothing else, I had no one to talk to. Sam was only so good; he listened but he couldn't give me any advice. If Dino was right, he'd be home in two more days. I figured I could wait it out.

When three days passed, I wasn't overly worried. Sometimes his work took less time and sometimes it took more. But the next day, when he wasn't in the cabin when I got home from work, I began to worry. We still didn't have a phone, so there was no way he could have called to tell me he needed to be away longer. When I went to bed that night, I told myself I needed to stop wishing for a different life, and just be content with Dino, who I knew still loved me.

On the fourth day, I knew something was wrong, so because it was my day off, I drove over to the speakeasy—but during the day, there was no one there I could talk to. I was uneasy all the next day, and when Ramona asked me if everything was all right, I did my best to assure her it was. When I drove up to the cabin, though, Dino's car still wasn't there, and I knew he was in trouble.

There was no one I could talk, and I didn't want to go to the club again and make a pest of myself. I knew I would just have to wait and see what happened.

That next week, when I opened the door to let Sam out, I saw a slightly crumpled brown bag on my porch. Sam sniffed it and turned to look at me before he took off around the cabin toward the creek. Before I even looked in it, there was no doubt where it came from, and my knees buckled.


They were paying me off. I remembered Dino saying if anything ever happened to him, they'd take care of me, and this was what that meant. Five hundred dollars was a lot of money as a payment.

Part of me didn't want to touch it, but opened it and hid the contents in my underwear drawer. I then crumpled the bag up and threw it into the fireplace.

"You look pale as a ghost," Ramona said when I walked into the diner that morning.

"I don't feel real well," I said.

"Do you need to stay home? I'm sure I can handle it."

"No, I'll be fine. Work will take my mind off it, and I'll be okay."

"Okay, suit yourself,." She said, leaving me to it.

Even though the diner was busy, the day dragged on and yet after work, I couldn't go back home. I knew I'd be intruding on Ruth and Jack, but I stopped by there anyway after I left the diner.

I knew she could tell by the look on my face that something awful had happened. "He's dead," was all I could say. I saw two things in her face; one was compassion for me and the other was relief. She took me in and made me a cup of hot chocolate, and we sat at the kitchen table.

Then I told her what Dino had told me, and about the bag with the money in it.

"I didn't want the life we were living, but I didn't want this either."

And then I cried.

# CHAPTER THIRTY SEVEN

It snowed again, and I welcomed the change in scenery. I didn't think I'd ever grow tired of seeing the snow-laden evergreen branches, for they allowed me to forgive the bare trees of fall. I checked the feeders, and I hadn't filled them lately, so I made sure I did so before I left for the diner.

There'd been no funeral, for there'd been no body. There was to be no closure, and it was something I was going to have to accept and deal with. I had no idea what happened, or where Dino's body was, and I supposed in the end, it didn't really matter. He would most likely have been in such a horrific condition, maybe even unrecognizable; I'd never ask, and I'd never know. I'd postponed telling Ramona about Dino, for I wasn't sure what I was going to tell her. But a week later, still unsure what I'd say, I made myself do it. I could have said he was killed in the line of duty, or even I have no idea how he died. But in the end, I blurted out, "Dino is dead. He died in an accident."

Ramona was surprisingly kind to me after his death, and I forgave her, her trespasses, just like I did the naked trees of the fall. Like Ruth had said, I was in no position to judge her or anyone else.

I hadn't been the best wife I could be. I only gave him half of me and not necessarily the best half. Had he ever been aware of that? I *did* love Dino, despite the life he chose, but I quickly realized I ended up resenting him for dragging me into his life. Somehow, he seemed to be able to turn himself off and then back on again. Off when he worked, and on, when it came to showing me the loving side of him. I looked down at my wedding ring and it reminded me of how he'd been so proud of himself, taking me to the Seeley Heart Trail and proposing not so long ago.

And then, without apology or considering him, I'd taken it upon myself to make sure we never had a baby. I figured it wouldn't be fair for a child to have a father who one day might not come home, and I didn't want to raise one by myself. That was just one of many selfish decisions I'd made.

No one from the speakeasy reached out to me, and truthfully, I hadn't expected them to. I would never go back there now; there was no reason. People who knew me, like Mr. Siegel, would only give me their half-felt condolences; after all, death was a hazard of the job. And from the times I was there, single women didn't show up at places like that unless they were looking for a man of few scruples, or to earn a living. I was neither.

The next month, there was another bag on my front porch, and I hid its contents in my drawer with the other money. I had no idea how long this would go on, and I wondered if it would depend on how much value they placed on Dino's life.

Most mornings, I'd lie in bed just thinking about my life, and waiting for the sun to rise—proving there'd be another new day.

I didn't rush to clear out his clothes; in a way I felt like if I waited, it would prove I *had* loved him. I waited for what I thought was an appropriate length of time to begin, and I quickly realized that he didn't have much. At a first glance in his wardrobe closet, I only saw two suits, two pairs of shoes, five crisply pressed white shirts, and a stack of winter sweaters and coats. If I included socks and t-shirts, it would all fill at most, two boxes. I would take it all to the same place I took Adele's clothes.

On my next day off, it rained, and the gloomy weather matched my mood. It was a perfect day to begin packing Dino's things. Confused, Sam just sat and watched.

"You're no help," I said, scratching him behind the ears. "But I love you, anyway."

I got everything but the sweaters and jackets into one box. As I pulled the sweaters out, I thought I might be able to wear a few of them, so I tossed them on my bed. When I got to the last of the coats, I packed them up and then noticed the floor of the wardrobe had a few loose boards. I tried to lift them with my fingers, but they were too heavy. With a butter knife from the kitchen drawer, I pried one board up then another, and there sat a shoebox I'd never seen. I pulled it out, almost fearful of what I'd find inside, and set it on the dresser before opening it.

"Well, here goes," I said to Sam.

Under his switchblade knife were photos of what must have been Dino with his parents, and then individual images of his mother, him, and what could have been a younger sister. He'd never talked about a family; in fact, I was never really sure where he was from—he'd told me two different places that I could remember.

There were two passports, each with different names, a pacifier, and a small stuffed teddy bear. Had these been the only two things he had left from his childhood?

Under all this is was what caught my breath. One by one, I counted four stacks of money wrapped in handkerchiefs, along with a note.

"Oh my god," I said, dropping down on to my bed.

I read the note first.

*Charlotte,*

*If you're reading this, then you already know something's happened to me. I know my life was one you hadn't planned on, and I'm sorry if I ever caused you grief. I tried to make sure you knew that I loved you, just like I always knew in your own way, you loved me too.*
*Take this, and make at least some of your dreams come true.*

*Always,*
*Dino*

When I gathered my wits about me, I counted out four thousand dollars! I didn't have to think about it twice. I hated myself for allowing Dino's death to fade into the background. And to feel this way made me see how I'd failed him again. It felt like betrayal, but I couldn't take my thoughts back.

It was still raining, but only two o'clock in the afternoon, so I quickly changed into something presentable, then drove over to The Tavern just to make sure there was no Sold sign nailed up. I must have driven by it and the real estate office a hundred times since the fire, and now I prayed someone was in the office. When I walked in, an older woman painting her fingernails was sitting at the reception desk.

"What can I help you with, dear?"

I took a deep breath to relax, but I still blurted it out. "I'm here to see about The Tavern."

The woman went back to finishing a nail before putting the lid on the bottle of polish and answering me.

"I see. Well, Mr. Westerbrook is out of the office right now—in fact, he's showing the property as we speak," she replied with what I took to be a mocking glint in her eyes—like she was saying to herself, *what in the world is someone like you doing here asking about that property?*

Even though I tried to stop it, a loud sigh escaped, and I knew she had me where she wanted me. And I was too late!

"You can leave your name and number if you wish."

"No, that's fine," I said. "I'll check back in later."

And with that, I walked out. I'd show her; I would go to the property and see for myself if someone else was interested. Even though the rain stung my face, I walked down to The Tavern and stood outside for a few moments, gathering my thoughts. I tried to calm the pounding in my chest by taking a deep breath. When I finally built up the courage to go in, there were two men standing there talking about the damage. In that second, I knew it was everything I could want. I loved the worn wooden beams, the weathered stone foundation, and the charm. I could picture it as a once-thriving gathering place, now sitting empty but with a lot of potential. There was even a bandstand where we could play music and I could sing again. I closed my eyes and envisioned a crowded room full of customers, eating and dancing, and I just knew if I could get it cleaned up, it would be perfect.

Finally, I cleared my throat.

"Good afternoon," one of the men said, glancing around the room. "It's a shame, isn't it?"

"Yes, it is," I said, looking around. The smoke residue was slightly overwhelming.

"Can I help you?"

Had I sensed he was debating whether or not talking with me would be worth his while? If he thought that, at least he wasn't as rude as the woman in his office was.

"Yes, at least I hope so."

"Well, let me finish up with Mr. Wilson here, and I'll be right with you." As he turned to the other man, he said, "Let me know when you have some figures for me, then."

"Will do. I'll get back to you in a few days," the other man said, shaking the real estate man's hand and acknowledging me with a slight tip of his hat.

"Now, how can I be of help, young lady? George Westerbrook's the name. Selling property is the game."

I was determined to hold my own, so I calmly said, "I'm interested in knowing more about the building.

"I see," Mr. Westerbrook said, thoughtfully. "Would it be for you and your husband?"

"No," I replied confidently. "I'd like to open up a diner."

"I see," he said again, nodding his head.

"It's a thousand dollars."

"And what would that include?"

I could tell Mr. Westerbrook was intrigued.

I took a deep breath and said to myself, this is your chance. The place was perfect for me.

"Well, it would include the building and the land, and everything you see, although you can see the fire caused a lot of damage. But I think it's mostly superficial. It'll definitely take a lot of elbow grease to get 'er back up and running. That's what I was having Mr. Wilson look at."

"I'd like to make an offer then," I said with as much confidence as I could muster.

I could see Mr. Westerbrook was taken aback.

"You mean, yourself? Ah...by yourself? Not that I want to be rude or anything, but can you afford it?"

"Yes, I can," I said, pulling my shoulders back. "I have cash."

I could see the wheels turning in his mind. Then, as though it was a second thought, he said, rubbing his chin, "Well, I do have someone else interested. . . but let me see what I can do."

I wanted to believe he was just trying to pull my leg, but my heart sank anyway. While it was cold outside, I was perspiring profusely.

"Why don't we go back to my office, and write up an offer," he said.

"Sounds great," I answered with more conviction that I had.

"Is this your car?" He asked when we walked past it.

"Yes."

The rain had stopped, and we sidestepped puddles on the way back to his office. When we walked in, his secretary, or whatever she was, must have seen us coming because she was acting busy on the typewriter.

"Hell, Mary. How many times have I told you not to use that damned polish in the office? It stinks up the place."

Mary turned twelve shades of red, and I inwardly I gloated.

"Now have a seat Miss. . . ah, what's your name again?"

"Charlotte Hayes."

# CHAPTER THIRTY EIGHT

An hour later, I just about jumped out of the car before I even put it into park, and without knocking, I burst through Ruth's office door.

"I bought The Tavern!" I couldn't decide whether to cry or scream. So I did both.

Ruth came running from their rooms; of course, she had no idea what I was talking about , and then I could hear Dorothy begin to cry.

"*What?* Are you all right?"

I took her by the shoulders and said, more calmly, "I bought The Tavern. Dino left me some money, and he told me to do something to make my dreams come true. So I did. I went and did it!" I tried to pull myself together, but I wasn't doing a very good job of it.

"Slow down and tell me," Ruth said, shifting Dorothy to another hip and dragging me to the kitchen table.

I told her about finding Dino's note and the money, and how the secretary made me feel like I wasn't worth her time, and about the nail polish and how Mr. Westerbrook gave her hell when we came back in to the office and it smelled like nail polish. If she hadn't told me to slow down, I would have rambled on.

"I'll get us a cola," she said, going to the icebox.

I was bouncing in my chair, ready to jump out of my skin, when she returned and sat back down.

"Now tell me again, but this time more slowly, so I can follow you."

So I did. I started at the beginning. About packing up Dino's things and finding the box with the money in it. And how I counted the money and decided to go look at The Tavern, praying someone else hadn't bought it.

"Mr. Westerbrook might have been playing me when he told me someone else had been interested in the property, and he *was* there with a man who was going to give him a price to work on the interior. But I decided I wouldn't let anyone buy it out from under me, so I offered him what they were asking, plus I threw in a hundred dollars for him to tuck in his pocket. I got my diner, Ruth," I said now, tears filling my eyes.

Now that Dino was dead, the air had cleared between me and Jack, and it was a relief not to have that weight on my shoulders. He'd told me several times how sorry he was, and I knew he meant it in all earnestness. I waited until Ruth told him about The Tavern before I asked her to see if he would help me refurbish the interior. He still did handiwork around town, and if he came to look at it with me, he'd be able to tell if it was something he could handle.

While the paperwork was still being done, Jack, Will, and Ruth came over to look at The Tavern with me. My hands were shaking when I tried to unlock the door, knowing this building held the future of my happiness. When we finally got inside, everyone looked at each other and then at me, surprised by the heavy smell of burned ash and lingering soot. I tried to act as confident as I'd felt when I saw the space originally, but it had been closed up for a week and I had to admit I felt chopped down a few notches.

I left the front door open to let the air circulate while Jack and Will made their way into the kitchen.

"Hmm," Jack said with a slight twist of the mouth.

I didn't take that as a positive thought.

"Since this is where the fire was, I knew we'd have the most work to do in here," I said, trying to make them believe I was aware of what I'd gotten myself into.

Jack began making a list, and I left him and Will in the kitchen while I went into the main dining room to survey the situation. When they eventually came back out, Jack said, "Well, there's nothing time and money can't solve, and I think we can take care of everything for you for about five hundred dollars."

I thought I'd die when he said that. I knew there was a lot of work to do, but I couldn't back down now, and it had to be done. There wasn't anyone more honest than Jack, and I knew he and Will would get me back up and running.

"When will the property be yours? I'd like to order some materials beforehand."

"It should be another week," I said. "And then we can get started."

Ruth said, "I can help you wash all the dishes and silverware so you don't have to buy new. . . maybe get some new pots and pans is all."

Before the next week passed, the Warranty Deed was all signed by the county and The Tavern was officially mine. When Mr. Westerbrook handed me a new set of keys, I wanted to hug and kiss him, but I didn't. I left his office and almost skipped down the street to The Tavern and opened the door to my new diner. I don't know why it shocked me that the smell of smoke still assaulted me.

I'd made my list, like I had at Adele's cabin, and I tried to remind myself everything could be taken care of, but then reality sank in. For a slight moment, I wondered what on earth I'd done. I'd already ordered a new stove and icebox, and Jack had all the lumber ready to build new storage shelves and a new counter. He'd helped me lay it all out, and he was ready to start work.

"If you have the budget, now would be a perfect time to replace the linoleum flooring in the kitchen," he suggested. "It's what we'll use for the counters and I can order enough to do both."

I'd already used up more than half of what Dino left me, but I still had my savings and the cash I was getting from the speakeasy. And Jack was right, now was the time to do anything else that needed to be done. I told him to go ahead and do it.

Extra workmen came in to clean and oil the wooden walls, and the tables and chairs, and when everything else was completed, they refinished the wood floors.

Ruth and I went down to the Sears in San Bernardino and bought new pots and pans, cooking utensils, and twelve dozen white fabric napkins. Before we left, I wandered into the fabric department where there were bolts and bolts of material, and I was especially drawn to a bright red plaid that I thought would look wonderful on the front windows. I hadn't originally planned on curtains, but when I saw the colors, Ruth read my mind and said she'd sew them. I guessed at the window size and then, before we left, I bought drapery rods.

The only things I had left to do was order a new sign for the front of the building and print a menu. I took my favorites from the diners in Texas and Lake Arrowhead, and added a few ideas of my own, and then asked a couple of local merchants if they wanted to put their store or business name around the edges of the menu so people could take them as souvenirs. Originally, only a few took me up on the offer, using the depression as a reason not to, but when I convinced them this was an excellent way of getting their name out to tourists, more of them jumped on the bandwagon. The local printer ran five hundred copies, which seemed like an outrageous amount, even to me, but when I figured if I served twenty-five tables a day, not to mention once we started having entertainment, that would last less than a month.

Of course, I was setting my goals sky high.

I also had a phone installed.

I had half a mind to write Miles and Finn to see if they could come up to celebrate the grand opening, but I knew they'd have a hard time being out of the club. Plus, I wanted to change things up a little. I figured locals and tourists from the camps wouldn't be interested in the easy listening music we'd played, so I put an ad in the mountain newspaper and the San Bernardino paper looking for a different type of band. Swing was popular, and that was the kind of music I could sing to, although if a band already had a singer they were used to working with, I'd be interested in that as an option too. The other idea I had was to bring in country western music. Over the years, it had also become popular, and some of it made for good dancing.

I heard first from a group calling themselves The Traveling Cowboys, and when they came up and auditioned, I knew they'd be a hit. Two of the men also sang, so I was relieved I wasn't going to have to learn new music. They agreed to play two nights a week, on Fridays and Saturdays, and I rented one of Ruth's cabins for them to stay in. A local motel would have been handy, but I knew Ruth and Jack could use the extra money and it wasn't too far of a drive for the guys.

By then, it was the end of April, and we set an opening date. For the locals who'd been following my progress, we were already serving breakfast, lunch and dinner, even though I warned them we might be a little slow getting up and running. Thankfully, everyone was very patient with us—they were all just happy we were there. I put another ad in the newspaper and they ran an article on the opening, which I hoped would bring a lot of new customers. The only thing left was for the sign to arrive and it was to be hung by the end of the week.

Anticipation for the new sign to be hung was almost killing me, and on the afternoon it arrived, I made sure the sign maker covered it until we were ready to unveil it. The band had finished setting up, and precisely at five, just like the newspaper ad said, we were ready to open. A crowd of onlookers gathered around and from inside, the band did a drum roll. The sheet dropped, and the crowd applauded.

"We've done it Mama," I cried.

I didn't think she'd mind the slight change of plans.

We opened Flo's Stockade and Diner.

# CHAPTER THIRTY NINE

As it turned out, the western band was a hit. The locals loved it, and we started getting people in from Lake Arrowhead, Blue Jay, Twin Peaks, Cedar Glen and even as far away as Running Springs. I always asked people where they were from, and it gave me a good idea of where I should be advertising. When the local campers started coming in, I had an idea. I'd noticed Big Bear had been using white trucks they called buses. They were open on the top and sides, and had four rows of seats behind the driver, and they carried passengers up to the mountains.

I found the company that made them and asked if they had any used buses for sale. They said they didn't, but they referred me to a company that might, and I was able to get my hands on one for a reasonable price. We were just turning a profit by then, and it only made sense to see if we could bring campers from the campsites to town and bring them back after the band quit playing. I had some fliers printed and school kids delivered them to the camps on Fridays and Saturdays. I had to admit there were times I wished we were bringing in liquor; we could have made a fortune. But I was satisfied with what we were doing, and we didn't need any trouble. Plus, after that first summer, we'd made enough money to pay for the bus and then some.

The Traveling Cowboys came to me one day and said they were putting too much wear and tear on their vehicle, coming up and down the mountain every week, and I thought for sure I was going to lose them. Even though I'd been listening and memorizing the words to their songs, there was no way I was going to be able to replace them; they were a big part of our success. They admitted they were making so much money, with what I paid them and tips, they'd consider moving up to the mountains if they could find regular work during the week.

There were so many new cabins being built, and knowing Jack had built their own cabins way back, I asked him if he had any ideas.

"I have one," he said. "I've been wanting to do more building, but I can't do it by myself. I hate to admit I'm getting older, but it's the truth. If the boys are interested in learning how to build, I can teach them, and it'll be profitable all the way around."

"Hell yeah," the guys said.

A week or so later, they started working with Jack and they stayed in their cabin for another few months until they could find something larger.


One Saturday afternoon, when the band was rehearsing a new song for the show, I recognized the words and started singing along. It was a catchy tune and as I was sweeping the floor—and thinking no one was watching me—my broom became my dance partner. We swayed and my steps were light. When their song was over, I tilted the broom back like a dance partner would do, then stood back up. The guys clapped, and I thought I was going to die of embarrassment.

"You've got a great voice, Charlotte," one of them said. "And good moves, too. Ever thought about stepping up and joining us for a few songs every now and then? I think customers would love it."

"Didn't she tell you she used to sing in L.A.?"

Ruth was standing in the open doorway, holding Dorothy by one hand, and the baby in the other arm. She was meeting me for lunch.

With a half smile of acknowledgement, Buzz, the lead singer, raised his eyebrows and nodded. "You never said."

"*Ruth,*" I said in surprise.

"Oops. I would have thought you'd said something by now. Sorry." She apologized, but she didn't look like she meant it.

In December of 1933, prohibition ended, and our business blew up. Beer and whisky were being served everywhere, and the more people drank, the more they spent on food. The campers could now bring their own liquor up, but it was much more fun to drink in a place like The Stockade and Diner, where they could also dance.

I sang for the band and the guys agreed I'd be a good addition to the group. I didn't know all the songs they played, and some were just made up, so I'd only come up on the stage for a few hours a night. That suited me fine, for I still needed to welcome customers and make sure there were no bar room fights.

One half of my life was in order. Even though I came home in the early hours of the morning, the exhaustion was worth every drop of effort, and I'd proven every challenge had worthwhile. The Stockade provided everything I needed—security, a sense of accomplishment and a steady income. On the surface, it looked like I had it all; a good reputation and stability, but everything else felt empty. My nights were lonely, and my success never filled the silence I felt the moment I opened the door to my cabin.

I was missing love.

Almost a year after Dino died, I met Ruth for a quick lunch at the diner in Lake Arrowhead. A while back, Ramona had sold out to a man named Earl Stanley and there was no longer any history to keep me from going in there from time to time. Ruth had the kids, so we sat in the back, and after looking at the menu for a few minutes, we ordered.

Earl wasn't a bad-looking man, probably in his early fifties, and he sported the still popular crew cut. He dressed like a city man, with cuffed corduroy pants, a white shirt rolled up to his elbows and suspenders.

"At lease his boots are suitable for mountain living," I said to Ruth. I added, "He's done a wonderful job combining his city background with a twist of the mountain look."

She gave me the eye.

"What? I can look, can't I? At least he's not a customer."

It was the first time I'd seen someone I could become interested in, but I knew nothing about him. Was he married? Why had he moved to the mountains when he was so obviously a city boy? Did he come from money?

Earl was attentive, but I couldn't tell if he even noticed me for being anything other than a customer. When we were finished with lunch, even though he was our waiter, I felt awkward leaving him a tip. He smiled for a second as we got up to leave, and I knew then I would be coming back in.

We'd had a lot of snow that winter, and berms were still high along the streets, and understandably, business slowed down. I hired a young man to come in every day to make sure the sidewalk and street in front of The Stockade were clear of snow so people could come and go freely. I was always thinking of ways to improve business and I remembered how we'd done so well at the diner in Texas when we started selling cookies, so I asked Ruth if she'd like to start baking for us. She came in twice a week and baked a variety of cookies, seasonal cobbler pies, and bread pudding. Customers went wild, and word quickly spread that we had the best desserts in town. I took that as a compliment, although we were the only diner in town!

I never saw anyone drop off the money, but I was still getting bags on my front porch. The amount was always the same, five hundred dollars, and it went straight into the bank. I didn't take it for granted—I figured they'd continue paying me off for about a year, and I was right. I guessed that was the value they placed on Dino's life. One year equaled six thousand dollars.

I didn't have a place to go to celebrate the remembrance of Dino's death—no church or gravesite—in fact, I had no idea when he actually died or if he'd even been buried. So early one morning, during the anniversary week of his death, for a change of scenery, I had breakfast at the diner in Lake Arrowhead. I'd thought about asking Ruth if she wanted to join me, but I wanted to be by myself. Why I chose the diner, I wasn't sure.

When I opened the door, Earl acted happy to see me, and while I didn't need to be shown to a booth, I followed him to one in the back.

"I've missed seeing you and your friend," he said.

"I have a place over in Crestline, so I'm not always able to get away."

When I told him it was The Stockade, his eyes widened in surprise.

"I've heard great things about that place. Good for you."

"As you know, running a restaurant is a lot of work, and I added entertainment, so there are a lot of working parts and it can be a challenge to keep everything working smoothly."

"I'll bet. What can I get you this morning? Are you a coffee drinker?"

"No, I'm fine. For some reason, I never got hooked. I'd like iced tea though, no lemon."

He no sooner walked away when an attractive woman with two small children came through the front door.

"Daddy," the children called as they ran to him.

Although there'd been no real reason to think there was anything more than a man just being friendly with a customer, it was clear that nothing was ever going to happen between us. It was still a dull kind of letdown, and I couldn't help but feel the sting of rejection. I shouldn't have felt that way, but I did.

So I ordered French toast with lots of butter and powdered sugar and bacon, and after gorging myself, I drove aimlessly around the lake until I took the Crestline road towards home.

It was my atonement for not mourning the death of my husband, the man I married, and for even thinking about getting out there and finding a new love.

It wasn't through the lack of men asking me out that I didn't have a social life—there were many—but I had a strict policy of not getting involved with customers, which eliminated most of the men I knew. Some of the campers from L.A. came up in groups of single men, and I stayed away from them, too. Who knew if they had a wife and kids at home?

I proved my rule right when I went out with a man who lived a couple of towns over. He'd been coming in for a while, and we'd hit it off. He was divorced and had older kids down the hill. He was a moderate drinker and a good dancer. We went to dinner, also out of town—hoping no one would recognize me later—and that was it. He did everything I hated. He dominated the conversation, bit his nails at the table, held his knife and fork like he'd never learned table manners, and chewed with his mouth open.

I didn't even finish the meal.

"I've made a mistake," I said as I picked up my purse and left.

I never saw him again at the Stockade, which was a shame. We'd lost a good customer.

I just kept telling myself Mr. Right was going to walk through the door one day, and I'd know he was the one for me. So that left just me and Sam.

I didn't dream a lot, or at least most of my dreams were bits and pieces of things that made no sense—even if they woke me up, they didn't take long to forget. But one night, my dreams were filled with images of me at home in Texas. My mother was still alive, and I was helping her in the diner. We'd just brought in a batch of cookies and she looked to make sure we were by ourselves in the kitchen before she handed me one.

"One day, we'll have a diner of our own," she said before I woke up.

I wondered what she would think of Flo's Stockade and Diner. I knew it wasn't what she'd had in mind, but she would have been proud of my accomplishments. From the start, I knew it wasn't going to turn out exactly like what she'd been thinking; instead once I saw the building, it was my interpretation of what it could become that inspired me. And I'd accomplished what I'd set out to do.

One thing that bothered me, though, was that already we'd become known as The Stockade, instead of Flo's.

I loved the sound of snow crunching underfoot, and when the patches of snow finally started melting, the air was still crisp but no longer biting cold. On the sides of the roads and along the path to my cabin, green shoots of this spring's daffodils began to push through. At first they were tight bulbs, but soon, they started to bloom brightly in the melted snow.

I wanted to see them as a sign the seasons had changed again, bringing with them new hope for the future.

Low clouds rarely made it to Crestline, and one morning, when I woke to fog so thick and dense I could barely make out the green branches of the trees in front of my cabin, it surprised me. Even if I didn't have to travel far, I hated driving in that kind of murky fog when it was dark, gloomy and thick enough it reduced visibility. Thankfully, the sun began to rise as I was getting ready for work, warming the air, and it turned out to be a beautiful day.

I'd taken in two abandoned kittens, and their eyes were just opening. They were both males, so I named them Abbott and Costello. I still couldn't leave them alone all day without feeding them, so I dropped them off at my neighbor's, who'd graciously agreed to watch and feed them. I was surprised Sam took to them so quickly; it was almost as if he had natural maternal instincts. He kept them warm by lying with them next to the fire, and when he did that, I missed his warm body next to mine in my bed. When they mewed, he whined, as if I didn't already hear them.

It was particularly rainy the beginning of March and a lot of customers stayed home until Friday and Saturday when rain or not, they were tired of being cooped up inside. Any nights the band played were our most profitable, and when the weather started warming up by the end of the month, everyone was ready for it. One of our regular customers said, "It's like the old saying, March comes in like a lion and goes out like a lamb." I'd never given it much thought before, but it seemed to be what had happened up in the mountains, at least.

With the warmer weather, the dogwoods had started to bloom and throughout the mountain towns, the trees with their white blossoms lined the roads and they were quite a spectacle. Most of the daffodils had also poked through the rest of the snowy ground, and the rest of the trees that had lost their leaves were now sporting tiny new green leaves. Soon everything would come to a peak, and the mountains would be as beautiful as I remembered on my first day here.

When someone filled for me in the mornings, I loved to sit on my porch and just listen to the sounds of the mountains, whether it was the wind in the trees or the birds singing their songs. Sam loved it too, so I usually let him wander. One particular morning, I saw movement to my left, and it was a beautiful red fox. My neighbor Liz told me she sometimes saw one or two, but mostly they were late afternoon visitors, being nocturnal by nature. He must have felt safe on my property, and I assumed he was looking for something to eat. I sat still and watched until Sam broke the silence with a deep bark; he must have seen the fox as well.

I wanted to scold him when the fox scampered away, but he was only doing his job. Protecting me, the kittens, and the house. It was sad I had no one I could share the experience with.

I decided, then, to take one day at a time, remaining hopeful that everything would turn around for me and love would find its way back to me. It might come gradually and unexpectedly, or it might return like the daffodils breaking through the frozen ground, filling the empty space in my heart.

I once read, "*Love is never lost…*" . I couldn't think of the ending, but I thought of a perfect one; *it was only waiting to be found again.*

Kind of like that last green spout of daffodils I saw just outside the walkway to my cabin.

# Joe

Back in 1912, when I was growing up in Watts, California, no one thought to lock their front doors *or* their cars. Just outside Los Angeles, Watts was still a relatively unknown small town known for farming and ranching, and housing was affordable. The Pacific Electric Railway came through, connecting to L.A., and my father was an electrician for the railway. He'd always hoped us boys would grow up wanting to follow in his footsteps, or go to college. When he was growing up, he wanted to go to college, and he got a scholarship to USC. *His* parents had immigrated from Italy to the U.S. and his mother was a proud woman who considered a grant, charity. She wouldn't allow him to accept it.

In junior high school, my two older brothers took an interest in the business, and this appeased my father for a while. He'd take them with him on weekends, and once Antonio, my oldest brother, graduated from high school, he decided to become an electrician and follow in my father's footsteps. My father worked long hours, weekends included, and it provided a good income for our family. Antonio was the most practical of us boys.

We all had paper routes and mowed lawns to earn extra money. Lorenzo and Antonio saved their money to buy better bikes, but I was happy with riding their old ones, so I always had more money than they did. My mother went with me to open a savings account at our bank, and I could hardly wait to make the weekly deposit to see what my new balance was. Looking back, it was one of the few things I did as a young man that could be considered being responsible.

After he graduated, the second eldest, Lorenzo, decided what he wanted to do. A neighbor down the street worked as floor runner at a Hollywood film studio, and Lorenzo thought if he worked in Hollywood, he'd have a shot at becoming a movie star. My father did his best to discourage him, but my mother said, "If that's what the boy wants to do, then let him do it."

When Lorenzo wanted to be called Larry, my father barely heard him before his fists curled at his sides. But instead of striking out, he shouted, "You changed the name your family gave you? You might as well slap me in the face. How could you do that?"

So when Lorenzo came home bragging about seeing famous movie stars and how important his job as a runner was, my father would walk out of the room.

"We'll see how long *that* lasts," he said to anyone who would listen.

My younger sister was a princess. After three boys, my mother still wanted a girl, and she figured the only way to be guaranteed she'd have one was to adopt one. At first, my father put his foot down; not only could they barely afford three boys, he'd said, they plain old didn't need another child. My mother won, as she usually did, and within a few months, they brought home a baby girl—they named her Laura, or Lolly, as she later preferred to be called. It turned out Lolly also wanted to become a movie star, but she settled for becoming a teacher, getting married and having children.

My birth name was Guiseppe Rossi, but I hated it and I went by Joe. "No one has that kind of name," I said when I started school.

Again, my father was outraged. "But you're Italian. Where's your sense of pride?"

When I argued they'd name my sister Laura, which wasn't Italian at all, and she wanted to be called Lolly, I had them over a barrel. And when I told them I'd already told my teachers and friends to call me Joe, they backed down. Plus, by that time, they were so busy doting on my sister, they figured they had more important things to do rather than worry about me and my name.

When I was around twelve, an Italian man named Sam Rodia moved in a few streets over, and he became quite the talk of the neighborhood.

Divorced, which was rare in those days, everyone wondered why. He was relatively slight in build, had hairy forearms, and even though I was certain he shaved every day, dark stubble always shaded his face.

He raised quite a stink with the neighbors when he started building metal towers on his property using steel rebar and concrete. Kids in the neighborhood were his biggest fans as we watched the structures grow, and we collected bottles, ceramic tiles, seashells, and broken pottery that Sam used in creating his mosaics for his structures.

Sam would tell us stories about old Italy, and about his work as a tile mason. Every once in a while, he'd take us with him as he walked the Pacific Electric Railway to collect railroad ties and other materials he could use on his towers.

It wasn't long before people outside the neighborhood heard about Mr. Rodia, and on weekends, cars from all over would be lined up along the street, waiting for their chance to drive by and see what the fuss was all about. Many years later, when I drove through my old neighborhood, the towers still stood, protected by the city's Cultural Affairs Department.

I was in my late teens when The Depression hit the country, and it made a big impact on our way of life. Even though my father had steady employment, neighbors were suddenly without work, cars with no gasoline sat idle in driveways, and one neighbor drove the streets in his pickup truck selling knife sharpening services along with live rabbits he'd slaughter on site. Meat and fresh produce were becoming scarce, and my mother, who'd always had a large garden, started bartering at our corner grocery store. When she baked our bread, she baked a few extra loaves and gave them to our neighbors. They, in turn, would share butter and milk from their cows. My father bought six chickens and built coops in the backyard, so we always had plenty of eggs. When he figured out we needed a rooster to have more chickens, he brought one home, and it wasn't long before we were all annoyed by his morning crowing.

We were more fortunate than many people, but we still ate a lot of beans and potatoes.

We could also still drive into Compton to buy clothes and shoes. Some of the neighbor kids wore patched and mended clothes to school, and every now and then, one of my friends would come over wearing something I no longer wore, and my mother would say it looked just like something she remembered me having.

We *did* have to make do with some things that weren't a necessity. Like in the past, when we complained our towels were threadbare and had holes in them, my mother used to turn them in the rags, and buy new ones. Now she said, "they'll dry out faster when I hang them on the line when they're that way."

My bicycle was still my only mode of transportation and one day when riding our bikes after school, a buddy of mine and I saw a trailer filled with furniture in front of a neighbor's house around the corner.

"What do you think is going on?" I asked naively.

Another neighborhood kid had stopped also and answered, "They're moving. Mr. Alonzo lost his job."

"Oh," was all I could think to say.

We watched a few more minutes until the daughter Angela came out carrying a pillowcase full of something.

"What are you guys looking at?" she asked bitterly.

I could hear the indignation in her voice and I could feel the weight of her anger deep inside me. Then I felt like a fool. What do you say to someone who has had their life upended? I wanted to know where they were going, but I knew better than to ask, and for once, I kept my mouth shut.

"Let's go," I said to my friend as I turned and rode off.

That night, I asked my father where someone might move if they lost their job here.

"Probably, they'd move back to where they came from. Could be the Midwest, although right now if they can't make it work here, they'd have a heck of a time making a living there too."

What would we do if that same thing happened to us? If my dad lost his job, would we have to move too? I was still at an age where I took everything so seriously and I was getting a glimpse of how crappy life could be.

Mr. Cranston was the neighborhood grocer, and one of the few local businesses that were still surviving. We did our best to support him and his wife, and if she didn't need to do a major shopping, my mother would send me down there to get the little things we needed, like milk, and sometimes canned goods. We had a few lemon and orange trees, and if we had more than we needed, it was my job to take them over to the Cranston's and trade for butter, sugar or, if we didn't need anything, candy bars. Mrs. Cranston started a side business of selling Avon—known then as the California Perfume Company—and my mother began ordering lipstick from her.

If Mr. Cranston didn't sell all his newspapers, I'd collect them and once a week take them over to the town vet, who'd pay me a nickel to clean and line the animal cages. Once he had a box with a batch of kittens, and I tried to get my mom and dad to let me bring one home, but my dad said there was no way he was going to feed another mouth. I didn't dare think about them being put out on the street, and fortunately, when I returned a week later, they'd all been adopted, and I felt a huge sense of relief.

I didn't particularly like school, but summers were still boring. The days were long and hot, and sometimes even *I* could smell myself if I'd been outside riding my bike all day. I tried to get cleaned up before dinner, but as she grew older, Lolly spent what seemed like hours in our one bathroom, and unless it was my father, no amount of pleading could convince her to let us in. More often than not, there'd be a line waiting to go to the bathroom, and that's when us boys learned to take a pee out in the backyard.

By then, my brothers were interested in cars and when I tried to help, they told me I only got in their way. Antonio was interested in girls, and he started shaving and wearing aftershave. Lorenzo had a buddy who lived down the street, and they were always off doing something that didn't include me. I was friends with a few guys in the neighborhood, too, and over the years, we'd been repeatedly told to stay away from the riverbed, but we thought we were old enough to take care of ourselves, and we went there every day. When I came home with wet pants, my mother took one look at me and knew where I'd been.

"Giuseppe!" She never called me Joe when she was mad at me. She pinched her thumbs and fingertips together and shook her wrists in Italian fashion. "Ma, sei scemo! Are you an idiot? You're going to get it! Wait until your father comes home. How many times have I told you to stay away from that riverbed? There are hobos down there, and you could fall down the embankment and kill yourself. We'd never know where you were."

I knew I was in trouble, but like an immature child, I shouted back, "There's nothing else to do!"

Sure enough, when my father came home, my mother told him where'd I'd been, and even though I felt like I was almost an adult, he took his belt to me. He never hit any of us hard enough to hurt us; he just wanted us to know he meant business, and I knew he was proving to my mother he was indeed still the man of the house.

While my brothers had decided what they wanted to do with their lives, I hadn't given my future much thought. When I was fifteen, Arnold, my friend down the street, who was three years older than me, had his driver's license and a Model A. My parents had no idea I was hanging out with him, and if they knew, they would have killed me. But my father was always working, and my mother spent her days either with my sister, or drinking coffee with the neighbor ladies; there was always someone at our kitchen table talking about all their troubles— once, my mother claimed to have fixed over twenty marriages.

Arnold's father worked at a brewery in Los Angeles and he would regularly re-stock their extra icebox with ill-gotten beer. His father never suspected him of lightening the stash by a few bottles at a time, and so by the time the weekend came around, Arnold collected enough to get drunk. I never touched the stuff myself.

Arnold was a big instigator, and I didn't need much convincing when he wanted to do something wild. We'd take his Model A out and cruise around with no purpose but to get into trouble. One time we were driving down main street and someone cut us off. We chased the guy and when we caught up with him, Arnold got out of the car and beat the crap out of the poor guy.

Sometimes we'd go out looking to steal things from cars, and when Arnold found a car he liked, I'd stand there as a lookout while he climbed under the car and stole something he either needed or thought he could sell.

When I had saved enough money to buy a car of my own, we alternated who drove, and yet Arnold still called the shots. If he wanted to steal something, we stole it. If he wanted to beat someone up, we beat them up. I found I was quickly developing a temper. One night when it was my turn to drive, even though it was during prohibition, we went to a bar out of town so no one would recognize us. We went in, and Arnold ordered a beer. He'd already been drinking, and I just wanted a root beer. Taunting me and calling me a wimp, he began pushing me, almost challenging me to fight him. He ordered another beer and wouldn't let up on me, so I hauled off and slugged him in the face.

A guy in the bar yelled at us. "Get the hell out of here. Go home." I walked up to him and slugged him, too.

Another time I drove, Arnold convinced me we should chase after a guy on a motorcycle and beat the crap out of him. I tailed the guy until he finally pulled over. I got out of the car, pumped to start a fight, and when the guy got off the bike, I realized he was twice my size and height. I didn't stand a chance in hell of beating him in a fight.

"What's your problem, buddy?" he asked, taking off his gloves. I could see it in his eyes—he was raring to have a go at me.

I had to think quick on my feet.

"Ah, right. Nothing buddy," I said back. "I just wanted to have a look at your motorcycle."

I had another friend, Charlie, who, when I was seventeen, was already married with two kids. He cheated on his wife, and not only did he steal car parts, he'd pocket things wherever we went.

A group of us would take our cars out to the L.A. riverbed and race. Charlie was a madman and would attempt daredevil stunts, like driving down into the riverbed, or going top speed and driving right up alongside another car. He was crazy, and I often wondered how he didn't get killed when he drove so recklessly.

I turned eighteen the day I graduated from high school, and my parents decorated our patio with streamers and hanging lights. We barbecued chicken and steaks, and my mother made up a batch of spaghetti and meatballs. I brought over a girl I'd started seeing, named Lucy Williams, and when we came out onto the patio, my mother looked around behind me.

"Where's everyone else?" She asked.

I'd spent so much time with Arnold and Charlie, I didn't really have any friends my age.

"This is it," I said, trying to sound more confident than I felt.

"Oh, okay," she said.

I introduced Lucy to the rest of my family, and then found my mother in the kitchen.

"Now don't go asking her a lot of questions. It's not like we're getting married or anything," I said.

She just swatted me away.

That night, when I dropped Lucy off, just as I built up the nerve to kiss her, she told me her parents were going to move back to South Dakota to help take care of her grandparents.

I felt like I'd been socked in the face.

When I turned twenty-one, I felt like a grownup and I celebrated with Charlie and Arnold. We went to a place Charlie knew where we could get a drink. I'd only had a beer now and then, so I was what they called a lightweight. There was a pretty girl in the bar, and even though I was always doing something rowdy, I was shy when it came to girls. In fact, I'd never been on a date. As a way to build up the courage to talk to her, I drank one beer after another, and in no time, I was what the guys later called shitfaced. When I finally went up to the girl to talk to her, her eyes narrowed just slightly, and she gave me the once-over.

"You're just a kid," she said. "I'm looking for a man."

Well, that knocked the wind out of my sails. Without telling the guys I was leaving, I just turned and walked out the door. I found my car in the parking lot, climbed in, and took off. I'd never driven after drinking, and I was yelling at myself for being stupid enough to approach that girl. My vision was blurry, and I had a hard time staying in my own lane. I came to an intersection, and didn't see that the light was red until it was too late to stop. Another car came from the right, and I swerved, but not before it hit me.

The impact nearly threw me out of the car and when I sat back upright, I almost felt dizzy. The minute I came to my senses, I looked over at the car that struck me, and the guy inside was moving. I jumped out and rushed around to the passenger side of his car.

"Are you all right?" I asked, still feeling queasy.

"I think so. Where the *hell* did you come from?" he asked, rubbing his forehead.

Neither of us was injured, and although we could still drive our cars, both of them were damaged. There was no way I could deny it; I was responsible.

There's nothing like a shot of adrenaline to sober you up. I gave the man my name and phone number at home.

"I'll pay for the damages," I said. "And I'm really sorry."

Adrenaline kept me sober enough to drive home, and even though it was two in the morning and everyone would have been in bed a long time ago, I came in the back door. Lorenzo and I still shared a room, and I didn't want to wake him and deal with his stupid questions, so I took my shoes off in the kitchen and edged my way into our room. Without bothering to take my clothes off, I crawled into my bed and covered my head with my blanket. When my parents saw the car the next day, I had hell to pay.

Despite jobs being so scarce, I'd been lucky enough to get work at the filling station in town, and even after paying my folks some rent, I was still making deposits into my savings account. I ended up using most of it to pay for the repairs to the car I'd damaged, but there was enough left to start working on mine if I wanted to. Instead, I just left the car sitting in the driveway, to remind me what an idiot I'd become.

Not long after that, Arnold was arrested for drunk driving and manslaughter. He'd run the same red light I had, but he struck and killed a pedestrian. He ultimately went to jail.

About a month later, Vinnie from down the street came up to me as I was working on my car. I was doing some of the body work myself to save some money, and I had a shop lined up to finish it off and paint it.

"Hey, Joe," he said, standing on the opposite side of the car.

He was a cop and the first thing that went through my mind was, could he connect me with somehow with either Charlie or Arnold?

He continued, "I've known you since you were a kid, and I've watched you do some stuff you probably didn't know I knew about. We all do things we eventually aren't proud of, but there is a way for you to turn your life around."

I didn't need anyone coming up with ways for me to change my life, so I said, "Thanks, Vinnie, I appreciate your concern," I said. "I'm figuring it out on my own."

"I'm sure you are, but I had an idea that could help you do it sooner than later."

He waited for me to think before I answered.

"What's that?" I asked.

"We could use a few guys on the force, and if you're interested, I can see if I can get you in."

"What?" I threw my head back and laughed nervously.

"You heard me. I see what's going on, and I think I can help you out. If you don't figure it out soon, you're going to end up in trouble, like Arnold."

The tension in my neck was killing me, and I rubbed the back of my neck to try to relieve it.

"You think about it, and stop by my house when you're ready," Vinnie said, giving me a salute. He then turned and walked back down the street.

There was no way I was going to become a cop.

I went back to work on my car.

Like an idiot, I went to visit Arnold in jail. I don't know why it surprised me that not only was the building itself cold and unnerving, but the high walls and barbed wire removed any doubt this was a place of confinement. I should have turned around in the parking lot and gone back home, but I was curious. Inside was just as intimidating. I handed over my personal belongings, and they checked my ID and searched me. The guards led me to a waiting room, where I sat among mothers, wives, and families, waiting to be called into another area.

Eventually, I was escorted into a room with glass dividing the visitors and inmates, and all communication was through phones, which were filthy. When they finally brought Arnold in, the lighting made him look like he was deathly ill. I tried to focus on our time together, but my surroundings kept drawing me away, and the sound of a ticking clock drove me crazy.

"Hey, man," Arnold said, trying to force a grin.

"Hey yourself," I said, trying to figure out what I was going to say.

"Don't be stupid."

"What?"

"Don't be stupid and do something that gets you into a place like this."

"I don't plan to."

"That's all I gotta say."

And with that, Arnold got up, and a guard came to get him.

Emotionally, I was sapped. I felt guilty for leaving him, but there was nothing I could do to help him, plus he wouldn't even talk to me.

Walking out of the building was like walking out into freedom, which it was. I was free to come and go, and Arnold wasn't, because he'd killed someone. I went home feeling even more mixed up than I had been before.

When New Year's Eve came around, I was still keeping to myself when I heard Charlie died. He'd rolled his car into the riverbed when a group of guys were drinking and racing. I pictured him laying there broken and bleeding, and then I could only imagine what his wife and children were going to do without him.

They fixed up his face for the funeral, but there was no disguising his left eye had swollen closed, and he'd broken his jaw. I couldn't figure why anyone would allow the casket to be open. There weren't many people at the service, and his wife cried the entire time. When the preacher gave his eulogy, he only talked about Charlie being a good man; a good husband and father. And I knew this was far from the truth. I'd been there when he cheated and stole. And then I asked myself—what kind of person did that make me?

The first of February, I drove by Vinnie's house, and his car was in the driveway. I parked a few doors down and then just sat there. I watched as his kids came and went. His wife came home with a trunk full of groceries, and Vinnie helped her bring everything in. I wasn't so far away he wouldn't have been able to see me if he looked up, and I prayed he wouldn't, for I wasn't ready for him to see me give up.

I had no idea what everyone else was doing that summer, and I really didn't care. I was still towing the line, but I had no motivation. I'd quit my job at the filling station months back, and I knew I could always go back there, but putting gas in cars wasn't exactly what I was hoping to do for the rest of my life.

"You'd better do something," my father eventually said, dropping the newspaper off on my bed. "You can always come to work for me."

I knew I didn't want to do that, so I looked at the want ads. The telephone company was looking for workmen, and the oil company in Huntington Beach was hiring. Neither of those sounded interesting, so I tossed the paper in my trash can and went back to bed.

"Marianne next door inherited herself a new dog, and she wanted to know if you'd be around today to walk it for her," my mom said from outside my bedroom door.

"Do I look like a dog walker?" I wanted to call back. But I was beginning to lose my muscle mass because of all the lying around I was doing, so I went next door to check out the dog. He was a handsome German Shepherd named Ozzie, and I said, "Hey fella. Wanna go for a walk?"

At least it gave me something to do two times a day while I was figuring out what I wanted to do with my life.

One day, when Ozzie and I were out, before I could stop him, he peed on Vinnie's lawn.

"Hey, there," he said. "Can't you control your dog?"

"Sorry, man," I said, pulling Ozzie's leash.

"How's it going?"

"Okay."

"You know, we're still looking if you're interested," Vinnie said, taking a swig of soda.

"What's all involved?"

"There's a lot of training up front, but once you get past that, it's maintaining public safety and all that. We have a new class coming up in about a week. I can see if I can get you in."

I didn't want to sound too anxious, so I said, "Yeah, I guess."

A week later, I stood in line with about twenty other young men who were waiting to get their heads shaved.

Like all other young officers, I spent my first few years walking a beat, controlling traffic, and enforcing parking and driving laws. I had my fair share of bringing drunks into jail after confiscating their alcohol and pouring it down the sewage drains, and then there was the constant filling out mounds of paperwork.

Eventually, I was interested in doing something more meaningful, so the next time I saw Vinnie, I asked him about any other opportunities. He told me they were organizing a Gangster Squad to deal with prohibition and organized crime in Los Angeles. I asked if he'd put in a good word for me, and a couple of months later, I was knee deep in training to go undercover. I moved into an apartment in L.A. and waited.

Eventually, the call came, and I met Vinnie at a local coffee shop where he was going to brief me. A new operation had come to town and their involvement in Los Angeles was growing.

"I've been inside for a while now," Vinnie said. "And the captain wants to upgrade his accommodations. They're looking into a floor at one of the hotels. They need a driver who can assume more responsibilities, and I've recommended you."

"Holy shit," I wanted to say. The few sips of coffee I'd drunk turned in my stomach.

"You'll be fine. Just say 'Yes sir,' and keep your mouth shut. Have you memorized the hierarchy?"

I knew it by heart, but I didn't recite it, for fear I'd sound like a know-it-all.

The Boss, who was the head of the family, the Underboss, who was the second-in-command, and the Consigliere, the advisor, were all back in Chicago. The Captain, Paulie "Knuckles" DeGrazia was the fourth in line and the man I was going to work for. He ran local operations—the one responsible for all enterprises and reported to the boss. Soldiers carried out the orders, and then there were people like me, who provided a service and kept to themselves until they proved their loyalty and capability.

I had to look the part, so Vinnie went with me to The Broadway department store, and I bought three suits, white shirts, cuff links, ties, shoes and socks. "Holy cow," I said when I looked at the bill. It was a good thing the store billed the department.

My first assignment was to drive Tony the Bagman. He collected money, so we spent the day driving to neighborhoods I was familiar with, but to places I never knew were there. They were involved in loan sharks, gambling dens and bookies. According to Vinnie, they'd just bought a warehouse and started bootlegging. I was told to stay in the car when we got there, so I didn't get a chance to check out the operation, but I hoped down the road I'd be trusted to go inside. There were two houses of prostitution, and one day I drove Tony and a woman to a doctor's office in a rundown building, which I quickly learned was where women could have an abortion. Every night when I got home, I made detailed notes about where we'd gone and what we'd done. We were on a fact finding mission.

I fit in, and eventually Mr. DeGrazia promoted me to becoming his driver. I took him everywhere, and since they were buying more properties, he had me go to the building department and planning commission to make sure everything was in order.

Once the hotel suite was remodeled, we had very stylish headquarters. There was no doubt the hotel knew the nature of their latest permanent guests, but they welcomed them and catered to their wishes during the remodeling. This was now where everyone met with Mr. DeGrazia; where he entertained and where he lived.

Over the next few years, I witnessed extortion, corruption of public officials, loan sharking, and murder. Some things didn't bother me as much as I thought they would. But I would have been lying if I said it was easy to look the other way when they felt they had to rough someone up or go to the extreme of murder. But I couldn't say anything or interfere if I wanted to keep my job. What I found interesting was there was such a strong family structure built on loyalty and I saw firsthand the severe consequences of betrayal.

I was always on call and had little free time, but one evening when I had a break, I went down to the hotel cocktail lounge and listened to some music. Not wanting to stand out, I'd slip into one of the back corner booths and sipped on a club soda with a twist of lime. Drinking anything stronger wasn't an option.

It'd been almost a month since I'd been in last, and I gave the waitress a nod to bring me my usual. The group was on a break and they were sitting in a booth by the stage. I noticed a woman was with them. She was gorgeous. Her hair was up in a twist, and her lips were ruby red. I was surprised when a few minutes later, she joined the three guys as they took their places, and they began to play a new set. I'd always found the base, sax and piano a comfortable relaxing sound, but the woman's voice brought them to an entirely different level. She softened the sound, smoothed out the edges. I was mesmerized.

When the waitress came back around, I ordered another club soda and just sat there and listened.

I was sure it was because I wanted to see the woman again that I was being pulled in every direction. That next week I drove the bagman twice, and then I drove Mr. DeGrazia out to the factory to meet with the foreman.

"Stand outside the car and keep your eyes and ears open," he said when I opened the car door for him to get out.

They were thinking about buying another commercial building just outside of town, and I sat in on the meeting with the contractor and the building inspector. From the outside, the building would seem to be refurbished and rented as office space. To Mr. DeGrazia, the bottom floor would become a revenue generating speakeasy with offices for businesses they controlled or had an interest in, and the rest of the space would be turned into apartments for those who worked in the speakeasy. Once the plans were approved, overseeing the reconstruction became one of my responsibilities.

Although we kept in touch by phone, I hadn't been back down to visit my parents often in the years I'd been gone. They'd moved from Watts to Lynwood, and when I finally made the time to go see them, I was taken aback by how much they'd aged. My father's persistent back pain had slowed him down to a snail's pace, as he liked to say, and he was working less and less. While he'd preached using protective gear, like gloves, helmets and insulated footwear, his hands were now gnarled with arthritis, and I noticed the shoelaces on his shoes were loosely tied.

"Makes it more comfortable for my feet," he explained when he saw me look down at them. I knew he'd broken his left foot several years back, and I wasn't sure what was wrong with his right one.

My older brother, Antonio, had taken over the business, leaving my father with answering the phones and doing the bookkeeping. Thankfully, my mother didn't appear to have as many physical problems, although she'd gained a lot of weight and her shoulders were more slumped over, creating a worsened curvature of her spine.

My sister was married and going to have another baby. I hadn't seen her since her wedding, and I was sure someone would say something, but no one did. Antonio was also married and had two boys.

"You still need to put some weight on," she said, giving me a hug.

"You remember old Mr. Rodia who built those towers? Before we moved from Watts, he gave his property to his neighbor and moved to Martinez, California, to live with his sister. Of course we haven't been back, but I don't think anyone ever heard from him again.

My mom made us lunch, and we sat outside under a sagging patio cover and ate with paper plates and napkins. Every so often I'd jump in my chair when I heard a creak coming from the wood beams up above us. I could just imagine it falling down and crushing us. Eventually, we finished, and I tried not to look too eager to help clear everything up and put it in the covered trash bins over in a corner of the yard.

"Lorenzo's doing good at the movie studio, and he's dating some starlet," my father said, raising his eyebrows.

"Now leave him alone," my mother said. "He'll get married when he's ready—although I would love to have more grandchildren." I caught the message loud and clear.

I had to work that night, so I needed to leave. I promised to not wait so long to come home for a visit, and I genuinely meant it when I said, "It was great to see you both."

I made it a point to drive by the old house and towers, and a combination of fresh and drooping bouquets of flowers laid at the base of the largest tower, which led me to believe Mr. Rodia had most likely passed away.

I knew I was risking trouble when I continued to sit in on the sets when Charlotte sang with the group. I told myself it was just a way to wind down either after a rough day or to take a break from a stressful evening. And that was partially true. The music offered me the temporary escape I needed, and listening to her somehow made me feel less alone. She could hold her own with the customers too, which was impressive. I'd been there in the lounge the night Fat Tommie Marino approached her. Even though the music had stopped, I couldn't hear what he said to her; but I *could* tell he made her uncomfortable. Against my better judgment, I readied myself to get involved if I needed to. But she politely put him in his place, and she returned to the stage, and Fat Tommie backed down.

One night, though, I did raise my glass to the group, and Charlotte acknowledged me. I knew then, it was too late for me to change my mind.

Once Charlotte and I began seeing each other, I knew I was serious about her. I'd been with a few women before, but none of them were candidates for any type of commitment. Right away, I knew Charlotte and I could be different. But I had two problems. I could never tell her about what I was doing, and I could only share parts of my life with her. She told me about living in Texas, and about losing her mother. She'd been on her own and I admired her strength.

When she was called into service to Mr. DeGrazia, I wasn't sure she could handle it. The truth was, I didn't want her to take the job, but I couldn't tell anyone how I felt about her. Eventually it became clear, but in the beginning, I couldn't show favoritism. And it crushed me when things started going south; over hearing men talking about some of the things they needed to do, and then the shooting of the real estate developer. I knew she'd met him before, for she'd told me about being in his suite with Clara.

I tried to protect her as much as I could, trying to reassure Mr. DeGrazia she was strong enough to handle it all, but I was terrified she'd lose it. And if that happened, there was nothing I could do to protect her without blowing my cover.

In my heart, I knew she was going to leave, and when she did, I understood. She was there one day, then gone the next. I figured Miles, Finn, and even Clara knew where she was, but I honored their bond with Charlotte and I never went there.

Our relationship had been complicated, and if I could have done anything differently, I would have. If I knew I was going to love her as much as I did, I would have stayed away,—I said that now, but even when I first laid eyes on her, I knew I wanted her to be part of my life.

I quit going down to the club—I couldn't sit there and wish it had all been a mistake and think she'd walk back through that door any minute. And I knew if I did go in, it would have caused an uncomfortable disruption with the guys. How would they have been able to continue playing when they saw me?

I knew without a doubt Charlotte was the one I wanted to spend the rest of my life with, and I missed everything about her; watching her sing, listening to her laughter, and smelling her perfume. Most of all, I missed her in my bed when I woke in the morning.

It took over a year for me to figure out how I could get myself out. It had to be done so that I wouldn't jeopardize my job, and Vinnie played a large part in the planning of it all. When it finally happened, when I faked my death, Mr. DeGrazia had to believe I truly died. Vinnie found an unidentified corpse, and we dressed him in my clothes and placed him in my car. I was there, but I couldn't watch as two men I didn't know shot the unknown man enough times to make it look like a gang shooting, which included rendering his face unrecognizable.

I never looked back at him, but I puked anyway.

It had been over a year since Charlotte left, and so much time had passed; had she gone on with her life? Would she have found someone new—it would have made sense. It was too late now to change my mind, even if it was too late to find her. I had to give it my best shot, and I had a feeling I knew where she was.

# AUTHOR'S NOTES

I thought Dear Noah was the end of my series set up in the Lake Arrowhead Mountains, but when a friend and reader in Crestline, Ca, (Maria Harmon) said she'd like to know more about Charlotte, I laughed and said to myself, "*Who is Charlotte?*" It turned out she was a minor character in book four, *The Maidservant in Cabin Number One*, who helped Ruth Landry escape from a life she refused to return to.

"I'll just have to write Charlotte's story," I said. "And I set it in 1930s Crestline." What started out as a Novella has now become a book, and hopefully you've enjoyed reading another piece of my character's stories about starting over in the idyllic Lake Arrowhead Mountains.

As usual, I've taken creative liberties to fit actual events into the timeline of my story. Many eyes have scanned these pages before printing, but typos still seem to evade me, and I'd love it if you'd let me know if anything jumps out at you; I'll correct it for the next printing.

I'd like to thank my original first readers, Myrt Perisho, who just celebrated her 90th birthday, Pat Aldridge and Susan Denley. I'll never forget sitting with them at Myrt's dining room table after they read my first manuscript, and it was their kindness and encouragement that boosted my confidence to continue with my writing. Thanks for being honest but kind with your critiques!

Sue Jorgenson's task has been to find my typos, so if there are still some here, blame her! And continued thanks to Pam Sheppard, my original developmental editor, who also helped me figure out which path to take with my books. And I can't leave out readers Diane Streich and Ferne Knauss, who have graciously given me feedback both before and after my books were published.

Again, to my wonderful husband Larry, who, after over forty-seven years, is still the wind beneath my wings. Thank you! You give me the courage to just keep writing when I doubt myself, and you always have great ideas about cars, knives and guns. He's given himself a new nickname, "My financier." Since my books are indie published, he's waiting for the day when I earn enough money to buy him a Porsche!

**Book Clubs**: If you're interested in reading my books, reach out to me; I'd love to hear from you and if you're in So. California, I can most likely plan to come to one of your meetings. If you're not local, reach out to me too; I have a wonderful book package I can offer you. Just let me know.

I'm constantly amazed to hear from readers everywhere, and I've made some great friendships with some who've continued to communicate with me. One of them is Maria Harmon, from Crestline, Ca. who inspired me to write about Charlotte, who coincidentally, she ends up there! (Her husband Joel reads my book too!)

Check me out at chrysteenbraun.com for free bookmarks, and email me at chrysteenbraun@gmail.com ; I'd love to know what you think.

Thanks for reading,

*Chrysteen*

P.S. Leaving great reviews is the best thing you can do to help authors. Amazon loves it and so do I!

**Where you can buy my books:**
If you'd like a signed copy of any of my books, email me at <u>chrysteenbraun@gmail.com</u> They're $15 including shipping, and I accept Zelle.

If you're in the mountains, **Timberline in the Glen** also carries signed copies, and not only will you be supporting a small local business, it's a wonderful store full of treasures.

And of course, all my books are available on **Amazon.**

## History of Simon Rodia, Watts, California

The town of Watts was originally part of a Mexican land grant, and the land was used for grazing and beef production. In 1907, it was incorporated as a separate city, and in 1926 it was annexed to Los Angeles.

The Watts Towers (also known as Towers of Simon Rodia, or Nuestro Pueblo in Spanish) are a collection of 17 interconnected architectural towers, built from 1921 to 1954 by Sam Rodia, (Sabato Rodia, an Italian immigrant construction worker), on the site of his personal residence in Watts.

The towers have been designated as a National Historic Landmark, and a Los Angeles Historic – Cultural Monument. They're listed in the National Register of Historic Places in Los Angeles.

## Heart Rock. Camp Seeley

Nestled in the San Bernardino Mountains, Camp Seeley is owned by the City of Los Angeles. You'll find camping, the heart-shaped hole and the waterfall where Dino proposes to Charlotte.

## The History of Crestline & Lake Gregory

Mormon Springs, Camp Lincoln, Pine Mont, Crest City, Summer in the Pines, and Valley of Enchantment were just a few of the names used to describe the camping spot that was to become the town of Crestline. In Joe's story, his father worked for the Pacific Electric Company, and they actually built a vacation camp for its employees where families lived in tent houses and enjoyed the use of a swimming pool, community dining room, social hall, and could partake in mountain sports activities. By1920, almost 150 people per week came up, but the development of Crestline as a community began as early as 1906, when a syndicate of San Bernardino investors purchased 630 acres for $11,000.

Far above the heat of the Los Angeles and the Valley, they laid out streets, put in water mains and Henry Guernsey built himself a house.

In 1906, they held a contest to officially name the town, and "Crestline" won. A man named S.W. Dillin created the Crestline Tavern out of an old cement warehouse, and in my story, I called it Flo's Stockade and Diner. Chip Anzalone, who bought our first cabin up in Skyforest, owns the real Stockade, which is actually a thriving business today. And the food is yummy!

The **First Drowning in Crestline** was my imagination, not an official recounting of an event.

## Big Bear Lake

Big Bear Lake is a reservoir in the San Bernardino Mountains and is a snow and rain-fed lake, with no other means of mechanical or natural replenishment. For approximately 2,500 years, it was home to the indigenous Serrano people who survived on berries, nuts and wild game. They considered the native grizzly bears as ancestors and would not eat the meat or wear the hides. (Unfortunately, by 1906, the unregulated hunting of the grizzly made them extinct.)

In 1859, a prospector from Indiana discovered gold, and with the onset of the automobile, tourism began. Hollywood soon discovered Big Bear, and it became a popular region for filming.

Big Bear Valley is known to have twelve to fifteen bald eagles. Since around 2012, the installation of a webcam made an eagle couple famous. Jackie, the female, has a Facebook page with over a half million followers. The nest is protected by closing the surrounding area to the public.

# HOW TO LEAVE A REVIEW

If you enjoy my books, please take a moment to leave a review. It's a wonderful way to let other readers learn about new authors and books.

**Amazon.com**
1. Go to the product detail page for the book
2. Select Review this Product
3. Write a product review in the Customer Reviews section
4. Select a Star Rating (4 or 5 stars)
5. A Green check mark shows you've successfully submitted ratings
6. Follow my profile to keep up to date with my new books

**BookBub.com**
1. Click on the book to go to its BookBub page
2. From this page, select Review to give the book a star rating or to leave a review
3. Afterward, if you'd like to share your review, visit the book's page on BookBub and scroll down until you see your review.
4. Follow my profile to keep up to date with my new books

**Goodreads.com**
1. Click on the book to go to its Goodreads page
2. Write your review in the Give Feedback form
3. Leave a Star Rating (4 or 5 stars)
4. Check the "Post Review to Goodreads"
5. Submit your review
6. Follow my profile to keep up to date with my new books

# THE MAN IN CABIN NUMBER FIVE, BOOK ONE

When Annie Parker discovers her husband's infidelity, she doesn't let it destroy her. She packs her bags and heads to Lake Arrowhead, California, the mountainside town where her family used to summer. Immersing herself in the restoration of seven 1920s-era cabins, Annie begins to put the pieces of her life back together. But starting over is never easy.

Alyce Murphy needs closure. When she discovers her father did not die from a heart attack, as she's been led to believe for the last 30 years, but in a murder/suicide, she is determined to uncover the truth of his death. But when she visits the cabin where her father ended his life, Alyce has to accept she may never know the true story.

Annie is looking toward her future while Alyce needs to put the past to rest. In parallel stories, both women are drawn to the rustic mountainside cabins as they search for the missing pieces—but they soon discover that the cabins have their own stories to tell.

# THE GIRLS IN CABIN NUMBER THREE, BOOK TWO

In book two of the Guest Book Trilogy, eighty-one-year-old Annie Parker recounts taking on, against the wishes of her new love Noah, an out-of-town design project that leads her down a path that is more than she bargained for.

Back in Lake Arrowhead, California, a long-awaited mystery is buried in Cabin Number Three. Annie meets Carrie Davis who wants to update her childhood home on the lake and feels a tie to Annie's cabins. Apparently, Carrie's parents stayed here during the Roaring '20s when Bugsy Siegel ran an underground speakeasy and distillery. Unconvinced, Annie decides to investigate and finds their names in the old guest books—Elizabeth Davis and Thomas Meyer. As exciting as that sounds, it's only the start of a winding tale that Carrie and the new man in her life uncover. The pair unravel a family history filled with gangsters, working girls, and a surprising twist to a family tree.

*The Girls in Cabin Number Three* combines women's fiction with romance, cozy noir mystery, and suspense—all wrapped up in the majestic environs of this lovely lakeside haven.

# THE STARLET IN CABIN NUMBER SEVEN, BOOK THREE

Return to picturesque 1980s Lake Arrowhead, California where another cozy cabin sheltered amongst the sweeping pine-lined vistas holds a long-buried secret, waiting to be divulged.

In this third installment of The Guest Book Trilogy, a young Annie Parker is struggling to overcome her grief over the recent loss of her sister, when a childhood friend unexpectedly turns up seeking refuge from an ill-fated marriage. It would have been easy for Annie to sink deeper into sadness, but when she learns her newest design client, Hudson Fisher, is the son of the late film actress Celeste Williams, her curiosity is peaked. As it turns out, the Roaring 20s starlet was no stranger to the Lake Arrowhead cabins—and this revelation sparks the unraveling of a scandalous story from Hollywood's bygone era. Did an illicit romance between this leading lady and her dashing costar take place in Cabin No. 7? What really went on behind-the-scenes during the filming of that silent picture? Will discovering a piece of the past bring closure to Annie's present?

A heartwarming tale of friendships, forgiveness, and a touch of old Hollywood glamour, *The Starlet in Cabin Number Seven* will have readers captivated from beginning to end.

# THE MAIDSERVANT IN CABIN NUMBER ONE: THE BEGINNING, BOOK FOUR

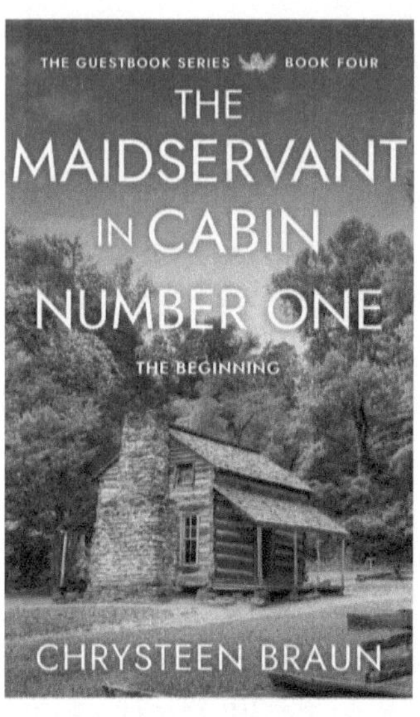

After her father's death in 1923, when Ruth Ann Landry is just ten, she joins her mother as a maidservant for a wealthy Seattle family. The hours are long, the rules are strict, but she and her mother desperately need her wages to survive.

By the time she's seventeen, they've moved into the house, and she's become a mistress to her employer. While accompanying the family on vacation, she sees an opportunity to start a new life, and leaves. Ruth eventually finds solace in the mountain town of Lake Arrowhead, California, where she stays in one of the cabins owned by a man who becomes part of her future.

*The Maidservant in Cabin Number One* is the beginning of the story of The Guest Book Trilogy, and of Annie Parker who eventually comes to own the cabins where Ruth Landry stayed.

# DEAR NOAH:
# THE CONCLUSION,
# BOOK FIVE

Now in her mid-eighties, Annie Parker reflects on a life shaped both by heartbreak and healing. Her journey began with a life-altering decision to start anew, dedicating herself to restoring a collection of 1920s-era cabins, each rich with its own story. Through this labor of love, she wove together the memoires of her past with the promise of her future.

In *Dear Noah*, Annie reflects on her passionate love affair with Noah Chambers, a relationship filled with joy and laughter but overshadowed by an ominous prophecy from an Indian fortune teller. As their love story unfolds, the prophecy casts a long shadow, leaving Annie alone and mourning.

Seeking refuge from her sorrow, Annie moves to Prescott, California, hoping for a new beginning near her mother. There, she meets Phillip, the charming owner of the local antique shop, who help her navigate the complexities of love, loss, and second chances. Through the stories embedded in the cabins and her evolving relationships, Annie discovers that life still holds surprises, and that healing is possible at any stage.

*Dear Noah: The Conclusion* is a tale of love, loss, and the rediscovery of hope in life's later years. It offers a poignant exploration of resilience and the enduring strength of the human spirit, reminding readers that it's never too late to embrace hope and love.